Janice Kaiser

Monday's Child

Harlequin Books

TORONTO • NEW YORK • LONDON
AMSTERDAM • PARIS • SYDNEY • HAMBURG
STOCKHOLM • ATHENS • TOKYO • MILAN
MADRID • WARSAW • BUDAPEST • AUCKLAND

ISBN 0-373-70642-1

MONDAY'S CHILD

"I feel like a piece of meat a couple of dogs are fighting over."

Bart patted Kelly's leg. "Just be glad I'm the dog who won."

"I am. But that doesn't do a lot for my self-respect."

Bart took her hand. "I'd say civilization hasn't been thoroughly destroyed if you can worry about your self-respect at a time like this."

Kelly stopped sniffling. "You're right. I guess you're a lot smarter than you let on."

He chuckled. "Thank you. That's the nicest thing you've said all day. But how could I possibly throw you to the wolves? You've got the best pair of legs I've ever seen."

She pulled her hand from his. "Well, that's a lousy reason. Are you saying that if you didn't like my looks, you'd have left me for the pirates?"

But Bart was gazing toward the village, not heeding her words. "Just what I was afraid of," he said. "Two guards now, with automatic rifles. That probably means they're thinking right along with us." He playfully cuffed her chin. "Well, my dear? Up to another game of hide-and-seek?"

ABOUT THE AUTHOR

After more than thirty romance novels, Janice Kaiser has become not only a reader favorite, but an innovative writer. *Monday's Child* is her second romantic caper for Superromance and a thoroughly entertaining read. Janice has as much fun writing about these characters as you'll have reading about them! She also has a deep appreciation of other cultures, having traveled to more than forty countries before taking up her present career.

A former lawyer and college instructor, Janice turned to writing in 1985, when she married her husband, Ronn, also a writer. The couple now resides in California.

Don't miss Janice's new single title release, *Private Sins,* available from Mira Books.

Books by Janice Kaiser

HARLEQUIN SUPERROMANCE
187—HARMONY
209—LOTUS MOON
224—MEANT TO BE
242—LOVE CHILD
256—CHANCES
287—STOLEN MOMENTS
403—BODY AND SOUL
494—THE BIG SECRET
541—CRADLE OF DREAMS
597—THE YANQUI PRINCE

HARLEQUIN TEMPTATION
462—BETRAYAL
466—DECEPTIONS

Don't miss any of our special offers. Write to us at the following address for information on our newest releases.

Harlequin Reader Service
U.S.: 3010 Walden Ave., P.O. Box 1325, Buffalo, NY 14269
Canadian: P.O. Box 609, Fort Erie, Ont. L2A 5X3

For Tim and Margo Scofield

CHAPTER ONE

BART MONDAY LEANED against the railing of the *Ban Don,*
watching as the coastline of Ko Samui slipped away. The
tufted crowns of the palms on the beach were beginning to
blend in with the vegetation in the background. And the
rich colors of the tropical plants, so intense on shore, grew
softer with each passing minute. Monday sighed with relief, then looked over his shoulder to see if anyone was
watching him.

A couple of Thai crewmen were loitering nearby, and the
steward with the gap-toothed smile seemed to be headed
for the bow. The captain was on the fly deck. But that was
all as it should be. Nothing was suspicious.

It had been a close call. Getting aboard the *Ban Don* had
been a stroke of luck. His choices had been limited. The
airstrip was being watched by the cops—he was certain of
that. Charter boats were out for the same reason. Thank
God for this rusty old tub. It was a far cry from the *Queen
Elizabeth II*, but it might prove to be his salvation.

He'd found someone with a launch willing to ferry him
out to the boat just before it set sail. It had cost him plenty,
but what choice did he have? The other passengers must
have wondered when he'd raced up the steps at the last
minute with the flight bag in his hand, then ducked into the
lounge, hoping to get under cover before he was spotted
from shore.

Now he was home free. Maybe. When the boat finished
its leisurely tour of some of the islands in the Gulf of Siam,

it would return to the mainland. He'd slip off the ship then and disappear into the back alleys of Bangkok.

He had already checked out the other passengers and decided they were benign. True, he couldn't pass for a tourist like the rest of them—not with his old tan bush shorts, faded blue work shirt and shabby sandals—but the crew was undoubtedly trained to mind its own business, and he could handle the passengers. The portly middle-aged Englishman had already tried to engage him in conversation. He'd put a quick end to that. Fortunately, the retired Australian couple had been preoccupied with their cameras. That left only the attractive blonde.

She'd been standing near the railing in her floppy straw hat and slim cotton pants and T-shirt, waiting for the cruise to get under way, when he'd come on board. He'd taken her in, noticing the way her legs seemed to go on forever. But he hadn't seen her since he'd boarded.

After another few minutes, with no sign of a pursuing police craft and Ko Samui blending into the horizon, Bart figured it was time for a leisurely tour of the boat. He made his way along the starboard deck. He was amidship when he spotted the blonde up at the bow, stretched out on a lounge chair.

She had changed into a blue-and-gold bikini that left nothing to the imagination. He smiled to himself, wondering what the crew must be thinking. Judging by the empty cola bottles on the deck next to her chair, the steward was being very attentive. He could hardly blame the poor bastard. He wouldn't mind helping her apply a little suntan oil himself.

Once he was within several yards of her he stopped and took up a station at the railing, pretending to stare out to sea. It wasn't only that the blonde was beautiful—she was one of his own kind. That made her special. God, it had been so long since he'd even spoken to a woman who wasn't Thai that he wasn't sure if he still remembered the protocol.

The local women were gorgeous, and most men he knew found them irresistible. But he was six foot four and liked tall women, someone with legs long enough to wrap around him—like the blond Valkyrie lounging a few feet away.

At some point he'd strike up a conversation with her. But there was no rush. She wasn't going anywhere. There wasn't any competition on board. Besides, he was dead tired. He hadn't slept more than a few hours each of the past two nights. A few winks would do wonders for his morale, and probably his appearance, as well.

Monday turned from the railing and slowly made his way to the stairs to go below deck. He wasn't sure why, but he felt a sudden sense of optimism. Maybe getting on this old tub would turn out to be the stroke of good luck he'd been hoping for.

KELLY WATCHED HIM LEAVE, just as she'd been watching him observe her for the better part of fifteen minutes—subtly, through her lashes. The way he'd ogled her, she'd been sure he was practicing come-on lines. That was damned annoying. It had been bad enough that the crewmen were leering; she didn't like having to endure it from a fellow passenger, as well.

Maybe sunbathing hadn't been a good idea. After all, this wasn't a cruise ship. But the secretary in the Bangkok office of Pan Pacific had assured her the cruise would be informal, like a floating party. Not that a party was what Kelly had been looking for, exactly, but she'd hoped to relax a little after a week of tough negotiating. Perhaps the best thing to do was get dressed. That would put a stop to the leering.

The steward came by just then, the same enormous grin on his face. He bowed. "Another cool drink, miss?" he asked, openly staring at her body.

Kelly was tempted to tell him not to bother coming by every few minutes on the pretense of being solicitous, but she'd never been good at being rude, even when it was deserved. "No, thanks," she said, wondering if putting the towel over her legs would be too obvious.

She pointedly turned back to her book and the steward took the hint. After he retreated, Kelly closed her eyes and tried to forget all of them—the steward, the uncouth passenger and the three men on the bridge who'd been watching her, one with binoculars. She inhaled the sea air and tried to focus on the sensation of the sun on her body. God knows, this would be her only chance to kick back a little on the trip. And two measly days off out of the two weeks she'd be spending in Thailand certainly wasn't much.

Kelly searched for a distracting thought, something to put her in a more pleasant state of mind. Funny, but it was several seconds before she thought of Duncan. That was embarrassing. He should have been on her mind all along. They'd been engaged less than a week, yet he seemed a million miles away. Wouldn't her mother have had a field day with that!

Kelly remembered their last conversation before she'd left Honolulu. Her mother had come over to her condo, supposedly to help her pack. Unfortunately, Beryl Ronan's real objective had been to proselytize. Again.

This time she wasn't too pleased with Kelly's decision to marry. Of course, Beryl took a dim view of many things Kelly did, from her choice of career to her engagement to her boss. And, as luck would have it, her mother wasn't shy about airing her opinions.

"You know, dear, I'd never want to interfere in your life," she'd said, "but I can't help wondering how you can get engaged to a man one day, then go traipsing off to Thailand the next. How romantic can your relationship be?"

Kelly had done her best to hold her tongue. She'd promised herself she wouldn't get into another argument with her mother—not over Duncan. That hadn't been easy. Kelly made her living arguing and she wasn't in the habit of backing down from a verbal battle.

"I'm sorry you feel that way, Mom," she'd said, folding a silk blouse to put in her suitcase, "but it's my engagement and it's my life."

"Well," her mother said as she plopped down on the big rattan chair in the corner of Kelly's all-white bedroom, "you know what they say... actions speak louder than words. I just know in my heart of hearts that your feelings for this man are far too cerebral for happiness."

"Cerebral?"

"If you feel any passion for Duncan Van de Meer, I've failed to see it."

"Why? Because I'm going to Bangkok without him? Get real, Mother. This trip has been scheduled for weeks. Besides, since when did you decide traveling was so undesirable? Aren't you the one who bought a yacht after Daddy died and sailed to Tahiti for the adventure of it all?"

"For heaven's sake, Kelly, I'm not suggesting that *traveling* is the mistake. The problem is not going with the man you love. It says something about your relationship. Don't you see that?"

Kelly gave her mother a tight smile but kept her mouth shut. She was proud of her reputation as a levelheaded, cool-under-fire litigator. If she could control her temper in court, then she ought to be able to handle her own mother.

Of course, Beryl Ronan was not your run-of-the-mill little old lady—in looks or temperament. Her glorious red hair was barely touched with gray, though she was in her sixties. More often than not, she pulled her hair into a loose knot on top of her head and skewered it with two fake ivory ornaments that looked suspiciously like chopsticks. And though Kelly favored tailored, conservative clothes, her mother always wore muumuus in a variety of strong colors. Her favorite had orange and red flowers on a purple background.

Kelly saw by her mother's expression that she was still waiting for a response. "Mom, my clients are in Thailand. I can't negotiate effectively for Pan Pacific from here. Duncan understands that. He *wants* me to go!" She paused to put her running shoes into her suitcase. "Don't you see, I have no choice?"

"No, I don't see. And if your father was still here, he wouldn't see, either. Why, we were practically inseparable for more than thirty years." She twisted her wedding ring. "I'm not trying to tell you what to do, dear, it's just that I want you to be as happy as we were."

Kelly stuffed a pair of navy low-heeled pumps into shoe bags. "I know you do. But I'm certain Duncan and I are well suited to each other. We both love the law."

Beryl Ronan rolled her eyes. "How exciting. Tell me the truth—when the two of you are alone do you talk about law?"

Kelly laughed. "Sometimes. Didn't you and Daddy ever talk about the swimsuit business?"

"Yes, but it wasn't the essence of our marriage. For heaven's sake, if you don't start off wanting to be together every minute of every day, where do you think you're going to end up?"

"On the Supreme Court?" Kelly teased.

Her mother smirked. "I'm serious. I think you should use this time away from Duncan to give some serious thought to your life. You're only thirty. Marriage to a man almost old enough to be your father will make you old before your time."

"Nonsense."

Beryl Ronan sighed. "All I'm saying is, treat yourself to some fun while you're there. With all the hours you put in, you deserve it. And it wouldn't hurt for you to think long and hard about your choice of husband. If Duncan is right for you, then you don't have anything to worry about. He'll be here when you get home. In the meantime, why not cut loose, have a last fling? Do it for me, Kelly. What could possibly be the harm in that?"

At the time she had dismissed the notion as another of her mother's machinations against Duncan. Still, a tiny part of her wondered if her mother didn't have a point in one respect—she didn't feel that kind of wild abandoned passion for Duncan that she'd always read about. But then, mature relationships weren't based on romance. They were founded on common interests, common values and common objectives. She and Duncan Van de Meer were perfectly matched in that regard.

And yet she had flown off to Ko Samui to take this cruise. She'd told herself she needed time away from business to relax. But it was almost as if there was a demon inside her, pushing her toward some... adventure, maybe. A last fling.

Of course, even if that was true, it didn't mean anything. A cruise to some far-off place would be good for a few laughs but nothing serious—even in her fantasies. And the real irony was that there'd be no party on this trip. Not with a passenger list that included one elderly couple, a stuffy middle-aged gentleman and the scruffy stud with the lecherous eyes. Even her mother wouldn't want her flirting with the likes of him.

Kelly hadn't gotten a really good look at the guy, but one glance had told her all she needed to know. He seemed like a man on the edge, the kind who survived by his wits. He was not someone she would have a drink with, let alone share a flirtation. No, on this trip she'd content herself with a good book. And before she knew it, she'd be on her way home to Honolulu and Duncan Van de Meer's waiting arms.

BART MONDAY MADE HIS WAY up the companionway to the main deck, curious to see if the blonde was still camped out on the lounge chair. The three other passengers had come below, their chatter having awakened him. But he'd gotten a few winks and felt a lot better. He'd washed up, but hadn't shaved because, in his haste to leave, he'd failed to bring his razor. The damned thing was so dull, though, it was probably just as well.

As he moved along the deck, he saw that the lovely lady was indeed still worshiping the sun. He took his sunglasses out of his breast pocket and slipped them on. Then he ran his fingers through his damp hair, went over to the railing where he'd been before, and stared at the water.

The Gulf of Siam was like a great lake, the water flat, the air heavy, humid. Only the movement of the boat made the wind stir. Ko Pong was in the distance. He'd asked the steward as he'd left the bath if they would put in there, but the man just shook his head. "Not Ko Pong, mister. You only look. Not Ko Pong."

Bart stared at the island's low, emerald profile, wondering why they'd come so far only to get a glimpse of the place. What was wrong with it, anyhow? Well, it didn't matter. The quicker they got to the mainland, the better.

He turned again to check out the golden one in her bikini and was greeted with a less than pleasant glare. He smiled.

"Nice day," he said.

She gave him a thin little smile but said nothing. Could be she was a bitch, or it could be she was shy. He hoped it wasn't a case of not liking men, because she was dynamite. What a waste that would be.

Never one to let a little adversity slow him down, he sauntered toward her, stopping at the railing a few feet away. He leaned back on it with his elbows and looked down at her, checking out every curve. Breathtaking.

"Is there something you want?" she said irritably, glaring at him once again.

"Nope. Is there anything you want?"

"Yes. To be left alone. I don't like being leered at."

He shrugged. "Sorry. I didn't know I was leering."

"I feel as though you were." She hesitated. "Maybe if you just went away..."

"And where do you suggest I go? It's a small boat, in case you haven't noticed." He laughed and turned to look out at the water. "No matter where I go, I tend to run into the same four passengers."

"Look—" she started to say, but was interrupted by a loud rumbling coming from the bowels of the craft.

They both looked back toward the bridge. The engine hesitated, coughed, then stopped. After that, the only sound was the lap of water against the hull of the boat.

Monday heard the captain shout, and there was a flurry of activity as crewmen appeared from nowhere and began scurrying about. The ship was slowing. They'd lost power.

"What's happened?" the blonde said. There was a trace of alarm in her voice.

"I don't know. Seems like we might have engine trouble."

The flurry around them continued. When he looked at her again, she was standing. There wasn't an ounce of fat on her body. The woman was lean and toned and had real muscles. His heart ached just looking at her.

"Do you think it's serious?" she asked, their recent animosity apparently forgotten.

"I don't know. They're checking into it now."

He leaned his back against the railing and watched the activity on the bridge. She was wearing sunglasses, so he hadn't been able to tell what color her eyes were, but he'd bet on blue. Yes, with that hair and swimsuit, she'd have to have blue eyes. He guessed she was in her late twenties, a woman, not a girl. And in her bare feet he judged her to be around five-ten. A perfect height for him.

"I ran to catch a plane once," he said. "Didn't make it. It later crashed. Maybe it was a sign from God. When I almost missed getting on board this tub, I probably should have figured this would happen."

She smiled thinly. "If I ever see you running for a plane I'm supposed to board, I'll make a point of delaying my trip."

He grinned. "My name's Monday, by the way. Bart Monday."

"Kelly Ronan," she said.

He extended his hand, still leaning against the railing. She hesitated, then took it. There were more shouts on the bridge, and they both turned their attention in that direction. The captain and crew were engaged in an animated conversation. He listened.

"Is it just me, or does this seem like a disaster in the making?" she asked.

"It's never good to lose power," he said. "But if you have to, I suppose we're better off on a ship than on an airplane."

She smiled broadly for the first time, pushing her sunglasses up into her short hair. "You have a point, Mr. Monday."

Her eyes were blue, all right. The softest, prettiest blue he'd ever seen. "Sorry about the leering, by the way," he said. "It's a weakness of mine. I get over it once I get to know a person."

"Had I known, I would have introduced myself earlier."

He pushed his sunglasses up into his hair, as well. "Does that mean I'm forgiven?"

"No, it just means I could have spared myself the experience."

"You're quick on the uptake," he said.

"Thank you. I think."

"The apology was sincere."

"And gratefully accepted," she said. "But at the moment I'm more worried about what's going on with this ship."

"Or what's not going on," he said with a laugh. He turned and stared across the water at Ko Pong. "You on vacation?" he asked without looking at her.

Kelly turned and leaned on the rail along with him. "Sort of. How about you?"

He shook his head. "Mind some advice?"

"No. What is it?"

"I'd get dressed if I were you."

"Why?"

Bart Monday continued staring into the distance. "Civilization can be very fragile in this part of the world."

She blinked. "What's that supposed to mean?"

"Last year pirates set on a disabled sailboat in these waters. Two French couples were on board. The women were raped, the men killed."

"Pirates?"

"Fishermen, actually. But the gold watches, cameras, jewelry, traveler's checks and women made them pirates, if only for the day." He paused and turned to her. "Ever heard of the Boat People?"

"Of course. But we're not exactly Vietnamese refugees in an old junk."

"No. You're a rich Westerner in a rusty old tub and you've got more gold in your purse than the net worth of an entire fishing village. *And,*" he added pointedly, "you're practically naked."

"Is that calculated to frighten me, Mr. Monday?"

He was amused. He liked women with sass. "Yes, as a matter of fact, it is." Then he shrugged. "But it's your body and your gold. God knows, I personally don't mind looking at you the way you are." With that, he sauntered away.

THIS TIME as she watched him leave she had an uneasy feeling. He'd been heavy-handed, but it wasn't the put-down that bothered her so much as the warning. Underneath the sarcasm there'd been a message that was dead serious. He wanted her to know there was danger. How immediate it was, she didn't know.

She turned and looked at Ko Pong. Surely small-time pirates didn't attack boats the size of the *Ban Don.* But telling herself that didn't seem to make a difference. Bart Monday's warning had had a ring of authority that was hard to dismiss. Maybe she *should* change. She'd had enough sun for one day, anyway.

Kelly went below to the lounge. The Australian couple and the Englishman were huddled together in the corner, talking quietly. There was no sign of Monday.

"Have you heard what the problem is?" the elderly Australian asked her.

"No. Engine trouble. That's all I know."

She went into the ladies' lounge, where there was a dressing room. The *Ban Don* had been designed as a ferryboat and was now used for day trips. There were no sleeping cabins for passengers, nor was there a need. Every other day it made a day-long tour of the islands with a stop at Surat Thani, on the mainland.

Unfortunately there were no shower facilities, which meant all she could do was sponge off a bit before slipping back into her blouse and pants and sandals. She decided to keep her bikini on.

As she finished dressing, Kelly thought about Bart Monday. Though he needed a shave and a haircut, he wasn't as disreputable as she'd first thought. Underneath the rough veneer was a man with a certain amount of intelligence and charm. Had he fallen on rough times? she wondered.

He didn't seem like an alcoholic or a drug addict, but their conversation had been too brief to get a reading on the man. If cleaned up, he could be rather attractive. He was somewhere in his late thirties, she estimated, very tall and broad shouldered. Kelly sighed. She did like tall men. Duncan was just barely her height, which meant she towered over him when she wore heels. Of course, that didn't matter. Superficial stuff like that was for kids.

The boat was still quiet when she returned to the lounge, so whatever was wrong with the engine hadn't been fixed. The other passengers, except for Monday, were huddled in conversation. She considered joining them but decided instead to find out what was going on, if she could.

Up on the deck there was an eerie silence. In place of her lounge chair on the bow, there was a crewman with an automatic rifle slung over his shoulder. His back was to her and he was staring out to sea. It was an ominous sign and she shivered.

Kelly decided to make a circuit of the deck. At the stern she found two more armed crewmen. Then, on the port side, she found Bart Monday, a bottle of Tsing Tao beer in his hand. He turned at her approach, then looked out to sea again. She followed his gaze to a small flotilla of boats several hundred yards away, between the *Ban Don* and the island.

"Pirates?" she asked, her mouth suddenly dry.

"Fishermen," Monday replied. "For the moment, anyway."

"Maybe they'll help us," she said hopefully.

"Maybe." He took a long pull on his beer, his head tilted back, the cords of his neck rippling as he swallowed.

She stared at the boats. "Surely the captain has radioed for help," she said after a while.

"Yes."

"Then the coast guard or somebody's on the way?"

"Yes. I spoke with the captain. They've dispatched a patrol boat."

Kelly felt better.

"But the closest is more than a hundred miles away," he went on. "Apparently most of the coast guard vessels are tied up in a large operation off Cambodian waters. We didn't pick a good day to become disabled."

"Aren't there any commercial vessels that can rescue us?"

"The Surat Thani ferry is a possibility. When I left the bridge, the captain was negotiating by radio with the company that operates it. The bad thing about all this is that every radio broadcast advertises the desperation of our circumstances."

Kelly traced his profile with her eyes. "How do you know all this, Mr. Monday? How is it the captain took you into his confidence?"

"He didn't. I speak some Thai." He grinned, showing even white teeth. "I got the uncensored version that way."

She turned and stared again at the fishing boats, thinking. The sun was sinking into a band of clouds. It was very beautiful—the color, the tranquillity of the sea. But with each passing moment the gravity of the situation was becoming more apparent.

"Are you concerned?" she asked.

"The captain has the boat better armed than I would have thought. I was pleased to see he was prepared. But that also tells me he had cause."

Kelly didn't know whether he was amusing himself at her expense or not. The crew's weapons lent credibility to what he said, though, so he couldn't have exaggerated much. The fishing boats were moving in their direction. She imagined them stalking the *Ban Don,* moving in for the kill. Whatever their intentions, they clearly weren't rushing to their rescue.

"What's happening now?" she asked, after watching for a while.

"I don't know. It looks like the fishermen and the captain are feeling each other out."

"Do fishing boats have radios?"

"If so, it's to eavesdrop on official communications. Those boys out there might be into fishing or they might not. There's no way to know at this point." He nodded toward the main cabin. "Maybe you'd be better off below."

"No. I want to stay."

The light was beginning to fade. When he put his sunglasses in his shirt pocket, Kelly got a good look at his eyes.

They were the color of burnt gold. She'd never seen eyes like that before. They were beautiful. Cleaned up, he'd be gorgeous. But with his old clothes, he reminded her of the irreverent, slightly-beyond-the-pale beach bums she'd known as a teenager.

Yet in spite of that, there was something about the man that was serious. Dead serious. More than anything he struck her as a square peg in a world full of round holes. "What do you do, Mr. Monday? If you don't mind my asking."

He finished the last of the beer and tossed the bottle into the water. "A little of this. A little of that."

"In other words, it's none of my business."

"Import-export," he said, as though it was easier to answer than respond to the challenge. "What do you do, besides cruise the Gulf of Siam alone?"

"I practice law."

"Really?"

"Is that so hard to believe?"

He shrugged, turning back to the fishing boats. "I would have guessed a tennis pro or a marine biologist—something that lets you spend time outdoors."

"If you're referring to my tan, I've lived in Honolulu all my life. I run and sail and surf and I belong to a canoe club. I go outside whenever I can."

"What brought you to Ko Samui? Vacation?"

"Sort of. I'm negotiating a corporate buy-out for one of my clients who's based in Bangkok, but I'm taking the weekend off. And you?"

He grinned sardonically. "I had to get away from the office for a few days."

Kelly scoffed. If she had to bet, she'd say Bart Monday hadn't been on the working end of an office in his entire life. She watched him stare across the indigo water for a minute before he spoke again.

"Maybe we'd best stop the chitchat, Kelly. I think it's time for you to go below." His voice was commanding, and she was a bit offended. Her impulse was to ask him who he thought he was, taking charge that way. But again, his tone had that ring of authority that demanded compliance.

She glanced at the boats. "Do you think they're up to no good?"

"Something doesn't smell right. I'm not a man of the sea, but I don't like this." He took her by the arm. "Come on."

They walked briskly around the deck to the stairway leading down to the main lounge. He didn't release her arm until they got there. She wandered to the table where the other passengers had gathered. Bart Monday headed for the storage cabinet at the back of the room. He opened it and took out the sports bag he'd carried on board, unzipped it and removed a pistol. Kicking the bag back into the cabinet, he wedged the gun under his belt. Then, without so much as a word, he left the lounge.

"Good Lord," the Englishman said. "What in God's name is going on?"

"They're concerned about pirates," Kelly said as she went to a porthole. Even as she uttered the words, she could hardly believe this was happening. Pirates! Things like that didn't happen in real life, at least not in *her* life.

Kelly turned back to the group as she heard the Australian woman begin to whimper. Her husband put his arm around her and made soothing sounds. Kelly turned her attention to the fishing boat closest to the *Ban Don*.

She saw the heads and shoulders of several men. In front of the face of one of them she saw a puff of smoke. Then she heard a round splat against the steel hull of the ship. Three or four seconds later there was a rapid series of pops. It sounded like a string of large firecrackers.

She dropped down to a bench, her hand covering her mouth.

"That's gunfire!" the Englishman cried.

Monday hadn't been exaggerating. The boat was under attack.

CHAPTER TWO

THE NEXT HALF HOUR WAS a nightmare. The *Ban Don* was surrounded. Bullets slammed into the side of the ship. The air was filled with the shouts of crewmen, the smell of gunpowder and the anguished cries of the wounded. Half of the portholes in the lounge had been shot out, sending shattered glass over the worn plank flooring.

Kelly huddled with the other passengers, keeping down so as not to be hit by a stray bullet. At one point, two of the crewmen dragged a comrade into the lounge, asking the passengers to do what they could for him.

The Englishman, who'd been a medic years before, tended the man until he died about ten minutes later. Kelly had tried to help, though the metallic smell of the blood sickened her. She wondered if they could hold off the pirates until help came or if it was only a matter of time before she, too, was lying on the floor, bleeding to death.

A few minutes later a second crewman was brought in. He was already dead. Kelly stared at the bodies, recalling the time her father had backed the station wagon over her puppy. She'd held the cocker spaniel in her arms as her father had driven to the vet's, but they'd been too late. Blackie had died in her arms.

Kelly crawled to the bench under one of the portholes and told herself that in the real world, the civilized world, things like this simply didn't happen. But it *was* happening and it was happening to her.

She hadn't seen Bart Monday since he'd left the lounge, though she thought she'd heard his voice once over the din. And at one point, when she'd taken a quick peek out the porthole, she'd seen a fishing boat come within a few yards of the *Ban Don* on the starboard side. Other than that, the action seemed to be on the port side.

The firefight became intense. Kelly sensed they were lost. She wondered if the pirates would spare her, or kill her for the sport. There was no doubt she'd be raped. She promised herself not to give up without a fight. But what could she do? She had no weapon.

The smoke outside was very thick and some of it was coming in the broken portholes. It was practically dusk. One fishing boat was on fire. The shouting seemed more and more desperate. Kelly crawled from one side of the room to the other, cutting her hands on the broken glass, trying to decide where she was safest.

Suddenly Bart came rushing down the stairs, pistol in hand. He made his way over to her. Without a word, he grasped her wrist and started pulling her back toward the stairway.

"Where are we going?" she gasped, stumbling behind him.

"Into the drink. We've lost. Our only chance is to go over the side."

Kelly dragged him to a stop, pulling on his wrist with both hands. "What about the others?" she asked. The Englishman and the Aussie couple were under a table in the corner, their arms over their heads.

"I'll come back for them, but I may not be able to save everyone," he said, his breathing labored. Perspiration poured down his face. His shirt was soaked. He smelled of beer and sweat and blood, though she could see no wound on him. His arm, though, was stained red—probably by someone else's blood. She swallowed hard, fighting down her panic. If she didn't make the right choice now, it could cost her her life.

Kelly looked into Bart Monday's eyes, not knowing whether she should trust him, not knowing whether she had a choice. Not once had the captain or any crewman come to them, except to die. Bart was the only one who'd shown concern.

Panic-stricken, Kelly followed him up the stairs. He still had hold of her wrist. His gun hand was poised at his cheek, the hammer cocked. When they got to the top of the stairs, he stopped and looked back at her.

"Do you swim well?"

She nodded.

"You may have to swim a couple of miles in the dark."

"Whatever I have to do, I'll do," she managed, her heart pounding so hard it was difficult to breathe.

"There are sharks," he said, "but if you stay here, I think it'll be much worse."

She looked at him desperately, beseeching him to help her. Monday read the message in her eyes. He understood. She didn't know how she knew that, but she did. He pulled her up the last step and put his arm around her shoulders. She started shaking her head, a feeling of helplessness coming over her.

"You can do it, Kelly," he said through his teeth. His tone was almost angry. "You can do it. Just do as I say."

There was an intense volley of fire, but it sounded as if it was coming from the far side of the boat. Monday stuck his head out and glanced quickly in each direction. Then he pulled back inside. His grip on her hadn't relaxed.

"Listen carefully," he said over the din. "One of the pirate boats is right against us. I think everybody on it is dead. When I give you the word, go over the side. Don't swim out in the open because someone might see you. Get on the far side of the boat and wait there until dark. Then swim for the island. It's your only hope."

"What about you?"

"I'll go back for the others. But don't wait for me. If I'm not there in ten minutes, start swimming whenever you think you can get away without being seen."

"I want to stay with you." A sob welled in her throat.

"No," he insisted. "Go now, while you still can."

Bart stuck his head out to make sure the coast was clear. Then he pulled her to the railing.

"Go on over!"

He gave her a shove, and that sent a shot of adrenaline into her. Kelly slipped off her sandals, climbed to the top of the railing, swung her legs over it and plunged in. Then she bobbed to the surface and looked up. Bart Monday gave her the thumbs-up, smiled and disappeared.

The cool water sobered her. The salt stung the tiny cuts in her hands. Kelly told herself she ought to analyze the situation dispassionately, like a lawyer. Which was worse, the pirates or the sharks? In the end she decided Bart was right. She was better off in the water.

The air exploded with gunfire. The boat bumped against the hull of the *Ban Don*. She began working her way around it. The wood smelled fishy, stronger than the sea. By the time she got to the far side of the boat, the gunfire had ceased. There was still an occasional shout, but Kelly sensed the battle had ended.

She heard an agonized moan from someone in the fishing boat. She hoped he was in bad enough shape that he could no longer pose a threat. After a minute she started to wonder what had happened to Bart and the other passengers. Would the pirates search for her? They'd seen her earlier, so they might. Bart was right, their only chance was to swim to the island.

There were more shouts, followed by a woman's scream. Then there were three or four shots. Kelly wondered if the others had been executed. Terror filled her.

She clung to the rudder as she searched the horizon, hoping she'd have the strength to make it to the island. The dark profile of the land was still visible. Should she start swimming now? Had ten minutes passed?

Desperation welled in her as she envisioned herself drowning or being eaten by sharks. She took a deep breath. Panic was her worst enemy. Panic and the pirates. She examined her cut palms. The bleeding had stopped, but she wasn't sure if there had been enough blood to attract sharks. Then she heard a faint sound. Her heart nearly stopped, but she made herself look around the side of the boat. A face was moving toward her. It was Bart Monday.

"I couldn't get the others out," he whispered when he came up beside her. Above them, on the *Ban Don,* they could hear the shouts and cheers of the victors. "The old couple refused to budge," Bart went on. "Somebody shot the English guy through a porthole. I barely made it out."

"What do we do now?"

"It looks like it's just me and you, baby. Feel like a moonlight swim?"

Kelly nodded. Anything he suggested, she'd have done. Right then Bart Monday was the most important person on earth.

The wounded man in the fishing boat groaned. Bart moved closer to her, slipping an arm around her waist. He held the rudder with his free hand. His lips were near her ear.

"You okay?"

She nodded again, though she didn't feel at all sure of herself.

"It'll take them a while to get organized, so we'd be smart to get out of here while we can."

"All right."

"But no fifty-yard freestyles. Do a nice quiet breast-stroke till we're a hundred yards out." He gave her a final squeeze. "Let's go."

Kelly began swimming as quietly as she could, wondering if a bullet would crash through the back of her skull at any moment. The thought terrified her. She didn't want to die out here in the middle of nowhere. But she knew that dwelling on death was not a good idea.

She forced herself to think of other things—the swimming lessons her parents had insisted she take before she even started kindergarten, the way her dad had held contests between her and her brother to see who could swim more laps. Skip had always won—he was older and bigger and stronger. Kelly gritted her teeth as she took a stroke, wishing she had his stamina now. Thank God she was in as good shape as she was. She needed to put as much distance between herself and the *Ban Don* as possible.

At first it was easy. Kelly felt she could swim a hundred miles. She had to rein her energies in, make certain she didn't kick too hard or splash. She could hear Bart's even breathing. She turned to look at him a time or two for re-assurance.

After a while she didn't have to hold herself back, but she was able to swim steadily. It seemed as though they'd gone much farther than a hundred yards. After another dozen strokes, she stopped to look back.

The *Ban Don* was some distance away, surrounded by the dark hulls of the fishing boats. Figures of a dozen men or more were moving over the flotilla. Even at that distance, an occasional shout of triumph could be heard.

"Do you think they killed the others?" she asked.

"Yes. Hopefully they spared the older lady any indignity before they did."

"God, they're beasts!" Kelly said bitterly. Now that she was far enough away to feel safer, her anger came to the fore.

They were treading water. Her arms began to tire. She could hear the increased pace of her breathing.

"How are you doing?" he asked.

"Okay. How much farther?"

"A hell of a long way, baby. Float on your back for a while. Rest your arms."

Kelly obediently rolled onto her back, filling her lungs and throwing her shoulders back. Her buoyancy in the salt water was good. She tried to relax her muscles, to tell herself she could do it, whatever it took.

"I'm no expert on sharks," Bart said, his head close to hers, "but they say the last thing to do is thrash around if one happens along. Turn sideways to appear as large as possible."

"Yes, I know."

"We'll vary our strokes. You set the pace. If you get exhausted, we'll do the dead man's float. Do you know how?"

Kelly nodded. "I'll be all right. The water's warm."

Bart put his hand under the back of her head to give her support. She regretted the unfriendly thoughts she'd first had about him.

"The next question," he said, "is whether or not you strip. The clothes could come in handy once we're ashore, but you've got to be able to get there. I'm taking off my shirt but keeping on my shorts. What do you want to do?"

Kelly's first impulse was to keep her clothes on, but she knew they would feel like a coat of mail soon. "I've still got my bikini on. Guess I'll take off the rest."

Getting stripped was a struggle. Bart helped, and when she was ready he suggested they swim freestyle. Kelly set off at an easy pace, keeping her strokes smooth. She routinely spent hours in the ocean at home. She reminded herself that shark attacks on humans were relatively rare. Time was her biggest enemy. Thank God she wasn't doing it alone!

After what seemed like a long time, they stopped to rest. Kelly tried to tread water, but when she lost her rhythm she took in a mouthful of water and coughed. Terrified that the pirates had heard her, she glanced back toward the *Ban Don.* Fortunately they were half a mile away. But when she looked at the island, she hardly saw a difference in its outline. Kelly felt a rush of pure panic. She was already tired. "How much farther?"

"A couple of miles, at least."

"Oh, Lord."

"Float on your back," he commanded. "After you rest for a minute, we'll do the backstroke. It'll be slower, but you'll be conserving energy."

Soon they were under way again. Several minutes later they shifted to the sidestroke. They stopped to rest again when they were about three quarters of a mile from the *Ban Don.*

"How are *you* doing?" she asked.

"Fine. Just a little out of shape is all."

"You're a good swimmer."

"I was a long-distance swimmer in my youth," he said, "but it's been a while."

Kelly wasn't sure whether being in the presence of an expert would make enough of a difference, but it did give her a bit more confidence. She knew he wouldn't be able to pull her along forever, though. Encouragement was the most he could offer.

"If I get into trouble, don't go down trying to save me," she said. "There's no point in both of us drowning."

He smiled as if amused. "If I'm going to end up on a deserted island, do you think I want to be alone?"

"It's not deserted, is it?"

"No, I don't think so. In fact, I think it's where the bad guys came from."

"You mean we're swimming back to their hideout!"

"The only other choice was the mainland, Kelly, and that's seventy-five or a hundred miles away. If you feel up to it, we can bypass the island and keep going."

"If I wasn't so damned tired, I'd laugh."

"Let's do the dead man's float for a while," he said.

"Yeah," she gasped. "Good practice for what lies ahead."

She took a deep breath and relaxed as best she could, floating facedown. When she needed a breath, she rolled her head to the side, taking in air while expending as little energy as possible. After several minutes her limbs had recovered some of their strength.

They resumed swimming again, varying their strokes, resting for a while, then swimming again. Kelly didn't want to let Bart down, but she was beginning to doubt she'd make it.

"Past the halfway point," Bart announced on a rest stop.

Only halfway? Her heart sank. "I don't think I can do it."

"Sure you can. Who knows, the fishermen's wives may have a stew waiting. We might get invited to dinner."

Kelly laughed in spite of herself. "Probably to be eaten ourselves."

"These guys are pirates, not cannibals."

"Let's get going," she said gamely. "Can't be late for dinner."

The next hour was sheer torture. By the end of it her arms and legs felt like lead. Once, while floating on her back, Bart towed her until he had to rest. It became impossible to do the crawl. The sidestroke, and lying on her back and kicking, was all she could manage. Even then, twenty or thirty strokes was the most she could do at one time.

The *Ban Don* became a small light on the silvery sea, though Ko Pong still seemed impossibly far away. Once Kelly went under. She came up choking, energized a little, if terrified. Bart held up her head as she sobbed.

"No more than half a mile, baby," he whispered. "Two lousy times around a track. You can make it."

She closed her eyes. The image that popped into her mind was of her goldfish when she was a child. When they became sick they'd float close to the surface, barely moving. She would rub their bellies to urge them back to health. It never worked. Kelly began sensing the inevitability of her own death.

Bart held her head now. He was treading water, supporting both of them. His breathing was labored. If he kept helping her, he wouldn't make it, either. That was becoming obvious.

"Go on," she gasped. "I can't do it."

Bart grabbed a fistful of her hair and yanked, sending a jolt of pain through her. "Yes, you can! Swim!"

Kelly tried again, but made almost no progress. When she stopped, Bart took her by the chin and held her face out of the water so she could see the island. There was enough moonlight to make out the green of the foliage. "There it is!" he said angrily. "Just there, Kelly. Don't stop now."

She rolled onto her back and began to flutter her feet. It felt as if she were swimming in molasses, but she kept on, knowing that at best she had only minutes left. One or two more attempts and there would be nothing left at all.

Every once in a while Bart would take her by the hair, or the base of the skull, and pull her along. Their progress was painfully slow. "Less than a hundred yards," he gasped after what seemed like another hour. "We're almost there."

For the first time since the halfway point, Kelly started to believe they would make it. She tried to listen for the surf, but she could hear nothing. She hoped there wouldn't be waves. Water near shore could be treacherous. Strong swimmers could drown within yards of land; she'd read that somewhere. How ironic that would be, to die virtually on the beach.

Suddenly she bumped against Bart. His arms went around her, and he lifted her six inches out of the water. "Bottom!" he exclaimed. "I'm standing on the bottom!"

Kelly managed to turn in his arms and look at the beach. It was only fifty yards away, and the water was practically flat all the way to the sand.

Her arms were around his neck as they waded toward shore. Soon it was shallow enough for her to stand. The sand between her toes felt like heaven. Bart half pulled, half dragged her ashore. Kelly was breathing hard, as much from excitement as exhaustion. She looked up at his face in the moonlight, knowing he'd saved her life.

"We made it!" she cried, pressing her face against his chest. "Thank God, we made it."

They dropped to the beach. Kelly was sprawled on her back, the sea lapping at her toes. Bart rolled onto his side, wrapping his arm around her. He drew his face close to hers. "You're all right, babe. The hard part's over."

He was gazing down at her, his damp lashes glistening in the moonlight. The air felt cool, but Bart was warm by comparison. She looked into his eyes.

"You saved my life," she murmured.

He leaned over and kissed the corner of her mouth. Kelly didn't know the man from Adam, but it didn't matter. She owed him her very existence. She lifted her rubbery arms and put them around his neck. Bart kissed her mouth. His lips tasted salty, swollen and dry. He pressed his face against hers and hugged her as she hugged him.

"Thank you," she whispered.

After a long time Bart sat up and surveyed the beach. "I don't see any signs of habitation," he said. "I guess we landed on a remote stretch."

Kelly managed to sit up as well, her strength returning a lot more quickly than she would have thought. "Do you think we'll be safe?" she asked, scanning the beach.

"I have no idea. All I know about this island is that it was a jumping-off point for the fishermen. I don't even know if it's inhabited by a regular population."

"What will we do?"

"Find a place to bed down for the night. It can get cool when you're practically naked."

His comment made Kelly aware of how cold she was. She knew that weakness had made her vulnerable to exposure. She shivered. "Now I wish I had my clothes."

"If you hadn't taken them off, you'd be at the bottom of the gulf. Besides," he said, pinching her chin, "you look damn good in a bikini."

Kelly looked out to sea. There were no lights on the horizon, no sign of the *Ban Don*. "Where's the ship?"

"They may have scuttled her. It would be the best way of destroying any evidence."

"Will someone still look for us?"

"I hope so. With no ship adrift, the authorities might look farther afield. Maybe they'll search the island." Bart got to his feet, shaking the stiffness from his legs. "Do you think you can walk?"

Kelly struggled to her feet. Her legs could barely support her weight. Bart put his arm around her and she leaned heavily against him. His body was warmer than hers, and it felt good to be next to him. He gestured toward the dark vegetation bordering the beach. "Let's see what we can find in there."

They trudged through the sand.

"Which is more you, Kelly, Robinson Crusoe or Friday?"

She turned to look at him. She was feeling stronger now. "Definitely Robinson Crusoe."

Bart Monday chuckled. "I'm definitely Robinson Crusoe, too." He kissed her temple. "I think ours is going to be an interesting relationship."

KELLY SAT DOWN, her back against a palm tree, while Bart gathered fronds to construct a shelter. They were twenty yards from the beach. She could see the white sand in the moonlight. Her mind was turning. Were the pirates still a danger? Would they be rescued? How long would she be in the jungle with a man she didn't know, but to whom she already owed her life?

She was hugging herself, shivering, when Bart returned with an armful of palm fronds. He dropped beside her, exhausted.

"I'm not up to building a tree house tonight," he said. "But I can probably manage a nest. Will that do?"

"Sure," she said wearily. "I don't care about anything as long as there aren't any snakes."

"Which lie do you want to hear—that there aren't snakes on this island, or that they're allergic to palm fronds?"

She shivered. "Don't even talk about it."

Bart winked. "I guess I'd better get to work if we're going to have our dream home ready by bedtime."

Kelly smiled. His jokes had kept her spirits up, maybe even kept her alive. He was a wonderful friend, and she still didn't know a thing about him.

Bart got to his feet. He was standing arms akimbo, his chest visible in the moonlight that filtered through the trees. He raised one hand to his chin and pointed with the other. "What do you think? Bedroom wing on the north or east side? You like morning sun?"

Kelly laughed. "You're not in the import-export business, Bart Monday. You're a stand-up comedian."

He dropped to his knees. "My football coach claimed life was easier if you looked at the bright side." He began digging in the sand. In minutes he had hollowed out a space the size of a single bed. Taking some of the fronds, he lined the hole, then piled the remaining fronds at the edge.

"Want to try the bed? It's firm. I can promise you that."

Kelly crawled into the nest and stretched out.

Bart took some of the extra fronds and covered her. Then he sat back on his heels, resting his hands on his hips. "It won't be as cozy as Granny's down comforter, but it'll hold in some of your body heat."

She sighed. "It's wonderful."

Bart crawled in beside her, pulling the remaining branches over himself. His side was against hers, from her ankles to her shoulders. His body heat felt wonderful. He put an arm and a leg over her.

"Logs burn better when they touch," he whispered. "Give me a hug and we'll warm up."

Kelly rolled into his arms, relishing his warmth. He held her close, rubbing her shoulders and back, warming her. She felt herself relax into his embrace as she snuggled into the crook of his neck. The stubble of his beard rubbed against her temple, but his long, hard body was a comfort. Her arms and legs grew heavy, and before she knew it, she felt herself sinking toward sleep.

CHAPTER THREE

WHEN SHE AWAKENED, the moon was directly overhead, its beams filtering through the trees. Cool air was coming from the side where Bart had been. Kelly sat up cautiously and looked around. She spotted him, crouched behind a palm tree five yards away, staring out at the beach.

"Bart?"

"Shh." He put his finger to his lips and turned back toward the water.

The wind had come up, and with it the waves. Kelly heard them tumbling onto the beach. She figured Bart had to be looking at something besides the water, but she couldn't see what, so she lay back down. After several more minutes Bart crept back to the nest. His skin was cool as he maneuvered himself near her.

"What was it?" she whispered.

"A couple of men walking up the beach. They're gone now."

"Pirates?"

"I don't know. Neither of them had a peg leg or a parrot on his shoulder."

Kelly groaned, knowing it was a serious matter despite his attempt at humor. "Do you think they know we're on the island?"

"Could be."

"Well, they didn't find us on the *Ban Don,* and they must have seen us before the shooting started."

"Several of them saw me during the firefight, that's for sure. A couple of them might even still be alive to discuss it, although they can't know we made it to shore."

Kelly remembered the dead crewmen and the Australian woman's scream. The carnage. She trembled at the horror of it.

"Cold?"

"No."

Bart put his arm across her body anyway and massaged her shoulder. She recalled the way he'd made her jump into the drink, and how he'd yanked her hair to make her swim. He could be hard, but she owed her life to that fact.

Her senses were much sharper now. Time and rest had helped to put the situation into perspective. She felt close to him, but that was purely a product of the circumstances. Except for the few words they had exchanged on the boat, and the strange intimacy of their death-defying swim, Bart Monday was a stranger, an unknown quantity. Yet she was clinging to him, practically naked.

His hand felt warm and strong. He seemed to enjoy touching her. Kelly breathed in his now familiar scent and snuggled still closer. Bart immediately began stroking her, more sexually than before. The stubble on his chin rubbed against her shoulder; she felt his warm breath on her skin. She soon became aware of his hard edges, the rough bone and muscle. Her body responded, but she told herself that it was just instinctive and didn't mean a thing. Confused by the jumble of emotions inside her, she gently pushed his hand away.

"Do you think someone will come tomorrow to rescue us?" she whispered, wanting to distract him.

"Maybe."

"I hope they don't give us up for dead. My God...what would we do?"

Bart rolled onto his back and gazed at the stars. "Survive as best we can. Sooner or later we'll have to take a chance that someone around here is friendly. Most Thais are law-abiding and peaceful. The trick will be knowing who to trust."

"How can we tell?"

"Things will look different by the light of day. We'll sort it out. Don't worry."

Kelly told herself she ought to concentrate on their plight, but it wasn't easy. She liked it when he touched her, and she'd started thinking of him in sexual terms. That wasn't good.

"I'm worried," she whispered, aware of the need to keep her mind, as well as his, on other things.

Bart leaned over and kissed her forehead in a friendly sort of way. Kelly searched his eyes as his hand trailed down her arm, taking her fingers and toying with them. His touch wasn't blatantly sexual, yet there was something terribly intimate about it. She felt a sharp twinge of uncertainty.

"I owe you a great deal," she whispered, "but I hope you don't misunderstand my gratitude."

He propped himself up on his elbow. She could see his smile.

"What are we talking about? Sex?"

She tensed, not expecting the directness.

"Don't worry," he said. "I'm not one to trade on that sort of debt. I just thought there might be mutual interest."

"I don't mean to sound ungrateful, but I'm not here by choice, Bart."

"We're in the same boat, honey. I just happen to be the type who likes to make the best of a bad situation."

She bristled instinctively. "Too bad you didn't have the opportunity to save two or three other women," she huffed. "At least that way you'd have had a choice."

He chuckled. "I'm content with you."

"Is that why you saved me—to have a companion when you got to shore?"

"It's warmer than being alone."

"I'm serious." Her voice had a definite edge.

Bart traced her lower lip with his index finger. "Do you want me to say something polite and socially acceptable, or do you want the truth?"

Kelly wasn't sure she wanted to hear what he had to say, but she didn't want to be a coward, either. "Yes. Tell me the truth."

"I was attracted to you the moment I saw you."

"And that's why you saved my life? Because you were attracted to me?"

"How noble do you want me to sound?"

Though his face was obscured, Kelly could feel his eyes on her. "God, what a strange conversation. You'd think we were in a pickup bar."

"The trouble is, you don't know how to go with the flow."

Kelly shut her eyes and groaned. He sounded just like her mother! That's all she needed—someone who thought an attack by pirates was a big adventure! Next he'd be telling her that surviving on this godforsaken island would be fun.

He touched her face, making her look at him. "I'm not pretending we're in a pickup bar, Kelly. I'm only doing what I feel, and telling you the truth."

His words sent another wave of caution through her. She wasn't used to direct talk about desire, sexual or otherwise. The men she'd dated had always been the serious sort who were interested in ideas—men who cared about their careers and the things they could accomplish. She'd always hated the Casanova types and had stayed clear of them.

Kelly considered Duncan Van de Meer the quintessence of her kind of man. He was serious, sophisticated, hardworking, clear thinking and mature. Duncan had been married when they met. And though she'd been attracted to his mind from the very first, she hadn't thought of him in romantic terms at all. Then, about a year ago, after he'd filed for divorce, he had taken her to lunch and confessed that he'd been halfway in love with her for months.

That had been a real shocker because she'd never so much as picked up on a hint of his feelings. But she was flattered. After all, he was a senior partner in the firm, well respected in legal circles and attractive—rather distinguished looking, actually. Lots of women would kill for a man like that, and he wanted *her!*

She'd been cautious at first. They'd played cat and mouse for weeks, neither willing to move toward intimacy. They were both conservative, used to hiding their true feelings. Their love had developed slowly, as the important kind did. In time, it became obvious that with all they had in common, they were destined to be together.

Now here she was, marooned on a tropical island in the Gulf of Siam with a scruffy, albeit charming, rogue by the name of Bart Monday. Embarrassing as it was to admit, she did feel a certain animal attraction to the guy. But so what? Logic told her there was no rational basis for feelings like that. Besides, the absolute last thing she wanted was to have unprotected sex, which could easily happen if she let herself get carried away.

As she thought about it, her vulnerability was undoubtedly a blessing in disguise—it would force her to use her head. She didn't need to use birth control with Duncan.

He'd had a vasectomy, and neither of them had even considered the possibility of sleeping with anyone else.

But then, when a person was lucky to be alive at all, things like birth control didn't seem too important. And yet, she couldn't dismiss the danger—not when isolated with a virile man who managed to set off a few sparks every time he touched her. She scooted away a few inches to put some distance between them.

"Going with the flow might be your way of living," she said, her tone reflecting the defensiveness of her thinking, "but it's not mine."

"What are you saying, that you never do anything spontaneously?"

"I'm not repressed, if that's what you're suggesting."

Bart fiddled with a lock of her hair. She shuddered, feeling an unexpected desire to press against him. They were facing each other, a few inches apart. He ran the back of his fingers over her cheek.

"Are you trying to seduce me?" she asked, figuring directness was called for.

"I'm not *trying* to do anything."

"I know," she said, "you're just going with the flow."

"Like it or not, Kelly, we're in a kind of a state of nature here."

"That doesn't mean we have to act like animals, does it?" Her words were brave, but even as she said them, her instincts were pulling her in the opposite direction. She couldn't help wondering if the passion her mother was always harping about wasn't the very thing she was feeling now.

Bart reached out and caressed the back of her neck, making the short hairs stand on end. Her heart began to lope, and she knew it would be up to her to stop him. But in the next instant he was drawing her close against him, her words evidently having had absolutely no effect on him. He was very strong, and that was somewhat frightening. But also exciting.

She didn't move when he brushed his lips against the corner of her mouth, tantalizing her. She wanted to kiss him back, but she told herself that would send the wrong signal. Instead she put her hand on his chest, intending to push him away. But it didn't work that way. Once she touched him, she didn't want to stop. She slowly drew her fingers down through the mat of hair, satisfying an uncontrollable urge.

Bart kissed her deeply then, and she kissed him back. Their tongues entwined and he took her derriere in his hand, drawing her against him until she could feel his swollen sex. She lifted her hand and sank her fingers into his tangled mass of hair. Desire roared through her and she felt herself letting go. She felt reckless, and it shocked her.

He peeled off the top of her suit and took one of her nipples into his mouth, sucking on it. Kelly arched against him. When he gently bit her, she felt herself grow moist. She knew it was insane, but she didn't care. Soon the bottom of her suit was off. Bart removed his khaki shorts and they were both naked, the moon casting mottled patches of light on their skin.

Bart kissed her, probing her with his fingers, rhythmically massaging her until she was ready. As soon as she felt a hot rush of liquid between her legs, he rolled on top of her, then they rolled again until she was over him, her breasts touching his broad, downy chest. He pulled her face against his and she bit his lip, hard enough that she could taste his blood. Bart kissed her even harder.

Then he moved on top of her again. She opened her legs and he guided his penis into her. She gasped. For an instant she grew rigid. Then she arched, driving him deeper.

At first he moved slowly, but Kelly didn't want to play at lovemaking. She wanted it all, and she wanted it now.

She urged him to move faster, thrust harder, get deeper. The pleasure was too great for her to control, so she went with it. She heaved against him, crying out.

Bart covered her mouth with his hand, but nothing could stifle her orgasm. She cried out again, her scream dying in his palm. When he collapsed onto her, she realized that he, too, had come. She began gasping for air and he lifted himself slightly, allowing her lungs to fill.

Her head rolled to the side and she moaned. "God..."

He pressed his lips against her neck. "I'm glad you didn't decide to pass this up."

She kissed his face, tasting his salty skin. "Don't get arrogant, Mr. Monday. I haven't decided how I feel about this yet."

"Let's hope you feel as good about it as I do."

She shook her head, though it was more in admonition to herself than to him. For a long time he held her. Then they uncoupled and rolled to their sides. Kelly listened to the pounding surf for several minutes, wondering what in the hell she'd done.

"I think I've decided," she finally said, pushing her damp hair off her forehead.

"Decided what?"

"How I feel. I can't believe we did it. My God, I don't even know you, Bart."

"It's too early to feel guilty," he murmured. "Enjoy it."

Kelly closed her eyes, wondering if he was right. No power on earth could change the fact that they'd made love. Regrets were a waste of time.

A soft breeze drifted over them. She felt the caress of the air, the soothing warmth of Bart's body. After what seemed like a long, long while, he began moving his hands over her again. Eventually he caressed her nub. She was soon throbbing, and when she touched his penis, she found him hard, ready.

This time he was tender, cradling her in his arms as he undulated. And when her climax came, he covered her mouth with his lips. Afterward, Kelly lay still, aware of the pounding of his heart. She had submitted, given herself without thought to the consequences. It seemed impossible that she had done such a thing, yet a tiny voice deep inside her asked how she could have possibly done otherwise.

KELLY WAS AWAKENED by the warmth of the sun and the buzzing of flies around her salty, parched lips. Bart wasn't next to her but she felt his presence. Sitting up abruptly, the palm fronds falling from her body, she saw him seated nearby, leaning against a tree. He was munching a piece of fruit, a grin creeping across his grizzled face. And he was naked.

"Hungry?" he asked, looking at her breasts.

Kelly folded her arms over her chest, inspiring an even wider smile.

"I foraged for breakfast." He picked up a couple of pieces of fruit. "Here's yours."

The desperation of their situation suddenly was all too clear. "I guess it wasn't a dream."

He wiped a trace of juice from the corner of his mouth. "Damned good one if it was."

She shivered in remembrance. "All those people being killed? The boat sunk? You call that good?"

"I was thinking of later."

Kelly looked away. The top of her bikini, caked with sand, lay beside the makeshift bed. She thought of her mother giving the suit to her the night she'd come over to help her pack. Over the years she'd worn hundreds of her mother's designs—some had been put into mass production later, others, like this one, were one of a kind.

Kelly searched for the bottom of the suit. She found it at her feet, under a palm frond and half-covered with sand.

"So, how do you feel?" Bart asked.

She didn't know quite what he meant, but on the off chance he was referring to the sex, she decided to ignore the question. Instead, her suit in hand, she sauntered into the undergrowth, certain his eyes were following her.

Once out of his sight, she did what she could to make herself presentable. She'd have killed for a bathroom, or even running water. Her hair, too, was caked with sand. Though her palms were still tender, she brushed herself off as best she could, bending over so that the sand fell from her hair onto the broad leaves of the knee-high plants.

After she'd gotten as clean as she could, she started to work on her suit. It looked pathetic, but it was all she had. When she was dressed, she made her way back. Bart was still seated at his tree, now wearing his shorts.

Smiling up at her, he tossed her the fruit. *"Bon appétit."*

It appeared to be some sort of mango. "What is this?"

"It's edible, that's about all I can tell you."

She wiped it with her hand before biting into it. The tangy flavor was unusual but tasty. She was more hungry than she had realized. Bart was looking her over.

"Come and sit down," he said.

Kelly plopped down, just out of his reach. Relishing her fruit, she continued to eat, regarding Bart between bites. "What happens next?"

"I'm not sure."

She smiled. "You got me into this. I expect you to get me out."

"It wouldn't be hard getting myself out, but you pose a more formidable problem."

"Why?"

"I could probably trade you straight across for a boat—maybe one with a motor."

"Thanks loads. Is that why you saved me? To have a bargaining chip?"

"Yeah, but I thought I'd use you myself first."

"If that's a snide reference to last night, you can forget it, Mr. Monday. It was an aberration."

His grin turned crooked. "Right. You aren't that kind of girl."

Put that way, he made her sound like a fool, and a trite fool at that. "My gratitude got the best of me," she said finally.

Bart picked up a twig and tossed it away. "We're square, so I guess you don't have to worry."

She was miffed by his cavalier attitude but wasn't going to give him the satisfaction of showing it. "Seriously, what are we going to do?"

"There was a plane out over the sea soon after dawn. It was pretty far out, but judging the pattern it was flying, it was a search craft."

"And it went away?"

"Yes, after half an hour."

She felt distressed. "Does that mean they've abandoned us?"

"That's what concerns me. I don't know if it was a cursory first attempt or if that was the whole show."

"Surely they'd make more of an effort."

"Who knows? They might have spotted debris and decided that was it, the entire crew and passengers lost. Or a whole flotilla might show up later. I'm afraid I'm not very knowledgeable about these things."

"Didn't the plane ever come near the island? They'd have to assume any survivors would head this way."

"You'd think so."

Kelly felt a well of frustration.

"Wasn't there a way for you to get their attention?"

"They were fairly far out. And I couldn't risk bringing the whole island down on us. Anyway, we need a surface craft to get out of here."

She almost asked if one would come, but that was stupid—he had no more way of knowing than she. So she finished eating and licked the last of the sticky juice from her fingers. "Great. Just great."

He smiled. "Don't despair. We've got each other."

She knew what he was thinking—it was written all over his face. She felt the color rise in her cheeks as he stared at her. "You need a shave," she said flatly.

"You could use a shampoo."

She brushed back her hair. "I know. I'm stiff and sore and I feel like hell. I don't suppose there's a stream or something where I could bathe."

"Not that I know of, but it might be a good idea to explore. At least that way we'll know what we're up against." Bart got to his feet. "You should probably stay here."

Pure panic shot through her. "What if something happens to you? I'd rather go along."

"The chances of being discovered are greater if we're out and about. If I don't come back, you'll know I'm in somebody's cooking pot."

"Thanks. That makes me feel better."

He stepped over and tousled her hair. "You aren't attached to me already, are you, babe?"

Kelly looked up at him. "You saved me, Bart. I won't forget that."

He extended his hand and, when she took it, he pulled her to her feet, putting his arms around her waist. "I'd hoped you'd remember something else."

Despite the grizzled beard, the dirt and sand, Bart and his golden eyes were damned appealing. She felt the first stirring of desire. Images of their lovemaking tumbled through her mind. Pulling her against him, he kissed her chin.

"Last night was one of the best I've ever had," he said.

She shrugged, trying to feign indifference. "It was the romance of the situation."

"No, I think it was you." He kissed her mouth.

After submitting for a moment, she pulled away. "I think we'd better not get into any bad habits," she said, managing to twist from his arms.

"What's bad about it?"

She let out a long sigh. "I made love last night without protection. I don't want to repeat my mistake."

"Maybe while I'm scouting around I'll spot a drugstore."

She leaned against a palm some distance from him. "Very funny."

"You only live once."

"Men wouldn't talk that way if they had to put in nine months carrying a child."

"Well, I didn't know. I assumed you were—"

"Well, I'm not," she interrupted. "Under the circumstances, I think one round of Russian roulette is enough."

Bart laughed. "It was two rounds, as I recall."

Suddenly they heard a shout from the beach. They spun around and saw three men in fishermen's clothing at the water's edge. Two of them had automatic rifles strapped to their backs. They were examining the footprints that led through the sand to where they were hiding.

"Damn," Bart said, crouching down. "I was so excited about seeing the plane I didn't even think about leaving tracks." He signaled for her to get down. "They're coming this way," he whispered. "It's time for us to get the hell out of here."

CHAPTER FOUR

BART LED THE WAY through the undergrowth, trying to make as little noise as possible. Damn, how could he have been so stupid as to leave tracks in the sand? It was a rookie mistake, and he hoped to God it would be his last. He wasn't only responsible for his own skin now, he had to think about Kelly.

They'd gone nearly fifty yards when they heard voices. He crouched again, pulling her with him. "I think they've discovered our camp," he whispered.

"Will they come after us?"

"I don't think they've spotted us yet. But we can't outrun them without shoes. Let's wait and see what happens."

He watched her face fall. He'd been pleased that morning when she'd sparred with him. It would be important to keep up their spirits, especially if they were there for the long haul. But she was no fool and she had to realize their situation was getting more desperate by the hour.

Trouble was, he was in a real quandary. Even being rescued could be dangerous—for him. He might be able to handle the Thai navy or coast guard without arousing suspicion, but he might not. As long as he could stay clear of the police, he'd be all right. But getting rescued at all was beginning to look problematical. They were faced with Hobson's choice: if they stayed near the beach to try to signal a search plane, they ran the risk of attracting the attention of the pirates.

It almost looked as if he'd have been better off staying on Ko Samui—at least there all he had to worry about were cops. But on second thought, how could he trade anything for last night with Kelly? She'd been pure heaven, a once-in-a-lifetime experience. No, some things in life were simply too precious to miss.

The voices were clearer now and more animated. He listened closely. Kelly watched him, searching his face for reassurance. When the voices died down, and the only sound was the chatter of the birds, she asked what they'd said.

"I couldn't hear very well, but my impression was they think someone from the ship made it ashore. I don't think they realize there are two of us. So even if they manage to capture me, they may not know to look for you."

"What'll we do?"

"We've got to scout around, see if there may be someone on the island who will help us."

"What do you suppose the chances are?"

"Your guess is as good as mine."

He changed their course so that they were walking parallel to the perimeter of the island. He looked back regularly to make sure she was able to keep up all right. She moved stiffly, which he could sympathize with because he was feeling the aftereffects of the swim himself. At least the soles of her feet were tough enough for a walk in the jungle. Probably from walking on the beach in Hawaii.

It was a miracle she'd made it this far. He'd known after one look at her in that skimpy blue-and-gold bikini that she was in great shape, but even knowing she was a swimmer he hadn't given her better than a fifty-fifty chance of surviving the swim. She had grit. She'd pushed herself to the limit, and then she'd given it a little bit extra. Quite a woman!

He was getting a bit too far ahead and stopped to let her catch up, noticing how carefully she picked her way along. "How are you holding up? Feet okay?"

"Were you kidding about the snakes, Bart?"

"Oh, *that's* it."

"I do not like snakes."

He chuckled.

"It's not a joking matter."

He looked down at her bikini-clad body, remembering with delight their intimacy of the night before. Strangely enough, their predicament almost seemed unimportant. If a man had to play the survivalist game, Kelly Ronan was certainly the sort of companion he'd want along for the ride.

She obviously didn't appreciate his bemused expression. "Why do I get the feeling you aren't taking this as seriously as I am, Bart?" she said.

"I prefer to look at the bright side of things."

"If there aren't any snakes on the bright side, I'll join you."

They resumed their trek. In places where the vegetation wasn't so dense, he let her take the lead. In thirty minutes, by moving steadily, they'd gone half a mile. It was hot. Both of them were perspiring. He was following her, watching a drop of perspiration slide down the indentation of her spine, headed toward her bikini bottom, when she stopped abruptly and turned on a dime, crashing right into him. If he hadn't stood his ground she'd have gone right through him.

"Snake," she wheezed, her voice laced with terror. It was all she said.

He looked over her shoulder and saw a small serpent glide into the foliage. He bit the inside of his cheek to keep from smiling. He put an arm around her waist and pulled her closer. "It's gone now."

She gave a tentative glance over her shoulder and visibly relaxed when she saw no sign of the snake. "God," she moaned, "I don't know which is worse. This or getting captured."

"Better the devil you know," he said.

They moved on. A bit later they found more fruit, but the taste was so bitter they didn't eat it. He wasn't too concerned about that. They'd found edible fruit once, they would again. The real problem was water. When he heard a gurgling sound from the jungle up ahead, he let out a sigh of relief.

"Is that what I think it is?" Kelly asked excitedly.

"Sounds like a stream to me."

A dozen more yards and they came to a rivulet. Nearby was a small pool that was covered with some sort of film and seemingly millions of insects.

"Do you think we dare drink it?"

"It's a cinch it's not full of industrial pollutants, but let's wait and see if we can find moving water."

They followed the rivulet upstream, away from the beach. Before long they heard the sound of a waterfall. They headed up a ravine to a place where the stream dropped over a four-foot ledge into a clear pool that looked to be two or three feet deep.

Kelly rushed to the edge of the pool. "I'm going to drink this," she announced. "I don't care what happens." She fell to her knees and began scooping water into her mouth.

He knelt beside her and took a drink. It tasted vaguely of vegetation but was otherwise all right. When he'd drunk his fill he wiped his brow and cheeks with his wet hand. It felt cool and refreshing.

"Can I bathe?" she asked.

"Sure, don't let me stop you."

She shot him a look of annoyance. "I guess it would be too much to expect you to leave, like a gentleman."

"I'm not a gentleman."

A large colorful bird flew overhead from one tree to another, cawing loudly.

"The jungle is full of eyes," he said sardonically.

"Right," she said. "What's one more beast?"

Kelly waded into the pool, trying to act indifferent to his presence. That made him smile. She removed her top as she went, flinging it onto the bank. Then she stepped out of the bottom of her suit and sank into the water. Without looking back at him, she tossed the bikini bottom over her shoulder, too.

When she sat down, the water came to her breasts, barely covering her nipples. He sighed. God, she was beautiful like that. Of course, if he told her that, she'd just get defensive.

He wondered then about her comment that morning. She'd sounded serious about not wanting to make love again, but she'd been eager enough last night. Twice. He'd have been ready for another round this morning if the fishermen hadn't shown up. But Kelly had been definite about not wanting to take risks. Was that an excuse? he wondered.

He wanted to ask about the man in her life. There had to be at least one. She was gorgeous and smart; she had courage and grit. He liked her sass even more than those long legs of hers, and that said a lot. No, there had to be a man in the picture somewhere.

He heard a rustling noise and looked up. Something was moving in the branches of a tree that hung over the waterfall. If it was what he thought it was, they might just have something to eat besides fruit. He started circling the pool, hoping to find a way onto the ledge by the waterfall.

He looked back and saw that Kelly was still bathing, oblivious to the fact that he'd left. She'd been rubbing water over her skin and dunking her head under the water to get the sand out of her hair. With luck, she wouldn't notice what he was doing. He was on the ledge, reaching for the branch, when she spoke.

"This is heaven, Bart," she said, apparently still ignorant of the fact he was no longer sitting on the shore. "You really ought to try it."

He didn't answer. Instead he inched a bit closer to the edge.

"Bart?" She turned around and, seeing that he was gone, called out again, an edge of panic in her voice. "Bart?"

"I'm up here, behind you," he said, realizing he had to keep her calm. "Don't worry about me."

"What are you doing?" She began looking around.

"You have heard of the giant Thai crocodiles that inhabit these remote islands, haven't you?" he asked.

"Very funny," she said.

"Just wanted to warn you," he said.

"Bart, where are you?" She hadn't yet looked up.

"Trying to be a gentleman. Just finish your bath, babe. I'll be with you in a minute."

She finally glanced up at the top of the falls and saw him on the ledge. From the corner of his eye he saw her flinch.

"For God's sake," he said, "whatever you do, don't scream."

The snake was almost within his grasp, but now that he was up close, he saw it was much bigger than he'd thought. And it was coiled tightly around the branch. It could be a struggle getting it loose.

"Oh, my God," Kelly said, apparently realizing what he was doing, "you aren't going to touch it!"

He reached for the snake, hoping to get it by the throat. "You want dinner tonight, don't you?"

"A snake? You've got to be mad! If that thing is poisonous and you die, I'm not going to feel sorry for you one bit."

He lunged, grabbing hold of it. The serpent hissed and writhed, jerking him around. It was much larger and stronger than he'd realized. The battle continued. Bart was being pulled to and fro when he lost his footing and went flying, landing in the pool with a tremendous splash. The water was deep enough to break his fall, but he hit bottom hard, and when he came up he found himself sitting a few feet from Kelly. Meanwhile, the snake beat a retreat into the foliage.

Kelly stared at him, as stunned as she was mortified. He'd recovered from his start and struck the water with the palm of his hand.

"Damn it to hell!" he shouted, angry and humiliated. He pushed his dripping hair out of his eyes.

She began laughing. "You got exactly what you deserved."

"That was your dinner!"

"Not *my* dinner."

"What do you want to do instead," he sputtered, "call Pierre's and reserve a table for two?"

"I kind of liked the fruit we had for breakfast."

Bart was annoyed by her teasing, but he knew he must have looked damned funny wrestling with that snake. He grinned and glanced down at her breasts. She noticed and crossed her arms over her chest. Her shyness amused him. It was rather endearing.

"Since I'm in the drink, I might as well bathe," he said. "You don't mind if I join you, do you?"

"It seems the crocodile thing was a joke, otherwise you wouldn't be sitting here so calmly, right?"

"Apparently this isn't one of the infested islands," he replied. "But I couldn't be sure until I saw you make it in without losing a leg."

She gave him a dirty look. "You were definitely right about not being a gentleman, Mr. Monday."

He unfastened his shorts, pulled them off and tossed them onto the bank. Then he scooted along the bottom until he was right next to her. "Do we know each other well enough to bathe together?" he asked.

"You are the most presumptuous man I've ever known," she replied, still hugging her chest.

"Why bother with pretense?"

"We may be in the jungle, but that's no reason to act like we belong here."

He put the palm of his hand on her knee. Kelly took it off. He gave her a woebegone look.

"You realize, of course, that if the engine of the boat hadn't broken down, I'd be back at my hotel by now, you and I wouldn't have spoken ten words and I'd already have forgotten you existed."

He took her jaw in his hand. "But that's not the way it worked out." He grinned. "Isn't fate wonderful?"

He leaned toward her, ever so slowly, giving her the opportunity to flee but confident she wouldn't. He knew the feminine mind well enough to distinguish pro forma resistance from the real thing.

Their lips touched and she didn't move. Then he kissed her hard, his tongue working into her mouth. For a moment Kelly struggled against the intimacy, but soon she stopped fighting him altogether.

When her tongue began probing his mouth in return, he cupped her breast. She moaned deep in her throat. He touched her inner thigh and she quivered.

Kelly pulled away from him then, squirming to the bank and onto the shore. She stretched out on her stomach, her feet still in the water. It was an invitation of sorts—at least, that's how he decided to take it.

He joined her, and within seconds he was running his hand down her back and over her bottom. She let him kiss her again. Soon he had her writhing under him.

As they made love on the grassy patch next to the pool, the birds kept up their chatter, making what they were doing seem a natural part of jungle life. Everything that had once mattered to him—running from the cops, escaping from the pirates—seemed irrelevant. The only thing he cared about was making her his.

When they had finished their lovemaking she clung to him as she had the night before. His heart was thumping. He was still inside her. If she was uncomfortable lying between him and the hard ground, she didn't show it. All she did was stroke his head. It struck him as curiously loving.

"Have you ever done this before?" she asked, running her fingers through his damp hair.

"You mean make love in the jungle?"

"I mean with a stranger, with somebody you didn't know." She paused. "Somebody decent, I mean."

He pulled his face back from hers and grinned. "Define your term."

She blushed, pushing him away. Bart rolled onto his back and laughed.

"Bastard," she said.

He laughed louder.

"I know why *you* did it," she said. "But I can't figure out why *I* did it."

"I'd like to think it's because I'm irresistible."

She looked at him. "I'd like to tell you you're an arrogant SOB, but I'm hardly in a position to do so."

"If it wasn't me, maybe it was the circumstances."

Another large red-and-green bird flew overhead, making a raucous sound. "Yes," she said, watching it, "you're probably right. It's the circumstances. God knows, you're not my type.''

Bart contemplated her, looking wounded.

"Don't tell me I hurt your feelings," she said.

"What would you have said if we'd gotten back to Ko Samui last night and I'd asked you to dinner?"

"I'd have turned you down."

He looked at her long and hard. "Definitely or only probably?"

"Does it matter?"

"Yes," he said, "of course it does."

Kelly rolled her eyes. "You men have the most fragile egos. All right, *probably*. There. Do you feel better?"

"Much."

"But even if I had gone to dinner with you, which is unlikely, it would've ended there. Consider this an accident of fate."

"So you're saying you'd have slept with anybody willing to save your life."

"No, of course not!"

Bart grinned again. "I'm special, but not too special. Suitable for the jungle, in other words."

Kelly turned red and looked away. Then she turned back, slugging him on the arm as hard as she could. "Men can be so insufferable about sex."

"What's his name, anyway?"

"Whose name?"

"The man back home. Unless you're ashamed to tell me."

"Ashamed?"

Bart shrugged. "Well, he wouldn't be pleased to know what's been going on, would he?"

She sat up, glaring at him. "You're really getting a kick out of this, aren't you? You act as though you're the only man on earth."

"At the moment, I am, babe."

Kelly pointed an accusing finger. "That's it, Mr. Know-it-all! I've had it. No more sex. The magic has definitely worn off. And stop calling me babe. I'm not your plaything."

"My dear Ms. Ronan, my intention isn't to offend you. I'm simply trying to keep things light. You know, of course, that we might be stuck on this island for a long time. Maybe for weeks or months. Who knows, maybe even for years. It won't pay to be at each other's throats."

"Don't be silly. Before long we're either going to be rescued or captured and killed by the pirates...if we don't starve to death first."

"Not if I choose a smaller snake next time."

Kelly glanced up at the branch over the falls. "I'm going to rinse out my suit and get dressed," she said as she crawled over to where her bikini was lying on the bank.

Squatting at the water's edge, she began to work the fabric in the water to get the sand and dirt out. He watched her, knowing she wasn't just another pretty girl. She was sharp as a tack and had sass galore. And she was beautiful, too, truly lovely.

He sighed. Kelly Ronan was soft curve and hard muscle. Tough and vulnerable. Strong, yet capable of submission. No, she wasn't just another pretty girl, she was very special.

"You know," he said, "if I live a hundred years, I'll never forget this image of you."

She glanced over her shoulder at him. "What image?"

"You there by the water, naked, with the jungle as a backdrop."

"I'm glad I please you," she said, returning to her wash.

"I'm serious. It stirs something elemental inside me."

"I've noticed. Animal lust."

He chuckled. "You don't seem immune."

"That's over now. I was serious. From now on this field trip is strictly business."

When he didn't reply, she looked back at him. He was on the ground, leaning back insouciantly, watching her. She wrung out the bottom of her suit and went to work on the top.

"Why can't people live like this always?" he said wistfully. "Be honest, isn't this better than the rat race at home?"

"Bart, I don't mean to disappoint you, but I'd give one of my toes for a bottle of shampoo."

"Come on, Kelly, where's your spirit of romance? Tell the truth. Haven't the past twenty-four hours been among the most exhilarating of your life?"

She rolled her eyes. "My God, you sound like my mother. I swear you do. She's a hopeless romantic, always ready for a big adventure. In my shoes, she'd be out dancing with the pirates. In a week she'd probably be their leader." She paused to wring out her suit. "Well, that's not me. This caveman stuff may appeal to you, but if by some strange twist of fate the bad guys went away, the good guys never rescued us and we did a Robinson Crusoe number here, I'll tell you what would happen. Within a few years I'd be a beat-up old hag, if not already dead from childbirth. You might find that romantic, but I don't."

Bart shook his head. She stood to put on her swimsuit. When she had it on she put her hands on her hips and continued. "Do you think it's an accident that women are the moving force behind civilization? If it was left to men, we'd still be in caves."

"I love you when you're angry," he said, knowing it was a cliché, but meaning it.

Kelly picked up a stick and threw it at him. He ducked, laughing. She picked up his shorts and tossed them to him. "You'd better get dressed."

"What? You aren't going to wash them for me? What kind of civilized woman are you?"

She shook her fist at him. "Not too civilized to give you a good pop, Mr. Monday."

"I can see now that man's first big mistake was agreeing to leave the cave. You women needed us then."

"Well, I need you now to get me off this damned island, if that assuages your ego."

"Will you be as nice to me in Bangkok as you are here?"

"You've already had your payment. In advance."

Smiling, Bart got up and took his shorts to the water. As he walked past Kelly, he patted her bottom. "You've got spirit, kid."

As he rinsed his shorts he heard chattering and looked up. There were a couple of small monkeys cavorting in the trees. Kelly saw them, too. She sighed audibly. "How are we ever going to get out of here, Bart?"

Her voice suddenly sounded so forlorn that he wanted to take her into his arms again. But it was a little too soon after her most recent lecture. He'd have to bide his time. "I've been thinking about it," he said. "If we don't find any friendly folks, we may have to steal a boat."

"You don't think the coast guard will come?"

"I don't know, and I'm not sure how long I'm willing to wait around and see. Anyway, searches at sea are usually brief. With the *Ban Don* sunk, there's not a lot of evidence of what happened out there."

"So what do we do now?"

"We find the enemy camp. And maybe something to eat."

"*We?*"

"You don't want to stay home in the cave, do you?" As he walked past her, he took her hand. "Come on, Jane, we've got an island to conquer."

CHAPTER FIVE

THE VILLAGE WAS NOT FAR from where the stream emptied into the sea and was less than half a mile from the waterfall. Bart and Kelly looked the place over from the edge of the jungle.

"What do you think?" she whispered, her chin resting on his shoulder.

"It looks temporary to me."

Kelly had to agree. There were no more than ten or twelve huts made of wood with corrugated steel roofs. There were a few men lounging about, smoking or sleeping in hammocks, but no women or children, no animals other than one or two mangy dogs.

"If I had to guess," Bart said, "that's a skeleton crew. The rest are probably out fishing or hiding from the authorities."

"Why do you say that?"

"Right before the fireworks started yesterday, I talked to a crewman. He said Ko Pong was mainly a way station for fishermen based elsewhere. I didn't ask if anyone lived here permanently. Now I'm sorry I didn't."

As he talked, Kelly noticed a plane out at sea, just above the horizon. "Bart, over there!" She pointed at the plane.

"Looks like the one I saw this morning," he said. "They're probably giving the search a last shot. It might even mean that surface craft are on the way. I'm not sure how these things work. I'm not a sailor."

"What *are* you?"

"Hey, look," he said, ignoring the question, "the plane's changed course. It's coming toward the island."

"About time."

"It's not going to see us hiding in the jungle."

"What should we do, run out onto the beach?"

"That would be fine if we could be sure it would spot us and there was a boat nearby to pick us up. The chances of our fishing buddies seeing us are a hell of a lot greater."

She groaned. "You're making it sound hopeless."

"If we're getting off this island, sweetheart, I think we'll have to do it ourselves."

They fell silent as the search plane came very near the island. The men down at the village noticed the aircraft and began stirring. They could hear shouts as those asleep were being routed inside the huts. Even the dogs were called in.

"These must be some of the boys who hit the *Ban Don,*" Bart said, "because they obviously don't want their presence known."

"Hell," Kelly said, "everybody's hiding from everybody else."

"It's a cruel world, my dear."

She sat on the ground, discouraged. "You and your damned philosophizing. All I want from life is a simple meal, a dress to cover my body and a pillow for my head. Is that asking too much?"

"No, but we're in the jungle. To survive, you've got to go get what you want."

Kelly rubbed her raw skin. "I'm tired, I'm hungry, I'm thirsty and I want to go home."

Bart tousled her short, unkempt hair. "I'll do my best."

The plane was close to the island now. It changed course again and began flying along the beach, disappearing from sight. Several moments later it roared directly overhead.

"So close and yet so far," Bart mumbled.

Kelly felt as though she could cry. "I hope you have a plan," she said.

"I'm working on one."

The sound of the engine faded and the futility of their situation began to sink in. Anger welled inside her, but Kelly didn't know who to blame. It was hardly Bart's fault.

She heard a dog barking and got back up on her knees and peered through the foliage at the village. One of the mutts had wandered to the edge of the cluster of shanties. It was barking, its nose pointed in their direction.

"I think he may have picked up our scent," Bart said.

"You see," she replied, "soap is not just a luxury."

"Come on," he said, "let's get out of here."

They went deeper into the jungle. After a while the dog stopped barking. They heard the search plane pass by a time or two before it went away. Bart stopped on a little rise where the jungle thinned and sunlight filtered into the clearing. Though it seemed as if they were in the middle of nowhere, they were probably no more than a few hundred yards from the village.

"Let's make this our camp," he said. "The stream's not far. You can rest while I forage for food."

"I'll come with you."

"No, your job can be to fix us a shelter. I'll help gather some branches and fronds."

"Great. Think you can find some pipe so I can install a shower?"

Bart winked and began removing the worst of the vines and undergrowth. After twenty minutes they'd cleared most of the top of the knoll and had accumulated a supply of materials. Before he left, Bart erected some branches to serve as the main supports for a lean-to.

He gave her a hug. "I'll be home later with dinner, babe."

"One thing, Bart. Don't bring a snake back with you. I'd rather have dinner with the pirates than watch you eat a snake."

He pinched her nose and took off.

Kelly experimented with the palm fronds until she found a way to tie them to the crossbar with vines. It was hot working in the sun, and she was soon perspiring. She wondered if, after finishing the shelter, she might be able to find her way back to the pool without getting lost. By evening she would be more than ready for another drink and a refreshing dip.

Within an hour she'd done everything she could. Using the last of the fronds, she lined the floor of the shelter, then lay down in the shade to rest. She was very thirsty, but decided not to leave camp until Bart returned. He hadn't said how long he'd be gone, and she hadn't thought to ask. What if he was captured? What would she do then?

If he didn't return by evening, she could be fairly certain that something had happened to him—if not the pirates, perhaps an animal would get him. Losing Bart, and being stuck in the jungle alone, was too horrible to contemplate.

It felt good to lie down, even if the ground was hard. It was amazing how everything was relative. At this point a few creature comforts would be a major luxury. A half-rotten piece of fruit would be heaven.

Kelly tried to get her mind off the buzzing insects and the incessant cawing of the birds. She thought of home, her life in Honolulu, her beautiful condo with the view of Diamond Head, her friends, Duncan. No matter how hard she tried, Hawaii seemed a world apart, a place from another life. Her career—her life's work—seemed about as relevant as a book she'd read in college. Reality now was the jungle . . . and Bart.

That notion didn't overly please her. She forced herself to picture Duncan Van de Meer's face, to remember what it felt like when they made love. Nothing specific came to mind. Instead she thought of Bart Monday and the way he had taken her down at the pool.

How ironic. Here she was thinking about a man she hardly knew when Duncan had been the center of her life for months now! They had started their affair slowly, having lunch, going out to dinner, sailing off Oahu's shore on the weekend. Neither of them had wanted to rush into anything. Even after they'd begun seriously talking of marriage, they'd still taken their time—methodically exploring their options, trying to decide whether Kelly should stay with the firm after they married or if she'd be better off affiliating with another practice.

There had been so many factors to consider—Duncan's children, the attitude of the other members of the firm. They had quietly and carefully worked through their laundry list of problems. And when they had finally announced their engagement right before she'd left for this trip, their planning had paid off. Everyone had been supportive. Everyone except her mother.

The worst part was that Beryl was impossible to ignore. In intellectual terms Kelly could dismiss everything her mother had said, but the underlying accusations haunted her.

Was it possible, as her mother had suggested, that she wasn't being true to herself? Had she rationalized her relationship with Duncan?

If she hadn't gotten marooned on this damned island, she probably wouldn't have given the notion a second thought. But what frightened her was the possibility that she had more of her mother in her than she cared to admit. Her whole life she'd been fighting it, struggling to define an identity separate and apart from the rest of her

family. Her older brother, Skip, had no such compunc-
tion. He, like their mother, enjoyed life on the edge. They
both reveled in the thrill of an adventure.

Kelly was more like her father, who hadn't been the free
spirit his wife was, though he'd loved that quality in Beryl
and reveled in her crazy ways. "It's nice to be levelheaded," he'd told Kelly some months before his death,
"but it doesn't hurt to let loose and howl every once in a
while. Your mother has given me that opportunity in life.
It was one of her greatest gifts to me."

Kelly understood that on one level, but she'd never truly
internalized it. Maybe she feared that side of herself, the
part of her that wanted to accept a dare, go for broke. Regardless of her reasons, the fact remained that she'd chosen a different way to live.

When her aunt Pearl had died, leaving both her and Skip
a substantial amount of money, Kelly had taken her share
and used it to go to Harvard Law School. She'd wanted to
be an attorney for as long as she could remember. She'd
been idealistic back then and had fantasized about working for women's and children's rights, but she'd changed
her mind when she got an offer from a prestigious firm in
Honolulu. Witt and Van de Meer specialized in corporate
law. They did a lot of Pacific Rim business. Her common
sense told her it was the chance of a lifetime.

So she'd returned to Hawaii and used what was left of
her inheritance to buy her condo. It was beautiful, far nicer
than anything she'd have been able to afford otherwise.
The view of Diamond Head and the Pacific was to die for.
The walls, carpets, drapes and furniture were all white.
Nothing competed with the view. Her mother was forever
telling her that the place was too sterile and lacked char-
acter, but Kelly loved it. It suited her.

Skip, on the other hand, had taken his money and
bought a plane. He'd started an aviation school for pilot

training and then had branched out to teach skydiving, as well. His business was prosperous, and he'd found a way to do exactly what he wanted and still make a living. A year earlier he'd married Patti, who was every bit as enthusiastic about taking risks as her husband. Neither showed signs of changing.

Well, that was fine for them. But there was no law that said you had to live on the edge to enjoy life. Negotiating an important settlement, pulling off an important court victory—those could be exciting, too. And Duncan felt the same way. He understood that.

Kelly listened to the cry of the birds overhead as she pondered her fate. The immediate uncertainty was if she'd survive the ordeal. And if so, then how would she deal with what had happened between her and Bart? Was making love with him the ultimate betrayal, or was it the understandable consequence of a death-defying experience? Ironically, she felt certain Duncan would understand—and even forgive her. And that said a great deal, both about him and about their relationship.

Still, Kelly couldn't help feelings of guilt. If only she'd stayed in Bangkok. If only she hadn't given in to the temptation to go looking for a little fun.

Mr. Kittikote, the president of Pan Pacific, was a lovely older gentleman, and he had a perfectly charming wife. They had taken her out to dinner her second night in town and she'd been touched by their warmth. If she hadn't taken this damned cruise, she might be spending the weekend returning the favor, entertaining them on behalf of the firm instead of building a lean-to and waiting for Bart to return.

Bart. All she had to do was think about him and she was consumed with images of their lovemaking—in the moonlight and again that afternoon by the pool. How slow she'd been to give up her chastity with Duncan. How eas-

ily she had abandoned it with Bart. Perhaps it was the
jungle, the brush with death. Or maybe it was just his
body.

Bart was attractive, all right, albeit in a raw, earthy way.
At a cocktail party at home, he'd likely have aroused her
curiosity, but no more than that. Of course, that was con-
jecture on her part, because she still didn't know him. Yet
in spite of that, she'd given herself to him as though he
were the only man alive. She could only hope it wouldn't
end up being her last mistake.

Kelly quaked at the thought. She didn't want to die, but
at the same time she wasn't at all sure they would survive.
She sat up, feeling anxious again. Where was Bart? He'd
been gone for at least an hour and a half.

She looked out the lean-to into the shadows of the jungle. "Please come back," she prayed. "Please come
back."

ANOTHER HOUR HAD PASSED. Bart still hadn't returned
and Kelly was beginning to worry. And her worry angered
her. She didn't like it that he'd assumed the role of caveman to her cavewoman. She'd always been independent
and self-reliant. What she wanted more than anything was
a drink of water and another dip in that pool by the waterfall. So why should she wait around? It wouldn't hurt
to have some water in camp, anyway, if she could figure
out a way to carry it.

Taking a large leaf, Kelly began experimenting with ways
to make a receptacle, finally fashioning a makeshift bowl
by tying the ends of a stick into a loop and folding the
outer edges of the leaf over it. She secured the leaf to the
loop by sewing it on with a stringlike vine. Then she was
ready to head off for the pool.

She knew if she followed the stream inland, she would
eventually come to the falls. Before leaving the camp, she

decided to leave a message for Bart. On the ground in the lean-to she wrote the word *waterfall* and took off into the jungle.

Knowing that the return trip would be much more difficult, she tried to memorize landmarks. Frequently she looked back to see what the route would look like when she was going in the other direction. It was an Indian trick she'd read about as a child.

It took longer to get there than she'd figured it would, and the rivulet didn't look familiar, but then she realized she was approaching it from a different angle. The first thing she did was to check the branch over the falls for the snake. A colorful blue-and-green parrot was the only creature in the tree.

Taking it as a good sign, Kelly went to the water's edge and took a drink. The taste was wonderful. She splashed water onto her face and tried drinking from her bowl. It worked perfectly, though water did drip through the holes where she'd lashed the leaf to the loop.

After drinking her fill, she put the bowl down, slipped out of her bikini and waded into the pool. She stayed in the water, listening to the jungle sounds. Bart was right about one thing; the past day had been remarkable—terrible and wonderful both. But it was getting toward evening and she knew she couldn't indulge for too long. She had to get back to the camp before dark.

Rising, she turned and was jolted by the sight of a Thai fisherman on the bank, watching her. A triumphant smile spread over his face. He lifted the muzzle of his automatic rifle and spat out several words, making it clear he wanted her to get out of the pool. Kelly froze. Even her nakedness seemed unimportant beside the horror of being discovered.

The man was small, boyish in size, though his demeanor was menacing. He wore baggy shorts that came to the middle of his skinny thighs, a short-sleeved shirt and sandals. Several long, wispy hairs were on his lip, a kind of mustache, she supposed. He had a large burn scar on the side of his throat. The wrinkles at the corners of his eyes told her he was no boy.

When he looked at her, a smile tugged at the corners of his mouth. Kelly crossed her arms over her breasts and sank to her knees. The fisherman gestured emphatically for her to come to the bank. Her eyes locked on his and she shook her head. Kelly knew she was as good as dead. She might be raped first, but she wouldn't get out of this alive.

The fisherman took a long knife from a sheath on his belt and signaled for her to get out. She refused. Slipping the rifle on his shoulder, he signaled a final time. Kelly held her ground.

Losing patience, he waded toward her, the weapon clutched in his fist. Kelly stopped breathing as he approached and grabbed her by the nape of the neck. He then laid the flat of the blade against her cheek, barking at her to get up. When she didn't respond, he lightly drew the edge of the knife over the end of her shoulder, drawing blood.

Kelly could hardly feel the steel cutting into her, but she moaned at the sight of the blood. The man tightened his grip on her neck, hurting her. When she still didn't move, he placed the edge of the blade against her throat.

She pictured him drawing the knife across her jugular vein and her body collapsing into the water, filling the pool with her blood. The image made her whimper. She didn't want to die. Her instinct for survival made her rise.

The fisherman placed the knife at the small of her back to urge her toward the bank. Kelly moved slowly. She contemplated breaking away and running, but she knew she wouldn't get far. He could easily shoot her. That might be the best outcome, but she wondered if it was possible for her to overpower him, perhaps grab the knife.

She was taller than he, and undoubtedly weighed more. But he was wiry and strong. His grip on her arm was formidable. He probably packed a hell of a punch—and he had weapons.

Once on the bank, the man gave her a shove, promptly sheathing the knife. By the time she turned her head, he'd lifted the muzzle of his gun. Kelly had missed her chance.

Her back was to him, but she watched him over her shoulder. He was grinning broadly. Kelly felt a dribble of blood run down her arm. The fisherman was babbling something, but the comments were directed more at himself than her. Judging by his tone, the words were licentious.

Then he indicated that he wanted her to turn around. She did as he ordered. He chuckled like a schoolboy examining dirty pictures. When he motioned for her to lie down, Kelly pretended she didn't understand. She wanted to draw him closer so that she could try to overpower him.

When he was close enough, she leapt at him, managing to grab the muzzle of the gun. But he reacted swiftly, shoving the weapon against her chest to push her off. Kelly brought her knee up but caught him on the thigh. Enraged, he swung the butt of the rifle against the side of her head. She was out cold before she hit the ground.

Kelly came to as he was lashing her wrists above her head. The face over her was grinning again, but it was blurry. Her eye was nearly closed. The man's breath washed over her face. He smelled of fish and tobacco.

Kelly was tied spread-eagle on the bank. She lifted her head to look around. She was in the same place she had made love with Bart that afternoon.

Bart! He might be her only chance. When the fisherman stood, Kelly began screaming at the top of her lungs.

The Thai struck her, nearly knocking her out again. She tried to keep up her protest, but he stuffed the top of her suit into her mouth, silencing her.

Her swollen eye was blurry and shimmering, but through her tears she could see the man step between her legs and unbuckle his pants. She panicked, writhing and pulling until she managed to get one ankle half free. The man cursed and bent over her, pressing one knee into her stomach and bringing the knife to her throat. She knew then it was hopeless. The fight drained from her. She closed her eyes, giving in to the inevitable.

He began running his hand over her breasts, making her skin crawl. When he knelt between her legs, she began to sob through the gag. She had never felt so degraded.

Just as the man touched her, she heard a terrible crash in the nearby brush, followed by a throaty cry. A body hurled through the air, and there was the crunch of bone on bone as the fisherman was wrenched from her and knocked into the pool.

Kelly strained to see two men thrashing in the water. Bart Monday was the first to emerge, pulling the fisherman up by the throat. Bart had a clear advantage of size, but the Thai was a skilled fighter. He managed a kick to Bart's solar plexus, but Bart was possessed. He lunged at the fisherman and pulled him down in the deeper part of the pool. They struggled again, the Thai delivering a stinging blow to Bart's head. They spun and flailed in the frothy water until Bart alone was above the surface. He held the Thai under. Seconds passed. Kelly heard the air bubbling out of the man. Even though he had intended to rape her, his death sickened her.

Dropping her head back onto the ground, she wept silently. In a few seconds Bart was beside her, pulling the gag from her mouth and cutting her free. Kelly put her arms around his neck and began to cry. He held her and stroked her head.

"Oh, Bart, why does the world have to be so ugly?"

"It isn't, babe. Only parts of it. Dark corners." He kissed her battered cheek.

Kelly clung to him. "Please, I want to get out of this place. Off this island."

He rocked her in his arms. "We'll be leaving at first light. I've found a boat."

CHAPTER SIX

BART SPENT A GOOD ten minutes just holding her, rubbing her back and arms, telling her everything would be all right. Thank God she'd rallied some at the mention of the boat. Shock could kill. But so could pirates, and he didn't think it was healthy to hang around there too much longer. If one fisherman frequented the waterfall, so did the others.

Bart knew he had a job to do and it wouldn't get any easier if he procrastinated, so he eased away from Kelly and waded back into the pool. Going to the spot where he'd drowned the pirate, he dragged the body to the far bank, trying to stay between Kelly and the pirate so that she couldn't see what he was doing.

After he'd stripped the body, he carried it into the undergrowth. His buddies would probably figure that he'd come to a bad end sooner or later, but if Bart had his way, he and Kelly would be off the damned island before that happened.

As soon as he finished covering the body with branches, he rinsed out the pirate's clothes, then returned to Kelly's side. He could see by the way she was squinting that her vision wasn't clear. He hoped she didn't have a severe concussion.

"Here," he said, handing her the pirate's shirt and pants, "I think you should wear these. I've done what I can to rinse them out, and they'll dry on you in this heat."

She started to shake her head and then winced. Obviously she was in a lot of pain. "No way, Bart. Not on your life."

He knelt and put his arm around her shoulder. "Just until we're off this island, babe. At least put on the shirt. It'll keep you warmer tonight, and it'll keep some of the sun off you during the day."

She started to protest, then sighed. She put on the shirt but drew the line at the pants. He knew she wasn't too pleased about wearing the dead man's clothes, but they had to make do, survive any way they could.

He made a cold compress from a pant leg torn from the shorts, which Kelly held to her battered cheek. Blood oozed from her shoulder, so he held another compress against it until the bleeding stopped.

"No telling how long before his friends come looking for him," he said. "We'd better get out of here."

She got up without a word. She was woozy and he had to help steady her. Kelly tossed the compress into the undergrowth. Bart grabbed the pirate's gun and knife, and they started off. They'd gone only a few steps when she stopped.

"My bowl," she said, looking around. "I made a bowl to carry water. Where is it?"

She scanned the edge of the grass by the pool and then went over to pick up her makeshift bowl. Filling it with water, she returned to him. He put his arm around her.

"I thought we might get thirsty during the night," she said.

"Think you can get that to the camp without spilling it?"

"I'm going to try."

"There's a surprise waiting for you, by the way. Dinner."

Kelly looked at him questioningly. "Something I'll eat?"

"No serpents, if that's what you mean. Just a little forbidden fruit."

"Good. As long as it's not disgusting, I'll eat anything. I'm at the point where it could come out of a garbage can."

He gave her good shoulder a squeeze. "That's the spirit."

Bart was relieved she was getting her sense of humor back. Maybe she was strong enough not to let this get her down. God, it must have been awful for her. If she hadn't left that message, he'd never have gone to the pool, never have found her in time. . . .

There was no use in dwelling on the worst, though. Darkness was falling and they had to get back to camp. Trouble was, the landmarks he'd picked out earlier seemed different in the failing light, though he was certain he was headed in the right general direction. By his reckoning they were about halfway back when Kelly tripped and lost most of the water in her bowl.

"Damn," she said as he helped her up.

"That's all right, we'll skip brushing our teeth tonight."

"Lord, what I wouldn't give for a toothbrush. Five minutes in a nice tiled bath would be heaven."

"Just think about all the folks at home sitting in their bathrooms, agonizing over extra cellulite or a ten point dip in the stock market."

"What are you, Bart, some kind of a backwoods philosopher?"

He grinned. "I guess you could say that."

She looked up through the branches at the blue-black sky. "Do you think we'll make it?" she asked in a quiet voice.

He pushed back the hair pasted to her forehead. "It's not far. If my calculations are right, our camp should be at the top of this little incline."

They heard a dog barking in the distance. A bird cawed overhead, seemingly in answer.

"That barking's coming from the village," he said. "That means we're close."

They started off again, but the slope dropped away and they had to double back. Finally they got to the camp from the back side. The shadows had grown dark enough that the silhouette of the shelter was barely visible. Kelly handed him the bowl and sank to the ground.

"Thank God," she said, "home at last."

He hollowed out a spot with his heel and set the bowl in it. Then he sat beside her. "Cheer up. It's time for supper."

She sagged against him, resting her head on his shoulder. He could feel her body quiver. He stroked her head.

"Everything will be all right," he said. "Tomorrow we'll be leaving for home."

She recovered after a few moments. The trembling stopped as suddenly as it had begun. "I wish I could believe you," she said, wiping her nose.

"Let's have dinner. Then we'll discuss my plan." They crawled into the shelter and he lifted a leaf covering three pieces of fruit. One was a sick-looking banana, the other two were the mangolike fruit they'd had that morning.

"Sad to say, but they look delicious," she said.

"Not exactly primo stuff, but they'll stave off starvation. I thought we could each have a mango and split the banana."

Kelly took a mango and bit into it. "Where did you find these?"

"The mangoes, in the jungle. The banana, in the garbage dump."

"You went to the village!"

"I scouted around it. The important thing is, I found a boat."

"A fishing boat?"

"No, this is smaller. A launch-type thing. I'm not sure what it's used for, but they've got a man guarding it. Probably around the clock. It's our ticket out of here."

"Do you know how to run the thing and where we'll go, if we manage to capture it?"

"What's all this logical thinking?" he teased.

"I'm normally a lawyer, not a water bearer." She paused. "I'm not being critical, Bart. I'm just suggesting we've got to be damn sure of what we're doing."

"I agree. But I didn't tell you the rest. I spotted a ship . . . a coast guard or navy vessel. It was probably either searching for us or for the fishing fleet. With luck, it'll be there tomorrow. If we get the launch and make it out to where the *Ban Don* went down, we stand a good chance of being picked up."

"God, I hope so."

"Don't worry, we'll make it. Just one more jungle dinner, and tomorrow it'll be real food."

Kelly took a last bite of her fruit. As he finished his, he saw her staring at the blackened banana. He handed it to her. "Go ahead. Eat it."

"Aren't you hungry?" she asked.

"Yeah. But I don't have the killer instinct of a lawyer."

He watched as she tried to peel the fruit. It practically fell apart in her hand.

"Maybe you should tell me what you do for a living, Bart, so I can make jokes about your profession."

"I already told you. I'm into import-export."

She stuffed a gooey glob of banana into her mouth. "I don't believe you."

"Why?"

"I don't know. Feminine instinct, maybe." She handed him the other half.

"Sure you don't want it?" he asked.

"No, it's all yours. I'm full."

Bart laughed. "Yeah, I bet. Here, let's share."

"No, I had my half. Really."

He shrugged and put a chunk of banana into his mouth.

"What I wouldn't give for a plate of spaghetti," she said wistfully.

His hand, coated with the last of the banana, was poised before his mouth. He hesitated. "Here. Have this. You can lick it off my fingers. That way you'll get it all."

"Bastard," she whispered. But she grabbed his wrist anyway and pulled his fingers to her mouth.

"That's no way to talk to your chief benefactor," he said as she ran her tongue over and between each finger, licking it clean.

"I bet you just love having a woman eat out of your hand," she mumbled.

"I must say, the sensation is pleasant enough. On balance, though, I think I'd rather have the banana." He laughed, but when Kelly nipped his little finger, he knew he'd pushed her too far. "Hope your pleasure was as great as mine."

She pushed his now clean hand away. "I'd have preferred pasta, but beggars can't be choosy."

"If we get out of this alive, Kelly, I'm going to take you to the Verandah at the Oriental in Bangkok. A ten course meal. Shrimp curry, steamed lobster, sweet and sour pork..."

"For God's sake, will you shut up? You'll have me gnawing on your leg in a minute."

He grinned. "Well, at least I can offer you an after dinner drink. How about some water?"

He got her leaf bowl. Kelly drank carefully. After she'd had about a quarter of the water, she handed it back to him. He took a couple of sips.

"You're an inventive lady, considering that basket weaving probably wasn't in the curriculum at law school."

Kelly lay back, moaning a little as her head touched the ground. "The one bright spot in all of this is that you have a sense of humor. I don't know what I'd have done if you were a bore."

"I mean to please."

She rolled onto her side, facing him. Her head was cradled in the crook of her arm. "You've been wonderful, Bart. I mean it. If you hadn't arrived at the waterfall when you did, I'd probably be dead by now."

He brushed her cheek with his fingers. "Let's not think about that. It's over."

"Yes, but..." There was a catch in her voice. "I feel so...violated."

He couldn't see well enough to tell if she was crying or not, but he gathered her into his arms anyway. "I'm sorry, Kelly. I didn't mean to be cavalier."

She cried softly. It was a long, long time before she took a deep breath and sighed.

"Sorry. This is just what you need on top of everything else—a weepy woman." She pulled away to wipe her nose on her arm. "It's just that I'm so damned miserable. This has got to be as primitive as it gets. I can see now I've taken a lot of things for granted. I felt so in charge of my life. I thought I was pretty hot stuff—lady lawyer making it in a man's world. Now look at me. I feel like a piece of meat a couple of dogs are fighting over."

He patted her leg. "Just be glad I'm the dog who won."

"I am. But that doesn't do a lot for my self-respect."

Bart took her hand in his, entwining their fingers. "I'd say civilization hasn't been thoroughly destroyed if you can worry about your self-respect at a time like this."

Kelly stopped sniffling. "You're right. Dead right." She paused. "I guess you're a lot smarter than you let on."

He chuckled. He could feel her warm breath on his chest. "Thank you. It's the nicest thing you've said all day."

"You're actually a very interesting man, Bart."

"Yeah?"

"Yes. What I said earlier was true. I probably wouldn't have gone to dinner with you back in Ko Samui. But now I realize I'd have missed something."

"The second nicest thing you've said today." He squeezed her hand.

"I'm serious. I appreciate the fact you haven't abandoned me. You've been loyal. I respect that."

"How could I possibly throw you to the wolves? You've got the best pair of legs I've ever seen in my life."

She pulled her hand from his. "Well, that's a lousy reason. Are you saying if I was fat and ugly you'd have left me for the pirates?"

"Maybe."

Kelly rolled over and turned her back to him, pulling the fisherman's shirt tight around her neck. "I take back all the nice things I said about you, Bart Monday. You're not a gentleman. You're a pervert!"

That made him laugh. "It's not just your legs. You're a hell of a companion. If a guy's got to be in a situation like this, I can't think of anyone I'd rather—"

"Oh, shut up, Bart. You're only making it worse."

He sighed.

"Good night," she said.

He didn't reply. He lay behind her, his body touching hers. He could hear her breathing and wondered what she was thinking about. Food, maybe. Or could it be the guy back home? He propped his head on his elbow and considered asking her about him. She hadn't given him an answer when he'd broached the subject earlier. But then it occurred to him that getting her talking about Mr. Wonderful wouldn't do much for his own cause.

For a while after that Bart listened to the night sounds and inhaled the womanly fragrance of her body. He'd been damn lucky that he'd gotten there in time to save her from the fisherman. Disaster averted. He knew the experience had upset her badly, if it hadn't traumatized her. But at least she was in one piece and all right.

He leaned over and kissed her neck. "Tomorrow will be better, Kelly. You'll see." He rolled over then, covered them both with palm fronds and fell asleep instantly.

KELLY SLEPT FITFULLY. It wasn't as cold as the night before, and the shirt helped, but her head was throbbing and she couldn't rid herself of the horrible image of the pirate as he was about to rape her. She tried to pull herself together, to remind herself it would have been much worse if Bart hadn't come along when he did, but that didn't help.

For a long time she cried silently so as not to wake Bart. God knows, she owed him a decent night's sleep. Finally she was so exhausted she dropped off. But her dreams were disturbing and she kept waking up, fearful they'd overslept and missed their chance to capture the boat.

The next thing she knew, Bart was shaking her awake. Kelly sat up, disoriented and confused. She clutched his arm. "Are they coming? Are they coming?"

"Who?"

"The pirates."

"No, it's time to break camp. We're leaving."

They were leaving! Excitement replaced her fear.

Bart had assembled their weapons—the automatic rifle and the knife—by a tree. The gun would probably make the difference in their escape, assuming they succeeded. Bart picked up the knife and rifle, then groped for her hand.

"You ready, kid?"

"I've never been more ready to leave a place in my life."

Kelly was sure he was smiling. Bart, she suspected, endured whatever befell him with equanimity. He might even be enjoying himself.

"I hope we don't get caught," she whispered, following him through the jungle. "All night long I heard people talking."

"You must've been dreaming. I didn't hear a thing and I slept with one eye open."

She had to repress her laughter. "One eye, maybe. Definitely your mouth."

Bart pushed through the thick vegetation. "Are you trying to say I snore?"

"It kept me awake."

"I've never had complaints before."

"Maybe I'm more delicate than your other women."

"Noticed the pea under the mattress, too, I'll bet," he said.

She was all set to give him a shove, but a dog barked. They stopped dead in their tracks.

"The village isn't far," he whispered. "Keep the talking to a minimum and be careful where you step."

"I can't even see the ground," she whispered.

"Do the best you can. Dawn will be in half an hour or so."

"Do we have to go near the village?"

"The boat is in a cove on the other side of it. There's no other way, unless we go deeper into the jungle."

Kelly sighed. "Lead on, Macduff."

They got near enough to the village that she could hear dogs whining. The smell of cooking odors and kerosene fumes was in the air. Despite the dense vegetation, she could see a light in one of the shacks.

When they came to the sandy beach at the edge of the jungle, just past the village, Bart stopped to survey the beach. Within minutes it would be light. The only sound was the waves breaking on the sand, thirty to forty yards away. He pointed to where the boat lay in the shadows. A red dot of fire was glowing against the blackened side of the craft. Apparently the guard was smoking.

Then a match flared, revealing a second face.

"Shit," Bart said. "There are *two* of them."

Kelly's stomach clenched. "So what does that mean?"

"It means I can't jump two guys and slit their throats simultaneously."

"There are two of us, too," she said. "Have you forgotten?"

He turned and she saw the whiteness of his teeth.

"I didn't know throat slitting was on your résumé."

She fought down her fear. "Is it on yours?"

Bart didn't reply.

"I know import-export is a cutthroat business," she said sarcastically, "but somehow I don't believe that's really what you do."

"Right now you ought to be wishing I was a contract killer."

"Are you?"

"No."

His answer had a ring of finality that Kelly wasn't sure it deserved, but it wasn't a profitable line of conversation so she let the matter drop. They stood there, listening to the surf and staring at the glowing cigarettes. With each passing minute the outline of the boat was becoming more distinct.

"Come on, Bart, there must be some way I can help. Granted, walking up to a stranger and slitting his throat isn't really me, but there must be something I can do. Distract them, maybe."

He sank to the ground. "Just be quiet a minute," he said. "I've got to think."

Kelly plopped down beside him. While he was calculating, she thought about the way he'd avoided answering her questions. Who was Bart Monday, anyway? A mercenary? A fugitive? She suddenly realized she'd never asked why he'd had a gun aboard the *Ban Don*. A legitimate businessman would carry a laptop, not a weapon. Until now she'd been too caught up in what was happening to them to analyze the situation.

Bart grabbed a handful of sand and let it run through his fingers. "We'll have to abort. Our best bet is to lie low and find a better opportunity—one where the odds favor us."

"There must be another alternative."

"Not a good one," he replied, the verve returning to his voice. "We'll head back to camp. It won't be too bad. We'll do a little remodeling, find something to eat. We'll have a gay old time, Kelly."

She didn't know whether to cry or get angry. A sense of humor was nice, but it wasn't going to help them escape. They needed to take action. But what? She forced herself to analyze the situation calmly, as he had. His conclusion that they should wait made sense. She didn't like it, but she knew he was right.

"Okay. If you're willing to go back to camp, I am, too."

Dawn was starting to break. The men near the boat were plainly visible. "Let's wait a couple more minutes," Bart whispered. "I want to see how well these guys are armed."

In another five minutes it was light enough for him to see what he wanted.

"Just what I was afraid of. Automatic rifles. That, and the fact that there are two guards now, probably means they're thinking right along with us. And our challenge will be to stay a step ahead of them." He playfully cuffed her chin. "What d'ya think, my dear? Up to another game of hide-and-seek?"

CHAPTER SEVEN

THEY TOOK A ROUNDABOUT way back to their camp. Soon they were past the village, though at a different angle inland from the one they had taken before. From the sound of it, there was a stream ahead. When they got to it they saw it was smaller than the one at the waterfall, but just fine for a drink and a quick wash.

Kelly's energy returned, and with it her desire to get some answers. "Bart, before we go any farther, I think it might be a good idea if we talked."

He blinked. "Before breakfast?"

"Well, I suppose we can forage for fruit and talk at the same time. But I mean it. No more delays. The time has come for you to tell me a few things."

"Sounds fair enough." He headed off into the jungle again. "Shoot."

"All right. For starters, are you married?"

He looked back at her and smiled. "No."

"That's a relief. I wouldn't want to have to face adultery in addition to starvation and torture."

He laughed. "And I'm not a misogynist, if you were wondering about that, too. My life-style doesn't lend itself to marriage, that's all."

"Yes," she said, poking her tongue in her cheek, "import-export must be very demanding of your time."

He nodded. "It is."

They were deeper in the jungle now, and the racket from the monkeys was getting louder. Kelly looked up. All of the decent-looking fruit was very high in the trees. She found a half-eaten piece on the ground and a couple of rotted ones that had fallen from the trees. "How old are you?"

"Thirty-eight."

"Where were you born?"

"Nebraska."

"Is your name really Bart Monday?"

"It has been ever since I turned up on the doorstep of an orphanage on a Monday morning. My mother didn't bother to pin a note to my diaper."

She was shocked. "Is that true?"

"Yes. But it was a long time ago. Don't waste any tears on it."

She gave him a long, hard look, trying to decide if he was telling the truth. She'd have bet he was. God knows, she'd spent enough time taking depositions and questioning people in court to have developed a sixth sense about whether someone was lying or not.

But at the same time she was sure that Bart was hiding something—not because he was dishonest so much as because he was secretive. And she damn well meant to find out why.

Duncan claimed the best technique to use when questioning the opposition was to ask innocent questions first, to put them at ease. Once they let down their guard, ask the tough ones. But she had a feeling that technique might not work with Bart. He was a hell of a lot smarter than she'd first thought.

He was a few feet ahead of her now, hunched over something on the ground. She knelt beside him and saw that he was in the process of digging up some kind of white tuber that was half-buried.

"We might be able to eat these," he said as he held one up to show her.

"Are you serious? They could be poisonous."

"Well, there's one way to find out. In the meantime I'm going to grab a few handfuls."

Kelly waited as he stuffed a bunch of them into his pockets. When he finished, they crossed the stream again.

"Oh, God," she moaned as they slogged through the water, "I hate nature."

Bart laughed. "You're too much of a city girl, Kelly. This little adventure is exactly what you need."

She gave him a dirty look. "Somehow I knew you were going to say that."

"See, you live with a guy for a while, and you start reading his mind. Another five years together and we won't even have to talk. We'll be able to do all our communicating by telepathy."

"I'm sure I will have killed you long before then," she said dryly.

He put his arm around her shoulder and gave her a quick squeeze. "I know this has been tough on you, especially on your pride, but I'm not sure either one of us can do much about that right now. I'll tell you this... I'd change things for you if I could.

"Oh, I'll admit it's not so rough on me as it is on you, but I still can't help being glad you're here. It might be easier to get out of here if you were a guy, but at the same time, I like being with you. I like being the strong one so you can be weak if you need to. And I like taking care of you."

She was surprised. He'd revealed a side of himself she hadn't expected. His tone was so thoughtful. That had knocked her off balance as much as what he'd actually said. A bird was making a terrible racket, but she hardly heard it. She didn't know what to say. She didn't even know what to think.

"Well," Bart said, a trace of humor returning to his voice, "the jungle can do one thing I hadn't realized—it can loosen the tongue. Am I right?"

"Yes, I suppose so." She idly pulled on a vine. The past few minutes had given her a very different sense of Bart. She wondered now if the humor was an attempt to cover his feelings so that no one would suspect he was vulnerable. Most men, even Duncan, didn't like to admit to weakness.

Suddenly Bart froze. "Shh! Listen."

She detected a faint throbbing sound. "What is it?" she whispered.

"A chopper. That's a chopper, babe. If it's the coast guard, we might be saved. Come on, let's get to the beach."

The roar of the engine grew louder as he forced her to move as quickly as possible. She stumbled after him. "Can't we slow down?"

"No telling how long they'll stay. This may be our last chance to be taken off by friendlies."

Friendlies? she thought. That sounded like military talk. But she wasn't going to worry about that now. Bart couldn't want to get off the island any more than she did.

It took them ten minutes to get near the beach. They ended up on the opposite side of the village from the boat. He moved parallel to the shore, inside the protection of the vegetation, and in the direction of the village.

Kelly couldn't hear the chopper. She wondered if it had already gone.

Suddenly Bart stopped. Kelly looked over his shoulder and spotted the helicopter. It was on the ground, close to the boat. A couple of men in gray uniforms were standing at the open door.

"Shit," Bart said.

"What's the matter?"

"That's a police helicopter, not the coast guard or navy."

"So what? What difference does it make?"

His expression was pained. "It's not the same, trust me."

"You aren't making sense."

He brushed the comment aside. "We can't tell what's going on from here. Those fellows are guards. The others must have gone into the village. Let's work our way around and see what we can."

That made sense. Kelly wasn't going to argue.

A finger of land separated the village from the cove where the boat and helicopter were. The area was slightly elevated and covered with palm trees and undergrowth. They crawled out to the edge of the plants, where they had a good view of both the village and the cove.

The village appeared deserted. A dog walked from one of the huts to a palm tree and plopped down. Kelly wondered what was going on.

"Where is everybody?" she whispered.

"Probably inside. And that's not good."

"Why?"

"It means this is a friendly visit, not a hostile encounter."

"Could they be interrogating the fishermen?" Kelly asked. "After all, there was an act of piracy in these waters a couple of days ago."

"Maybe."

"Well, why don't we go down and find out? After all, those are the police, aren't they?"

"Kelly, it may not be that simple. The situation is a little more complicated than you know. Actually, a lot more complicated."

She studied him but didn't say anything.

He sighed. "The fact of the matter is, you and I need to have a heart-to-heart talk."

The way he said it, and the look in his eye, sent a sick feeling through her. He stared at the village, biting his lip. "This isn't so easy to explain."

Kelly groaned as Bart scooped up a handful of sand and let it trickle through his fingers before slinging the last of it away. She stared into his golden eyes until she couldn't wait any longer.

"Damn it, Bart, just be straight with me."

He let his eyes close slowly, like a man in pain. Then he gazed squarely at her. With a couple of days' growth of beard, and his brownish blond hair tangled and dirty, he looked more like a rogue than ever.

"Bart," she implored, "speak."

He took a deep breath. "The police are looking for me," he announced. "I'm subject to arrest."

Kelly searched his eyes for a sign he was joking, but there wasn't any. She groaned. She'd expected something like this, but it hurt, anyway. And the worst part was, she'd let him make love to her—several times!

"What did you do?" she asked.

"Nothing, really. I'm not a criminal. The cops are the bad guys. Some of the key ones are on the take, and they consider it in their interest to eliminate me. We can't trust any of them."

She felt like crying. "Do you honestly expect me to believe that? The police are practically within spitting distance, ready to take me off this godforsaken island, and you say I can't trust them? What do you take me for, some kind of idiot?"

"It's the truth."

She looked at him in disgust. "Shit. Pardon my French, but shit!"

"Kelly, there's a perfectly reasonable explanation for everything."

"Oh, yeah? Then why didn't you tell me about your criminal tendencies earlier?"

"There was no reason to."

"Damn right," she retorted. "You were getting what you wanted. Why spoil it?"

"Listen," he said, losing patience, "we don't have time to bicker."

"All right," she said, propping herself on her elbow. "Let's hear it. The whole story."

"I'm involved in an undercover operation that's blown up in my face. If that was the navy or the coast guard, I'd march down there with a smile on my face. But there's only one reason the Thai police would be out here, and that's to find me. They're desperate to silence me. It's that simple."

Kelly rolled her eyes. "Do you expect me to believe that?"

"Why not?" He gestured toward the village. "You don't hear any shooting, do you? Cops and pirates playing bridge? Does that strike you as normal?"

"Maybe the police don't know they're pirates. Not every fisherman's an outlaw, you know. Besides, as I said before, maybe they're interrogating them."

He grimaced, apparently not liking her logic.

"What makes you so sure the police have come for you, anyway? Did they know you were on the *Ban Don*?"

"I'm not sure. I got out of Bangkok because it was too hot for me there. I barely got away."

Kelly was skeptical. "You said you're on a clandestine mission. Who are you working for?"

"I can't say."

"Oh, that's convenient!"

"The more you know, the worse it will be for you, Kelly. As it is, your life's in danger because you've been with me."

"That's convenient, too. Sorry, I don't buy it. If you've got problems with the police, it has nothing to do with me. I'm a tourist who's been shipwrecked and set upon by pirates. I'm not a criminal, and they will accept that."

"They won't."

Her eyes narrowed. "I hate to say this, considering you saved my life, but how do I know your story isn't a ruse to keep me out here? Maybe you're some kind of a perverted survivalist. After all, this is every man's fantasy, playing Robinson Crusoe with a half-naked woman."

"Please, Kelly, let's not get into that again."

"Damned right we won't get into that again." She rose to her knees.

Bart jerked her back to the ground. Her face went right into the sand, and she came up spitting.

"Shh!" he said. "They're coming out."

She was angry, but he had gotten her attention. Lying beside him, she looked down at the cluster of huts as she brushed sand from her face. Three or four fishermen had come out of one of the houses. With them were half a dozen policemen, including an officer who was talking animatedly with a fisherman who appeared to be the leader.

They were much too far away to be heard, but the fisherman kept pointing toward the jungle, then out to sea. It wasn't hard to imagine they were discussing her and Bart. The pirates had probably found their dead comrade, the one who had tried to rape her. But none of that proved anything—certainly not that the police were corrupt.

"You see," Bart said.

"See what? The fishermen might have convinced the police that someone else attacked the ship." She sighed. "Bart, that helicopter may be our only chance!"

"You go with them, you probably won't live to get to Bangkok," he warned.

She glared. "Why should I believe you?" she asked. "You won't tell me what your clandestine operation is or who you're working for."

"The American government."

"If you're in trouble, why didn't you go to the embassy?"

Bart sighed, closing his eyes again. "I couldn't."

She scoffed. "Next you're going to tell me the American embassy is full of criminals, too."

He shook his head, looking as though he wished he'd never left Nebraska.

"Well, are you?"

"Government officials can be crooked, too. A G-S rating doesn't guarantee sainthood! And we have just as many bad apples in our country as anywhere else."

Kelly laughed. "You're paranoid! Well, I've got news for you, Mr. Monday. I intend to get off this island— preferably in the next few minutes!" She started to get up but Bart stopped her once more. He had a tight grip on her arm and he looked worried.

"The more you know, the worse it will be. They'll torture you. Believe me."

"Not good enough. I intend to be on that helicopter when it leaves."

"Kelly..."

"I'll scream if you don't let go of me!"

He reached for her mouth, but she managed to get off a brief cry before he clamped his hand over her lips. She struggled, but he pinned her beneath him, using his weight to hold her.

"Damn! Now you've done it!" he said. "They heard you. They'll be here in a few minutes." He glanced down at her, his look intense. "Listen, Kelly, if I let go of you, will you run with me into the jungle? If we go now, we'll make it. Will you come with me?"

She shook her head. She could have lied, but it didn't matter now. He could run if he wanted to, but she was getting off the island in that helicopter.

Bart turned her around, pinning her but lifting her chin so that she could see the village. His hand was still clamped onto her mouth, his knee pressed into her back. She hated him then—hated him for hurting her, for lying, for making love to her under false pretenses.

"See!" he said, sounding more like a madman every second. "They're getting their weapons. They're coming!"

As the men started in their direction, Kelly knew Bart was running out of options. He must have read the situation the same way because he let go of her, a bitter, fearful look in his eyes. Despite that, she could tell he was still calculating. He turned his gaze back on her.

"All right," he said, his voice strangely calm. "They'll get one of us, but there's no reason it has to be you."

"What are you going to do?" she asked.

"Give myself up," he replied. "I'll tell them I'm a survivor from the *Ban Don* and that the ship was attacked by the fishermen. If they're honest, they'll question these guys. But I can tell you now it won't happen that way. If they don't kill me on the spot, you'll see some unorthodox police work. In any case, all you have to do is stay here and watch. The truth will soon become apparent. If I get a hug and a kiss from them, you'll know that I lied."

He didn't wait any longer. He stood upright. Kelly rolled onto her back, looking up at him, shocked. Why did she suddenly believe him?

Bart waved his arms and gave a high-pitched scream, trying to duplicate the sound of her cry earlier. Without looking down, he took the tubers from his pocket and dropped them next to her. "These will start tasting better after a few days. Don't forget to take the gun and knife. You'll need them before this is over."

Kelly reached out and touched his ankle. "Bart..."

"Remember, they don't know you're here. Only one fisherman saw you, and he's dead now." He rubbed his toe against her arm, a final gesture of affection. "Take care of yourself, beautiful, I've got to go."

He strode down the sandy dune toward the village. Kelly lay there, trying to make sense of what had happened. She tested the logic of his words. Then she rolled onto her stomach and watched him march toward the policemen, who'd stopped at the base of the slope, their weapons at the ready.

Kelly suddenly had a terrible sense that she had forced him into a rash and deadly act. Even if he was nuts, one thing he'd said made sense—she'd be able to tell a lot about the intentions of the police by the way they treated him.

As Bart reached the bottom of the slope, four policemen fanned out to encircle him. He lifted his hands in surrender, then came to a halt. He began talking, pointing out to sea, then at the fishermen's village. But the cops didn't listen. One of them stepped forward and swung the butt of his rifle, catching Bart on the side of the head and knocking him to the ground. Kelly winced and let her face drop into her hands. When she looked up again, two of the men had grabbed Bart's arms and were dragging him toward the village. By the time they were halfway back, she knew she'd made a terrible mistake. Even if Bart was a criminal, there was no justification for treating him that way. And if the police didn't take action against the pirates, it would mean that the rest of his story was probably true, as well.

A sick feeling came over her. The truth was beginning to sink in. "My God," she said half aloud, "what have I done?"

DURING THE NEXT HOUR the police tied Bart to a palm tree and took turns beating him. Occasionally one of the fishermen would also give him a kick. Kelly winced with each blow.

It took a long time, but Bart finally slumped forward, apparently unconscious. One of the policemen threw a bucket of water in his face to bring him to. They went through the whole routine again, but after a while the men must gave gotten tired of the sport, because they drifted away.

As the police official went with the chief of the pirates back into the hut, Kelly wondered what to do. She couldn't cope in the jungle alone, yet she didn't have many options. Should she surrender? At least she and Bart would be together that way. Torn by indecision, she waited.

After another twenty minutes the policeman came out of the hut. He shook hands with the head man, then rounded up his men and marched off in the direction of the cove.

Kelly was incredulous. Would they leave without Bart? That made no sense. She hadn't counted on that possibility.

That left her with a momentous decision. Should she run down to the helicopter and throw herself on their mercy, or should she stay behind with Bart? He was leaning against the tree, his head bowed and bloody from the beating.

Below her, the police contingent was nearing the area where the chopper had landed. She looked at Bart, then back at them. Obviously the police couldn't be trusted, and there was no way of knowing whether Bart would survive long enough to be rescued. She knew now what she had to do—she'd rescue him herself.

Her first task was to get back to their camp, where she'd be relatively safe. Kelly crawled toward the jungle with the rifle slung over her back, the knife in her teeth. Halfway back she heard the chopper lift off. She felt a well of emptiness knowing she was truly on her own.

She tried to tell herself that she was an intelligent woman and could do whatever was necessary to save Bart. But law school hadn't prepared her for a search-and-rescue mission. She didn't have the slightest idea how to go about saving anyone. Only one thing was certain—she needed a plan, and she needed it fast. No telling how long Bart could hang on, considering the way he was being beaten.

When she finally reached the jungle, she stopped to rest. With Bart there had been a thrill underneath the terror. That was gone now. There was only loneliness. But then she reminded herself that no matter how bad her situation was, Bart's was far worse.

She pictured him tied to the tree. His wounds had to be severe. Perhaps he was dead already. The thought made her sick, but she told herself she couldn't give up. She'd take action. Do something. Anything was better than nothing.

The rifle strapped to her back felt heavy. She didn't know why she bothered with it, except that Bart had told her to keep it, and so she would. Perhaps she could figure out how to fire it. She'd put her stereo system together and she'd even figured out how to operate her VCR. Could a gun possibly be any more complicated than a VCR? Probably not.

She came to the small rise close to their camp and sat down to rest and think. The logical first step would be to find out what the fishermen had done with Bart. That meant she'd need a closer view of the village. The real problem was, if she attempted a raid on her own, the consequences could be deadly. Still, a reconnaissance was as good a place to start as any. She could decide what to do when she got there. She rose and began to retrace her steps.

Half an hour later she'd managed to work her way around to the back of the village. When she got her first clear view, Kelly saw that Bart was no longer tied to the tree. Pure terror shot through her. Was he dead? Could they have already dragged his body off and buried it?

One of the dogs must have caught her scent, because it began ambling in her direction. It lifted its nose and gave a feeble bark.

"Damn," she muttered under her breath.

She wondered what Rambo would do. Probably toss the dog a slab of meat. But if she had any meat right now, she'd eat it herself.

The pirate dog was not more than five yards away, sniffing in her direction. When it whined, Kelly was glad for the semifriendly reception. She made a kissing sound, a sort of instinctive, nonthreatening overture. The dog wagged his tail. She smiled. A friend.

The dog inched forward. He looked like a refugee from a leper colony, but his friendliness was indisputable. She let him sniff her. His tail was wagging like crazy now, and he licked at her shirtfront. Then it struck her. The pooch was reacting to his master's smell on the shirt!

As she gave the dog a half-apologetic pat, there was a bloodcurdling scream. Bart!

As best she could tell, the sound had come from one of the huts. Kelly gritted her teeth, wincing at the thought of what the pirates were doing to him.

Fido, the pirate dog, began meandering back toward the village. Kelly was alone again but she'd learned one thing—Bart was still alive, at least for the moment.

By chance she'd discovered another, perhaps crucial, fact—at least one of the guard dogs held a special affection for her. With luck, the other one would, too. Because of the smell of the fisherman's shirt, she might be able to sneak back into the village in the dead of night.

Kelly smiled. Not even John Wayne's scriptwriters could have come up with that!

CHAPTER EIGHT

WITHOUT BART FOR WARMTH and companionship, Kelly didn't need an alarm clock to avoid oversleeping. During her night alone in the lean-to, she probably hadn't slept more than ten consecutive minutes. Each time her eyes opened, she'd check the moon to see if it was midnight.

She'd taken astronomy in college—one of those bone-head science classes for nonmajors—and had learned the easiest way to estimate time was by the full moon, since it moved at roughly 180 degrees to the sun. A full moon directly overhead indicated midnight. As the phase changed, the time when the moon was at the azimuth also changed, though Kelly couldn't remember how.

For the first time ever, she regretted daydreaming in class. If she got off the island, she would return to her alma mater and give a speech on the importance of paying attention to the boring stuff.

Kelly's best guess was that it was near midnight—time to head for the village. The distance was not great, but she knew she'd have to fight her inherent fear of the darkness. As a child, she'd begged to have a light on in her room at night. Her mother had never questioned her about it, but even if she'd asked why she was afraid of the dark, Kelly wouldn't have known what to say. If some traumatic event had taken place in the dark, she didn't recall it.

Because of her fear, she had almost elected to wait near the village. In the end, she'd returned to camp because she thought her chances of being discovered were less. God knows, the last thing she needed was to blow this opportunity. Bart was counting on her, and every minute she waited he was in peril.

She'd worried off and on all night about what shape he'd be in. Not good, that much was certain. She had tried to make the bed more comfortable for him, knowing he'd need to rest, so she'd spent the afternoon gathering fronds. She had also tried to close the gaps in the walls, especially near the ground.

Her other goal was to make the shelter snakeproof, but Kelly knew a determined reptile could get to her regardless, so she tried not to think about that. She laid in a supply of water to go with the tubers. She hadn't found any more fruit, but she had spotted some things that looked like crayfish in the water. She might try to catch some of them later. But the main thing was to get Bart back. She prayed he would be able to walk, because she couldn't carry him.

She looked at the moon again. It was beginning to have a distinctive after-midnight look about it. She couldn't arrive at the village too early, when the pirates might still be awake, nor could she arrive too late, when they might be awakening for the day.

Kelly was still without a definite plan, though she had several contingencies in mind. The gun was useless—with or without operating instructions—though it could come in handy for Bart. Accordingly, she had hidden it near the village for use later.

The knife, on the other hand, was a weapon she could use. All afternoon she had struggled with the question of how she would deal with a guard. Could she slit his throat? Her mind was filled with all the reasons she should, but she doubted she had the stomach for it. She thought she could kill someone in self-defense, but to slay an unsuspecting or sleeping man seemed an impossible task.

Kelly didn't know whether she would have to deal with that. *Everything* was unknown, including whether or not Bart had survived the torture. Still, this was her chance. For Bart's sake, as well as her own, she had to make the best of it.

She crawled out of the lean-to. It was darker than the previous night because of the waning moon. That might prove to be an advantage when she got to the village.

Wedging the knife under the band of her bikini, Kelly tried not to worry about what she might step on. Moving through the dense vegetation was difficult. At times the moon was blacked out by the thick canopy of trees. A couple of times she became mired in vines and had to back out of a tangle and try another route. More than once a vine slapped against her face, bringing her to the verge of a bloodcurdling scream.

At last she came upon the village. There was no sign of life except for a faint glow coming from the nearest hut, the one she thought Bart was being held in. Peeking in the window might be a good way to begin, she decided, but the huts were built on low pilings, some distance above the ground. Kelly spied an oil drum and thought she might be able to move it under the window so she could see in.

She worried about the dogs. Would she be better off to seek them out and renew their friendship, or deal with them as the need arose? Recalling the old saw, she elected to let them lie. Then, taking a deep breath, she moved into the open.

The only sound was the wind in the palms and the distant crash of the waves. Considering how fearful she'd been all day, her entry into the village almost seemed too easy. But, as Bart had pointed out, the pirates didn't know she was around, which meant she'd have the element of surprise.

Kelly reached the rear of the hut. As she'd suspected, the window was a good two feet above her head. Fortunately, the oil drum was empty, so she rolled it to the window. The trick would be to climb up on it without making any noise. Tumbling it over would be as subtle as setting off a burglar alarm, but she wasn't about to walk into the hut without knowing what was inside.

She put her right knee on top of the barrel. It was rusty but seemed sturdy enough. As she pulled up her second leg, her foot thumped the side of the barrel. The noise sounded like a cannon shot. Kelly froze.

There was a sound from inside. When she heard it again, she realized it was snoring. Her heart pounded as she prayed it was Bart. Kelly hadn't slept with enough men to know the variety of male snoring patterns, but the sound seemed familiar.

Suddenly something wet touched her ankle. Kelly stifled a scream as her leg recoiled in reflex, thumping the barrel again. When she looked down she saw two glowing eyes. It was Fido.

Kelly wanted to shoo him away, but she knew she dare not make a sound—the two thumps had been bad enough. She steadied herself and slowly rose. But Fido refused to be rejected. He whimpered and got on his hind legs, making a scratching sound on the side of the rusty barrel. Then he barked. Not once, but three or four times.

Kelly quickly looked in the window. The fisherman was on his side, curled up on his cot, apparently asleep. On the table next to him, glowing faintly, was a kerosene lamp.

Bart was on the plank floor, asleep, his hands bound behind him, his ankles tied, too. His battered face was visible, as well as the welts on his body where they'd beaten him. Kelly's heart constricted.

Fido yapped again. Kelly knew she had to shut him up before he woke somebody, so she climbed down. She sat on the sand and let him sniff his master's shirt.

At least the situation was clear now. She had to sneak inside the hut, awaken Bart without alerting the guard, cut the ropes and help Bart escape. She had the knife. All she needed was the courage.

Kelly told herself that if the guard were to awaken while she was inside, she'd have to kill him. The alternative was too horrible to contemplate.

The problem now was the dog. Given his friendliness, he'd likely want to go into the hut with her. That would never do. Realizing he was more enamored of the fisherman's shirt than he was with her, Kelly unbuttoned it and put it in the sand next to old Fido. He looked confused. He gazed at the shirt and then at her, sniffing each in turn.

When the dog decided the shirt was more interesting, Kelly crept to the corner of the hut. She was tiptoeing along the side of the structure when she saw a figure moving toward her from the far side of the compound. She froze, shrinking into the shadows.

Knowing he would see her as soon as he got close enough, Kelly squirmed under the hut, between the pilings. She was out of sight but was able to see him easily.

The fisherman headed up the steps, letting the door bang as he entered. Kelly cursed her luck, though she knew she ought to be grateful that he hadn't come along after she'd gotten inside.

The new arrival was talking loudly, awakening the first fisherman. A minute later the man who'd been asleep stumbled down the steps and off in the direction the second man had come from.

Kelly was sick with disappointment. How long would it be before the new guard fell asleep, assuming he intended to sleep at all? Disheartened, she rolled onto her back and stared up at the flooring. Then she noticed that she was able to see light shining through the broad gaps between the planking. The spaces varied, but averaged at least a quarter to half an inch in width—wide enough to slip a knife blade through!

The realization sent her heart pounding. She might be able to present Bart with a blade to cut himself free. True, that might not be easy if the guard was awake, but even if he didn't sleep, it was unlikely he'd sit there staring at his prisoner. It seemed worth a try.

Kelly worked her way across the underside of the structure. The farther in she went, the narrower the crawl space became, forcing her to slither on her stomach.

The ground was a combination of sand and litter. It smelled to high heaven. Worse, there were cobwebs. Kelly had visions of spiders hanging down from the planks, ready to crawl through her hair or across her face. The thought set her teeth on edge, but she told herself she couldn't let her fears stop her.

When she finally got to the point where she figured Bart would be, she noticed that a dark object obliterated the light. She'd calculated correctly. Now the question was how to get his attention without alerting the guard. She could poke him with the blade, but she had to be subtle.

Kelly tried to recall the position of his body. She couldn't tell much by what she was able to see through the cracks—only his perimeters. Eventually she'd want to stick the blade in front of his face. Once he saw that, there would be little doubt who was under the hut.

As she lay there thinking, Kelly sensed a presence. She turned her head slowly, horror rising in her gorge. Three feet away she saw the luminescent glow of two beady eyes. Rat's eyes. Sickness went through her like death. Every vile creature on earth was suddenly stalking her. Wasn't survival hard enough without this?

Kelly fought down her panic. She continued to stare at the eyes. They refused to blink, they refused to move. Would the damn thing be content to watch? she wondered.

The thought hardly registered before the creature moved. Closer!

Kelly had no idea if her eyes glowed back, but her size didn't seem to intimidate the intruder. Fortunately the thing didn't venture near her face. She wouldn't have been able to stand that. She would have screamed bloody murder, probably knocking herself unconscious trying to get out from under the hut.

Instead it went toward her lower body, moving very slowly. Kelly shook her leg, but that didn't bother the rat. When she lifted herself to see what it was up to, she clunked her head on the floorboards. It wasn't a hard clunk, but it was enough to frighten her. Her head dropped back to the ground. Then she felt it, a feathery tickle against her lower thigh. Whiskers! Rat whiskers!

She shook her leg again. The feathery touch stopped, but after a few seconds she felt a prickling sensation just above her kneecap. Feet! Rat feet!

Kelly moaned. What if it got on top of her and walked along her leg? The thought was too much to bear. She drew the knife from the band of her bikini and took a swipe toward where she thought the rat would be. She only hit the ground, but the attack was enough to send the animal scampering off, squealing hideously.

Kelly lay still for a second, trying to calm her pounding heart. In the silence she could hear Bart snoring, sleeping like a baby. Ironically, she would have traded places with him if she could. If it hadn't been for the torture, and the fact that it was her fault, she'd have given him a poke with the knife. As it was, she'd probably have to, anyway—to wake him up.

Kelly pushed the blade through a crack until she hit him. The reaction was a loud snore. She tried again in a different spot. This time there was movement.

She peered through the cracks, hoping to recognize a body part. Bart seemed to be turning over, and she saw what might have been his head. Poking the blade up, she ran it downward, to the first dark mass, a shoulder, perhaps. Movement again and sounds of awakening.

Though the guard could be watching, Kelly knew she had little choice but to continue. She moved the blade back and forth, in hopes that Bart would be looking at it. Then she withdrew it to await a reaction. There was more movement, and then she saw an eye peering through the crack.

She wanted to say something, but she couldn't risk it. All she could think to do was present the knife blade and let Bart take it from there. Gauging the position of his body, she put the knife through a crack at a point she hoped would be behind him, just below the waist. Then it would be up to him.

After several moments she felt a tugging against the blade. He was sawing the ropes on the cutting edge of the knife, just as she had hoped!

Finally she felt something give. Then she heard a voice. It was the guard. Kelly withdrew the blade. She heard footsteps, then more harsh words.

Suddenly there was a thud, a stifled cry, a crash. There were two or three violent thumps against the wood floor, then silence.

Kelly couldn't stand the uncertainty. "Bart," she said, "are you all right?"

There was a silence, then he said, "I'm untying my feet."

Her heart soared. She didn't need to be told to get out from under the house. As she reached the edge of the structure, she heard Bart descending the steps. A second later he appeared. He was half doubled over, holding his side. In the faint light she could see his badly mangled face. Sticking the knife back in the band of her bikini, she ran to him. Bart limped forward, almost falling before she got there.

He put an arm around her, and she did her best to support him. "Thanks, babe," he whispered. "I thought I was a dead man."

They began moving toward the jungle. Behind them, on the far side of the compound, the other dog barked. Fido stood at the back of the hut where Kelly had left him. The fisherman's shirt was lying in the sand. He yapped at the sight of them but didn't sound too unfriendly.

Bart was limping badly, and he groaned with each step. "How bad is it?" she asked.

"A few broken ribs, I think. Maybe a cracked bone in my leg. I can only see out of one eye."

They reached the spot where the dog stood guarding the shirt. Kelly paused to pick it up. Fido wagged his tail and yapped again. The other dog ran toward them.

"We've got to get into the jungle," Bart said.

Kelly worried that a bullet would crash into her before they made it to cover, but it didn't happen. As they reached the foliage, Bart collapsed. Kelly knelt beside him, and he reached up and touched her face. Despite the darkness, she was able to see his smile.

"I guess we're even now," he said. "A life for a life."

"Bart, I'm so sorry. It's all my fault."

He was wincing. "Does that mean the sex is not necessarily over?"

"Sex? How can you think about sex at a time like this?"

"You've got to think about something when you're trying to decide if life's worth living."

"And you were thinking about *sex?*"

"I wasn't thinking about import-export." He started to laugh, but the pain must have been too much, because the sound turned into a groan.

The barking dog had quieted down. Fido hadn't followed them into the jungle, but Kelly could hear him several yards away, whining sadly.

Bart noticed, too. "Seems like you made a friend."

"It's because of the shirt. I think the guy at the pool was his master." She took advantage of the opportunity to slip the shirt back on.

He took a painful breath. "Crawling under the house like that was brilliant, by the way. Brilliant."

"Actually, it was accidental. I was going to come in the door until they changed guards."

"Where's the gun?"

"I've got it hidden in the bushes. Shall I get it?"

"Yeah, if you can find it in the dark."

"I think I can. The question is whether you'll be able to make it back to camp."

"I'll have to try. The alternative is not very appealing."

"What happened, anyway? Why did the police leave you with the pirates?"

"I guess they liked the isolation of the spot. Instead of taking me back to the head man in Bangkok, they decided it would be better if he came here. They probably figured this would be a convenient place to dispose of me once they got what they wanted."

"Then it's true what you said about the corrupt police officials."

"That reception I got in the village wasn't a training exercise, babe."

"What is it they want, anyway?"

"It's a long story. Let's discuss it later. Right now we've got to get out of here. Why don't you find the gun and then we'll go."

Kelly crawled off then to search for the weapon. It took her a good five minutes to locate the right bush. When she got back to Bart, he was lying on his back, staring up at the stars.

The moonlight coming through the branches fell squarely on his face. The sight of his battered flesh made her heart go out to him. "Poor Bart," she said as she hovered over him, "you look dreadful."

"That's about how I feel, too."

He lightly touched her bruised cheek. "You're sure a sight for sore eyes. Prettiest damn thing I've ever seen, even with a shiner."

"I guess we make a real pair."

He kissed the tip of his finger and pressed it against her lips. "Two bookends, Kel."

"Come on," she said, "let's get you home."

Bart struggled to sit up, but stopped where he was. Judging by his grimace, the pain was terrible. "My body's not so sure about this moving around business."

"You want to rest awhile longer?"

"Just for a second or two." He studied her, managing to smile. "By the way, have you had any good meals recently?"

"I ate some of the tubers. How about you?"

"They gave me a few bites of rice. Just enough to whet my appetite."

"At least you got something."

Bart nodded thoughtfully. "How hungry are you, anyway?"

"About a step short of cannibalism. Why?"

"It was stupid, but I ran out of that hut and left a whole pot of rice behind. It was sitting on the table."

Kelly's eyes rounded. "A whole pot?"

"Enough carbos to last us a week."

She looked back through the foliage at the hut. Light still shone out the back window. "I take it the question is whether I'm hungry enough to go back and get it?"

"It would be for you more than me."

"What if the guard wakes up?"

"He won't be waking up in this life."

Kelly didn't have to ask why. She looked at the sleeping village, the hut with a dead man on the floor, and imagined what it would be like to have a stomach full of rice.

CHAPTER NINE

THE MOON WAS LOWER, but otherwise everything in the village appeared unchanged except that both dogs were looking at her now. The main difference was that Bart was waiting in the jungle and his guard lay dead in the hut.

In less than a minute Kelly was stealing along the side of the house, keeping to the shadows. When she reached the corner, she peeked around to survey the other buildings. There was no sign of life. Both dogs had followed her all the way to the hut, but only Fido seemed interested in what she was doing.

Kelly tiptoed around to the steps and quickly made her way to the screen door. A faint glow from the kerosene lamp lit the room. She stepped inside, her eye drawn immediately to the body lying in the middle of the floor.

Her first thought was to grab the food and get out. She lifted the lid and saw that it was two-thirds full. The sight was so enticing she couldn't resist stuffing a glob in her mouth. She chewed briefly and swallowed, smiling as the lump hit her stomach.

Carefully replacing the lid, she headed for the door, then stopped dead in her tracks. A fisherman stood at the base of the steps. He was slightly older than the others. He wore shorts—his sinewy legs hard as a kick boxer's—rubber-soled sandals and a sleeveless undershirt. His taut skin was unusually dark, emphasizing the whiteness of his teeth and eyes. He grunted something that had a distinctively malevolent ring to it.

"I know I wasn't invited," Kelly said, "but would losing a little rice hurt you all that much?" She didn't know where the comment came from, but it didn't matter. The man understood her about as well as she'd understood him.

He said something under his breath as his eyes focused on her legs. Then her shirt caught his attention. His eyes turned hard and his demeanor became instantly commanding. He motioned her back into the hut.

Kelly struck a defiant pose. The fisherman reached behind his back and drew a knife.

That familiar lost feeling came over her. Why did she keep running into little guys with excess testosterone?

As he started toward her, Kelly firmly planted her foot in the middle of his chest and gave him a tremendous shove. He went flying, landing hard on his backside. She dashed down the steps, but the fisherman caught her ankle, sending her sprawling. The pot clanked as she hit the ground.

Before Kelly could recover, the pirate had scrambled to his feet, shouting an alarm. She picked up the pot and swung it at him, catching him on the shoulder and knocking him to the ground a second time. That gave her a chance to make her escape.

Cursing, the pirate took off after her. Kelly knew it would be a footrace. The heavy pot put her at a disadvantage, but she refused to drop it. And although the ground felt like quicksand, adrenaline drove her legs.

She'd made it halfway to the jungle when the fisherman dived, catching her heel. She frantically rolled over, but by that time he was up again and coming at her. She recoiled at the expected jolt when a shot rang out, spinning the fisherman in midair. He landed on her legs with a thump.

Shuddering, Kelly pulled herself free. There were shouts from the village. The whole place seemed suddenly alive.

The dogs began barking excitedly. Kelly staggered to her feet and started toward the jungle.

"The rice!" Bart shouted from his hiding place.

Kelly stopped, went back, picked up the pot, then resumed her dash for cover. Tripping over a vine, she fell almost at Bart's feet, just inside the cover of the jungle. She was gasping for air. Incredibly, Bart was smiling.

"The tides of obligation have swung again," he said, bemused. "If I'm not mistaken, it's now advantage to me."

Kelly, breathless, slammed her fist into the ground.

As she scrambled to her feet, Bart squeezed off a few rounds, just enough to send the pirates diving for cover. Then he slung the rifle over his shoulder and staggered about ten yards before he sank to his knees. Kelly, still carrying the rice pot, was at his side at once. "Just give me a minute or two to catch my breath, babe. Then we can get the hell out of here."

"Do you think they'll come after us?"

"Not right now. Those shots probably slowed them down, and anyway, they can't see any better than we can at night. My guess is they'll wait until morning to come looking for us. Our main problem right now is our lack of mobility."

"You can say that again. Do you think you can make it back to our camp?"

"Yeah, but I won't be breaking any speed records." He took a deep breath, then struggled to his feet. Kelly helped him get his balance before she picked up the rice pot. "Damn good thing they make this stuff gooey. I bet you didn't lose a grain."

He groaned as a stab of pain shot through his ribs. She shifted the pot to her other hand and put her arm around his waist. It felt good to have the support, but even better to feel her body. The simple kindness of her touch was heaven. Bart knew, even if she didn't, that he'd never make it without her.

He had been certain he'd never see her again, never touch her or hear her voice. He still couldn't believe she'd come after him—that they were together again.

"Let's get out of here, Bart. I want us to live long enough to eat the damned stuff," she said.

He started to chuckle, but another stab of pain made him wince instead.

"You all right?" she asked quickly.

"Sure. A couple of broken ribs, a gimpy leg. I'll live to fight another day... I hope."

"Well, you may be a cripple, but at least you can shoot." She paused for a moment. "Is that another skill you picked up in the import-export markets, or did you shoot bear in Nebraska?"

"You've missed your turn at sarcasm, my dear. You're the one beholden right now, remember?" he said as they started off into the undergrowth. The pain in his leg was almost unbearable, but at least he was alive.

"This is a game I'm willing to let you win if we could just stop now," she lamented. "Why can't we call time-out and go off for a nice brunch at the Halekulani?"

"With me instead of Mr. Wonderful?"

"At this point, I'm not particular. I just want out of this nightmare."

When Kelly paused to see if anyone was following them, Bart took the opportunity to rest. He sank to the ground. She stood next to him as they both listened, but all they could hear were the night sounds of the jungle. No voices, no noise of men following.

Bart gingerly pressed his battered face against her thigh. It felt so good to touch her. He'd thought of this while they were beating him—what it was like to make love with her, spar with her, just look at her. And in a way, he was half afraid this was only a dream.

"By the way, Kel, thanks again for saving my skin. I was sure I was a goner."

"All part of the service," she said.

He patted her leg. "Maybe. But it must have been hell for you, doing that alone."

"I'll tell you this much. This hasn't been my idea of a fun vacation."

"Mine, either," he said. "Except for a few terrific moments, anyway."

She was stroking his head in an affectionate, almost maternal way, when they heard a dog bark. But the sound seemed to come from a distance.

"Are you sure they won't come after us tonight?" she asked.

"I don't think so. But the police will be back in the morning. Perhaps in force."

Kelly groaned. "Lord, you mean they're going to hunt us down like animals? How will we survive?"

"The same way we have till now."

He'd heard the hopelessness in her voice, but he understood it better now. Kelly got down, but she was tough—a hell of a lot tougher than he'd thought, even after she'd survived that awful swim. Dear God, it had taken guts for her to come after him like that. Even making her way alone from the camp to the village had to have been difficult for her. But she'd done it.

He ran his hand up and down her calf, partly to reassure her, partly to reassure himself. Her skin felt smooth and cool compared to his. It was comforting to touch her. It reminded him of his childhood in the orphanage, wishing he had a mother to hold him, and hugging his pillow instead because it was all he had. Well, he wasn't a little boy anymore, and Kelly wasn't a pillow. Best of all, he wasn't wasting time wishing for something he couldn't have. Kelly was exactly who he wanted and she was with him now. Somehow that made the world seem a better place.

"I think we'd best get you home before you collapse for the last time," she said. "You need to rest."

"You're the nurse."

"No, Bart. I'm the doctor."

He imagined a grin on her face, but it was too dark to tell. He got to his feet, and they started off again. Bart put more and more of his weight on her. He knew she wouldn't be able to support him like that forever, but it was the best he could do. Besides, even if they didn't make it to camp, he figured the closer they got, the better off they'd be.

Their navigation was surprisingly accurate, considering the darkness, and the proximity of the hillock to the beach made it easier than it otherwise would have been. Placing the camp on a hilltop had turned out to be one of his better decisions. When they broke into the small clearing, he collapsed again.

Kelly knelt beside him. "Get into the shelter, Bart," she told him. "We'll eat, I'll wash your wounds and then we'll get some sleep."

He didn't argue. He dutifully crawled into the lean-to, promptly rolling onto his back. His leg felt as if a truck had run over it. Kelly made him as comfortable as she could, then scooped out a glob of rice from the pot, formed it into a little ball and put it into his mouth. He raised his head to swallow, then lay back down again and said, "You eat. I'll rest for a moment."

Kelly quickly consumed three or four handfuls before she offered him another one. "I'll say one thing for those guys," she said between bites. "They sure can cook."

"Delicious, isn't it?" He smacked his lips.

"This proves the old saying that everything is relative."

Bart laughed but had to hold his side. "I sure could use a drink."

"Former Brownie that I am," she said, "I just happened to have a few bowls of water prepared."

"Ah, what an angel."

They each had another bite of rice before Kelly crawled out to get the water. She offered him a drink, using a folded leaf as a cup. After drinking, he lay back down. It hurt to breathe, but he told himself he would have endured much worse to spare her a similar fate.

Kelly began gently dabbing his face with a part of her shirt she'd torn off and moistened with some of the water.

"Why did they beat you? Were they sadistic or what?"

"That's part of it. They didn't like me killing that guy at the pool, but I think it was primarily to soften me up for the main event. Tomorrow I was scheduled for an official Thai police interrogation."

"I was surprised when they didn't take you back with them on the helicopter."

"They must have decided that discretion was in order. As best I can tell, these pirates are in the drug loop too, though rather remote from the people I've been involved with. The cop who came yesterday knew them. Thank God neither he nor the fishermen counted on my having help."

"Is that what this is all about, drugs?"

Bart sighed. "I guess you can't get into this mess much deeper than you already are." He hesitated for only a second before going on. "I've been operating undercover as a dealer, but I'm really working for the government."

"Then why were you so evasive earlier? If you'd just come out with it, you might not have had to go through that beating."

"I was trying to protect you, Kelly. I told you that."

"Protect me from what? The truth?"

"Can we change the subject?"

"No, we can't change the subject," she retorted. "Your credibility is already shaky. I still don't know what to believe."

"Would I go to so much trouble to save your sweet little butt if I wasn't firmly on the side of good and virtue?"

"On your lips, virtue is as slippery as that snake you wanted to eat," she murmured.

Bart laughed again, but immediately fell back in pain, groaning.

"Serves you right!"

"Oh, please," he moaned, "don't give me a hard time. Don't use your lawyer brain. Just pretend you're naive and trusting."

"That's the problem, Bart. I was naive and trusting. And everything you've done has undermined my trust."

"Don't tell me you're mad at me," he said with despair. He didn't feel up to an argument.

"I find you very annoying at times, Mr. Monday."

Bart put his hand on her thigh, rubbing it lovingly. Kelly took his wrist and moved his hand.

"Don't even think about it," she said. "Anyway, you're too badly injured."

"For what?"

"What you were thinking."

"Which was?"

"Oh, Bart, shut up! You know perfectly well."

She was still being defensive, but he sensed it was more token resistance than before. She *did* care about him, he could tell, though he wasn't quite sure how he knew. One thing was certain—it was more than just the fact she'd risked her life for him.

And yet, in spite of the way she felt, she was fighting him. He'd have discussed it with her, but he was fairly sure she'd get even more defensive. The problem was, she hadn't admitted her feelings to herself.

"Maybe we should get some sleep," he said.

Kelly was very still in the darkness. He wished he could see her face. He wondered what her expression might tell him.

"I'm sorry, Bart," she said softly. "I'm tired and jumpy and scared to death. Knife fights aren't normally a part of my daily routine."

"Come lie down next to me," he said.

She lay beside him, but immediately rolled onto her side and pulled some fronds over them for warmth. Bart scooted as close to her as he could, even though she turned her back to him. He put his arm around her and pulled her even closer, liking the feel of her body against his.

After a few minutes of silence she said, "It was difficult without you last night. I missed you."

"I missed you, too. I worried about you."

"Did you?"

"Yes, I knew what I was facing, but I didn't know what was going to happen to you. I didn't want them to kill you because of me, but I figured they would. That was the worst thing of all."

She half turned her head toward him. "You really believe they'd do that?"

"Yes," he said. Kelly settled back. He caressed her arm, running his hand along it. "Even now, I'm reluctant to tell you everything. If there's a chance they'll spare you, it would only be because of your ignorance."

She didn't respond, and that was okay because he was suddenly very tired. He craved sleep, and with her in his arms the world seemed to have found its balance again. His mouth was near the nape of her neck. He nuzzled closer, touching her soft skin with his parched lips. His pain faded into the background. He half consciously kissed her neck, and when Kelly didn't move he figured she'd already fallen asleep.

Bart felt himself begin to drift off. His last thought was that in the morning he'd tell her he loved her.

THE THROB OF HELICOPTER blades bored into her subconscious with the persistence of a morning hangover. Kelly wasn't ready to wake up, and it took several moments for her to realize where she was. Then it all came tumbling back.

She looked around. Bart was next to her, snoring, dead to the world. The throb of helicopter blades was so loud she wondered how he could continue to sleep.

She jostled him. "I think the police are back. Bart?"

He was zonked, unfazed by either the sound or her imploring.

"Bart! There's a helicopter up there, maybe half the Thai air force. Wake up!"

One wary eye opened a crack. "Huh?"

"A helicopter. Don't you hear it?"

The second eye opened. For the first time he seemed among the living. He raised his head. "What time is it?"

She rolled her eyes. "How should I know? The alarm didn't go off."

He raised himself to his elbow and looked through the ceiling of the lean-to. "Choppers."

"Yes. That's what I've been trying to tell you."

The pounding sounded as though it was directly overhead. Bart started to crawl out of the shelter, but he suddenly froze with pain. "Shit." He groaned. "Stick your head out and see if it looks like they've spotted us. Being in a clearing makes us sitting ducks for aircraft."

"Nice time to think about it." She crawled to the edge of the lean-to and stuck her head out. She immediately spotted two choppers. One was circling the hilltop at four or five hundred feet. A second one was farther away. "I think the closest one is looking this way," she said.

"Don't let him see you. Get back in here."

She pulled her head back inside. "There's another farther away." She took another peek. "No, make that two more. God, it's like a swarm of mosquitoes out there."

"Unfortunately we don't have the right repellent."

"What's that?"

"A surface-to-air missile."

"We do have a knife and gun," she said with pointed sarcasm.

Bart ignored the comment. "We slept too late."

"If you'd warned me that you wanted to get up earlier, I might have tried. At home my eyes pop open five minutes before my alarm clock every morning."

Bart shook his head with amazement. "There's tremendous talent hidden in that beautiful skull of yours, isn't there?"

She gave him a dark look.

The sound of the helicopters grew fainter. Kelly took another peek out the door, but could see nothing.

"I think they've gone."

Bart was thinking.

"So, what now, *mon général?*" she said.

"We have to assume they've spotted us. They'll land and come in here on foot. I'd say we have fifteen minutes at the outside."

"So what do we do, surrender or retreat?"

Bart grinned for the first time that morning. "What do you think, babe?"

CHAPTER TEN

BART DIDN'T WANT TO LOSE any more time. He grabbed the gun and knife while Kelly took charge of the rice pot and one of her handmade bowls. They each had a final drink of water and then they were ready to go.

By then one of the helicopters had returned, making it a certainty they'd been spotted earlier. Bart knew each minute of waiting reduced their chances of getting away before the ground contingent reached them. But if they headed out now, the guys in the chopper might shoot at them. They were damned, whatever he decided. And Kelly's fate was tied to his.

He studied her face to gauge her mood. She seemed anxious, fearful, but she was in control of herself. Bart cursed, knowing every minute was precious to them. It was his fault they'd overslept. Kelly was counting on him and he'd let her down.

Then, much to his relief, the helicopter suddenly headed back toward the beach. Bart immediately crawled out of the lean-to. He needed Kelly's help to stand, but once he was on his feet he felt pretty good—a hell of a lot better than the night before. "Amazing what a good night's sleep will do for a guy," he said, pinching her cheek.

"So nice that you're a morning person," she said. "I'd hate to have to put up with a grumpy disposition on top of everything else."

He savored the sight of her in the full light. Her eye didn't look so swollen now, and her bruises had faded to a pale green. He was sure she looked better than he did. Bart felt around his eye. He could see out of it, but it was swollen, and probably purple.

He gazed up at the still-empty sky. "Come on, Kelly, let's get out of here. Gotta follow that yellow brick road."

She grinned, bemused. "Think there'll be a wizard waiting for us at the end?"

"If so, let's hope he's not carrying an M-16."

He could walk without leaning on her, though he limped badly. His leg felt strong enough to support his weight for now, but even if the bone wasn't cracked, he didn't think he'd be able to walk on it for too long without it swelling. Kelly couldn't manage both him and the rice pot, and that meant they had to get as far as they could as fast as they could. With luck, it might be far enough.

Wasting no time, he left the clearing, plunging into the thick jungle. He took the lead, telling her it would be better if he set the pace, considering his leg. Kelly hadn't argued. In a way, she seemed more subdued than she'd been since this whole mess had started.

"Do you have any idea where we're going?" she asked after they'd been walking for a few minutes.

"I'd like to say Bangkok, but there's a little matter of a couple of hundred miles of open sea to contend with."

The undergrowth soon became dense and he had to pick their route carefully. They could hear the helicopter circling their abandoned camp.

"I have a hunch we got out just in time," he said. "The ground contingent should be arriving any minute now."

Kelly stopped beside him. "Will they be able to follow us?"

"They'll try, but tracking someone in the jungle isn't a picnic."

Kelly seemed somewhat relieved, but it was evident she wasn't going to follow him blindly.

"Seriously, where *are* we headed?" she asked, as if to underscore his very thought.

"The way I look at it, we've seen about three percent of this island. Who knows what the interior is like, or even the other side of the island? I figure we can hole up somewhere in the interior for a day or two, probably on the mountain. When I get stronger, we can scout out the place more thoroughly. A boat or some other opportunity is bound to present itself eventually."

"Assuming they don't use bloodhounds in the tropics."

He gave her a telling look. "Being a small, mobile band, we can use guerrilla tactics if need be."

"Small being the operative word."

They could hear helicopters again. Bart looked up through the high canopy overhead. "Aren't you having fun yet, Kel?"

She smiled sardonically. "You can't imagine how much I wish you were putting me on, Bart. I'd sleep with you for a month if you'd just get me out of here in one piece."

He cupped her chin in his hand. "You may live to regret that promise, sweetheart." He turned then, and resumed the trek.

They fought their way through thick undergrowth for about twenty minutes. The helicopters were constantly circling the area, but Bart was sure that so long as they stayed in the dense jungle they'd be impossible to spot from a chopper. The air search wouldn't last much longer, but the land search was another matter.

Unfortunately he was already starting to run out of steam. He was limping more severely, and he'd been forced to slow their pace. He knew he had to get his weight off his leg for a few minutes, so he suggested they rest. He sat on the ground, leaning against a tree. Kelly put down the pot and sat beside him. They were deeper in the jungle than they'd ever been; it was humid, a lot more humid than near the beach.

"You know," she said, "I'm beginning to resign myself to the fact that we aren't going to be leaving here anytime soon. It's a mistake to keep hoping and praying, only to be disappointed."

"It might help if you think of this as a nature excursion."

"I know you're making an effort to keep things light so that I won't flip out completely and go running off into the jungle, screaming, but maybe it's better to think in terms of sober reality."

"The problem is, it's not completely in our hands."

She shook her head, a sad expression on her face. "You know, I'm not used to that. I've always felt so in control of my destiny. And now I'm discovering how little power I really have and how much I've taken for granted all these years."

"Like the man said, there's no point in worrying about the things you can't control, so think instead about the things you can."

"What man was that? Thoreau? Emerson? Franklin?"

"More like Babe Ruth or Ty Cobb, I imagine. It's a baseball cliché."

She rolled her eyes. "I knew sports would become pivotal in my life one day... if I waited long enough."

He chuckled, patting her hand.

"Oh, God," Kelly said, turning her face toward the heavens, "what the hell am I doing here? I should be taking a deposition in some nice air-conditioned office, not running through the jungle half-naked, in fear for my life."

"I could use a gin and tonic myself."

Kelly gave him a punch in the arm. "You have a knack for getting to the bottom line, don't you, Mr. Monday?"

"It's all part of my survival technique. You can't start worrying about God and the true meaning of life until they've got you lined up before the firing squad and they're offering you a last cigarette."

"I don't smoke, so I guess I don't have to worry about that conundrum, do I?"

They exchanged smiles.

"So, tell me about your life in Honolulu," he said. "Where do you live?"

"I've got a condo, with a view of Diamond Head."

"And you drive a Jaguar."

"A Porsche."

"I was close."

She shut her eyes and took a deep breath. There was a slight smile around the corners of her mouth. Bart watched her for a minute.

"You have such a wistful expression on your face," he said. "What are you thinking about?"

"My bathroom at home."

"Your *bathroom?*"

Her eyes flew open. "Oh, yes, it has such wonderful white tile, and everything gleams when it's scrubbed. If I ever get back, I'm going to lie down on the floor and kiss the tile."

He pushed a wisp of hair off her face, smiling. "It's hard to imagine you as a proper socialite lawyer, all dignified with makeup and jewelry and..."

"Clothes?"

"Yes, clothes and a supercilious attitude."

"I'm not a socialite and I'm not supercilious."

He looked her up and down. "I guess, to be honest, I like to think of you just as you are now, this minute."

"Half-naked and unwashed. Yeah, this is my essence, all right."

Bart reflected. "So you own a big fancy condo in Hawaii and drive a sports car, huh?"

"The condo's not that big, just two bedrooms, and I use one of them as a home office. I inherited some money from an aunt. I used the biggest part of it to pay for law school, and I put the remainder down on the condo."

"You've lived in Hawaii all your life?"

"Except for three years in law school, yes. My parents were Californians, but they went to Hawaii on their honeymoon and liked it so much that they decided to move there. Mom was a clothing designer, and Dad had always wanted his own business. He scraped together every dime he could lay his hands on, and they started a swimsuit business."

"That took guts. I can see where you got your courage."

Kelly laughed. "Oh, they had courage, all right. They had some hard years early on, but they made a success of it. Daddy died just before I went to law school. Mother sold the business, but she still does free-lance designs. In fact, she brought me this suit I'm wearing the night before I left to fly to Bangkok."

"I must tell your mother that I admire her taste," he said.

"You mean, assuming you ever meet her."

"Oh, I'll meet her, all right. You don't think I'm going to fade into the sunset, never to be seen again, once we're out of here, do you?"

When she didn't reply he glanced over at her and saw anguish on her face. He realized immediately she wasn't thinking about him. More likely it was the guy back home. Evidently it had been a mistake to bring up the future and try to place himself in it. He imagined she was feeling guilty about having had sex with him, as well. Damn. That would teach him to speak without thinking. At least he hadn't been stupid enough to tell her he loved her. She probably would have laughed in his face.

He glanced over at her and saw she still looked thoughtful. He decided the wisest course would be to beat a hasty retreat. "What I mean is...Kel...people don't go through things like this without...keeping in touch. We'll probably have a reunion in ten years to tip a glass to the ordeal, don't you think?"

"I don't know," she said softly. "I haven't thought that far ahead."

"We've been through more together than most high school classmates," he said, trying to sound lighthearted.

"I suppose." She gazed off into the distance. The conversation had clearly touched a nerve.

"You're thinking of Mr. Wonderful, aren't you?" he asked quietly.

She blinked. "How did you know?"

"Lucky guess." He picked up a leaf and started shredding it. "You known him long?"

"Yes. Nearly five years."

"Then what took you so long...I mean, if he's so wonderful and all, why haven't you married?"

"Because until recently he was already married. But now we're engaged."

"Oh, I see...one of those situations." He tried to sound matter-of-fact, but when Kelly's head whipped around in his direction, he realized he hadn't succeeded.

"No, it's not one of *those* situations, Mr. Monday," she said pointedly. "Duncan and I did not have an extramarital affair and I did not break up his marriage. He didn't so much as leer at me until after he split up with his wife."

"Oh, I see. Duncan is the noble type, apparently. I can admire that."

"And I can do without the sarcasm."

"Hey, I'm not judging. Just trying to be supportive."

"Somehow it doesn't ring true, Bart. Let's just drop it, shall we? I'll worry about Duncan and you worry about whomever."

"My hands are full worrying about you, my love. No point in taking on additional burdens."

Kelly looked at him as if she wasn't sure whether he was being glib or tender. Ironically, he wasn't sure himself. After a long, uncertain silence she glanced around.

"Don't we have to get going?"

Bart groaned. "Yes. But you'll have to help me up." He reached out his hand. "Not being the noble type, I'm going to have to let you keep carrying the rice pot. The alternative is to carry me."

"I'll carry the pot, thank you very much." She helped him to his feet.

The pain in his leg was fierce. It had stiffened up on him while they rested, but there was no point complaining about it. Giving Kelly a smile, he started off through the jungle. She followed along behind, carrying the rice.

"So what does Mr. Wonderful do?" he asked as he continued to slog along.

"He's a lawyer. The head of my firm, actually."

Bart shifted the weight of the rifle slightly. "A lawyer marrying a lawyer."

"I know what you're thinking," she said. "Two attorneys in one family are a prescription for disaster. But that's not true. At least, not in our case. It depends entirely on the individuals concerned, and Duncan and I are both tolerant and understanding of each other's needs. And since we both care so deeply, we're going to try very hard to make sure it works."

"That's nice, Kelly. I'm pleased for you."

"You're mocking me."

"No, I'm not. I said, 'That's nice.' What did you expect me to say?"

"It was sarcastic."

Bart stopped and turned to face her.

"Just keep walking," she said. "I don't want to argue about something that's none of your business to begin with."

He turned without a word and headed deeper into the jungle, dragging his swollen leg. The throbbing was getting worse. Ten minutes passed before Kelly spoke again.

"Duncan understands my love for the law, and I understand his," she said. "That's why we're so compatible. It's not like having to explain to someone why it's so important to stay at the office late to prepare for a court appearance. We're both in exactly the same place."

"Sounds really romantic."

"You obviously don't understand how important things like that are," she said. "Day-to-day living is where a couple's happiness is made or broken."

"You mean day-to-day things like who carries the rice pot and who carries the rifle?"

"Very funny."

"Seems pretty elemental to me. By your standard, we'd make the perfect couple."

"Don't flatter yourself, Bart. In the outside world we probably couldn't get through lunch together without having an argument."

He stopped and turned around. Kelly put down the rice pot.

"With all due respect, Ms. Ronan, I think you've sold yourself a bill of goods about loving the law and loving your law partner. If *I* was the man you loved, I'd feel pretty bad if that was the best you could come up with in explaining why you were going to marry me."

Her hot, sweaty face turned bright red. Her eyes narrowed. "You are the most pompous, egocentric, self-righteous bastard I've ever met, Bart Monday! What makes you think I'd even try to explain my personal feelings for Duncan? You're the last person on earth I'd share them with! You couldn't possibly understand how I feel about him!"

"I beg to differ, my love. I think you've explained how you feel about him very well."

Kelly pushed past him and plunged into the jungle. "Go to hell," she called over her shoulder.

He began trudging after her. "If that's where you're headed, then I guess that's where I'm going to end up. We're in this together, babe."

"Yeah? Well, I've got the rice."

"And I've got the rifle and the best sense of direction."

"Ha!" she said.

"I thought you'd see it my way."

He shrugged and followed her. Fortunately her pace wasn't too fast for him to keep up.

"You know, Bart," she said a few minutes later, "sometimes you remind me of my mother."

"I think you said that once before. Something about life being one big adventure for her, wasn't that it?"

"You got it. She and my brother, Skip, like living on the edge, seeking thrills and new experiences at every turn. Not me. I like a nice, safe, conservative life."

"The kind you'll have with Duncan," he said sweetly.

"Yes."

"You think he'll still have you after he finds out you've been rooting around in the jungle with an old war-horse?"

She turned to give him a nasty look. "Duncan will understand that these are exceptional circumstances. He's a mature and sensitive human being, which is more than I can say for you!"

"Yeah, well, if Duncan is so wonderful, why did you come to Thailand without him? If he's head of the firm, couldn't he have managed to take the time off to come with you?'' he asked.

She picked up her pace a bit. "That does it! I'm not talking to you about Duncan again. Why people keep questioning the way I live my life is beyond me."

"Let me guess. Your mother said the same thing?"

Kelly stopped walking. She turned to him, her eyes narrowed. "Yes, as a matter of fact."

Bart gave her a lopsided grin. "Sounds to me like your mom is a lady after my own heart."

"Are you kidding, she'd absolutely adore you." Realizing what she'd said, Kelly turned an even brighter shade of red. She turned and started through the jungle again.

"Does Duncan know your mom doesn't like him?" he called after her.

"Shut up, Bart! Will you just shut up!"

He laughed to himself, but knew he had to be careful. He may have pushed her a little too hard. "Hold on, pumpkin," he implored. "Not too fast. This leg's complaining."

"It can fall off, for all I care!"

"Hmm," he mumbled to himself. "Seems I've struck a chord."

Bart stumbled along as best he could, walking much faster than he comfortably could, just to keep pace. He kept his eye on the sweet curve of her half-naked derriere, and that helped keep him going.

Ah, life was good, he thought. Sometimes at least. Now, if he could just get them both out of this mess. What he wouldn't give to have Kelly all to himself in a suite at the Oriental. They could stay in bed for a week—making love, living off room service. He rubbed his grizzly chin, contemplating her long legs.

Kelly was starting to pull farther away, causing him to momentarily lose sight of her. "Hey, Daniel Boone," he called, "you're veering off course. If you keep going in that direction, we'll be back where we started before too long."

She stopped and waited for him, her hands on her hips. "All right, kemo sabe, you lead, then."

"I wasn't being critical. It's just that I think we might be better off going more that way," he said, pointing.

"That's fine by me."

He tried to lift her chin to make her look at him, but she pushed his hand away. "I'm sorry if I said some things about Duncan that upset you. It's probably only jealousy."

She looked at him with surprise. Bart shrugged.

"The heat of the jungle makes people irritable, jealous, hungry, horny—you name it, the jungle will do it to you," he said.

"Nice try, Bart. But you might consider saving some of your material. If the undercover business goes bad, you could always try the comedy clubs. At least it's an honest living."

"You're angry with me," he said with mock concern.

"If I didn't feel you were my only hope of getting off this godforsaken island, I'd be gone in a flash. And you can take that personally."

"I *am* sorry," he said.

She sighed. "Well, let's forget it." She looked down at his leg. "Do you need to rest again?"

"I could use a drink of water," he replied. "How about you?"

"Yes. And a bath. And a nice chateaubriand with... lime sherbet for dessert."

"Lime sherbet?"

"It was my favorite when I was growing up," she said wistfully.

"I can't promise you a lime sherbet, but I might be able to come up with some water. If we head over that way, we might find a stream."

THE TERRAIN BEGAN to slope upward, and the density of the vegetation kept them from seeing very far ahead. Kelly started wondering if they were going in circles, despite Bart's professed sense of direction. She switched the heavy pot from hand to hand every minute or so as she followed him.

"Please tell me you were an Eagle Scout," she said, "so I won't worry that you don't know what you're doing."

"I was an army Ranger," he said without looking back.

"Really?"

"Cross my heart and hope to die."

"That explains a lot."

"If you're referring to the pirates I've been forced to eliminate, yes."

They continued trudging through the jungle. The constant raking of the vines and branches made their skin raw. The birds were ubiquitous, and they saw a larger species of monkey high in a tree, but no other animals. Kelly found herself thinking about Bart and his former profession.

"Mind if I ask you something?" she said after a minute or two.

He stopped. "Do you have to go to the bathroom?"

"No. And if I did, I wouldn't ask for permission. It's about when you killed those pirates. It's been three...since we've been here. That's a lot." She put down the rice pot.

His eyebrows rose. "You would have preferred I hadn't?"

"No, I was just wondering..."

"If it bothered me?"

She nodded. "Yes."

"I try to think in terms of what would have happened if I hadn't killed them."

She contemplated the answer, searching his eyes.

"Satisfied?" he asked.

Kelly shrugged. "I was just curious."

"If it makes you feel any better, before this trip, it was years since I killed anybody." He bent over awkwardly and picked up the cooking pot, handing it to her. "That drink of water is waiting, and I'm getting thirstier by the minute."

Before long the terrain got steeper and the jungle thinned a little. Kelly was glad for the change. At least she knew they weren't doubling back on their route.

Bart started moving laterally along the slope until they came to a small stream. The water was running rapidly and looked fresh. Seeing it, he took the makeshift bowl and scooped some up, handing her the vessel. She took a couple of gulps and handed it back.

Bart drank with enthusiasm. Then he took the rifle off his back and lay down. He sighed, gazing up at the sky. He looked utterly exhausted. She felt badly about being so harsh with him earlier and sat cross-legged beside him.

They could hear helicopters in the distance, but it seemed the air search was petering out. She wondered what the police were likely to do next.

Now that he'd gotten the weight off his leg, Bart looked content. More than once she'd suspected he was actually enjoying their adventure, which made her mad just on principle. His face was looking better, though it was becoming more discolored. She tried to remember the way he'd looked on the *Ban Don*.

Even then he'd had a couple of days' growth of beard, though he had definitely been appealing—handsome, in fact, and an accomplished lover. Despite their continual tiffs, she did like him—though not in a way that meant anything, of course. Still, the man could be amusing, not to mention tender and sensuous.

His eyes were closed, so she took the opportunity to check out his chest. He had an appealing physique—muscular, yet not to excess; masculine, yet not brutish. Duncan was far less robust. Though trim, there was a softness about Duncan that almost made him seem a little weak.

She'd always dismissed that as unimportant. It wasn't Duncan's body she loved—it was his mind, his soul, the person he was. She was an active, athletic and physical person herself. If Duncan fell short, it was only by the comparison she was drawing to Bart, a comparison that meant nothing.

"A penny for your thoughts," he said.

The remark caught her by surprise. Bart's eyes were open and he was looking at her. She turned away. "You don't have a penny. And even if you did, my thoughts aren't for sale."

"Judging by the blissful look, it was either Duncan or me."

"Very astute, Mr. Monday. It was Duncan."

He nodded, a Cheshire-cat grin on his face. "You see. A man who understands women is a man indeed."

That amused her. "Well, since you understand us so well, and since you have a certain...shall we say, appreciation...for my sex, how is it you've never married?"

"I told you, Kelly. The life I lead doesn't lend itself to long-term relationships."

"You mean you've never met anyone you wanted to marry?"

"I came close once."

He'd piqued her interest. "And who was she?"

"The daughter of my commanding officer at Fort Benning. Gorgeous creature with chestnut hair and a dynamite bod. Smart. Pretty as could be. I met her shortly after she graduated from Auburn University.''

"What happened?"

"We were sort of engaged. The rough plan was to marry when I came back from a tour of duty in Southeast Asia. But I was gone for quite a while and Carol Lee was not the most patient woman ever to grace God's earth. She met a socially prominent doctor from Atlanta, and my irresistibility faded with the peach blossoms.''

"That must have been rough.''

"I wasn't thrilled. I went on a three-day drunk, wrote her off and vowed never to fall in love again.''

"Did you succeed?"

He hesitated before answering. "For the most part.''

They fell silent. Bart again stared up at the sky. Kelly glanced at him occasionally, feeling considerably more compassion for him than she had before. Then her lawyer brain kicked in and she wondered if there'd been a word of truth to the story.

"Have you been back to the States since?" she asked.

"Not for long. I've been out here for years.''

"Let me guess. Your lady friends have been beautiful young things who've struggled as masseuses or bar girls, with perhaps the occasional innocent but desperate prostitute who is down on her luck.''

Bart grinned. "You're more of a woman of the world than I was prepared to give you credit for.''

"Your type is not all that mysterious, Bart.''

He nodded, as though respecting the potency of his opponent's punch. "That puts me in my place.''

She immediately felt contrite. "I didn't mean to be unkind.''

"No, that's all right," he said, rising with some effort to a sitting position. "It's good we each know where we are on the social register.''

"That isn't what I meant at all." She felt badly, whether that had been his intention or not. She had been a bit too pointed. Sometimes it was difficult to remember not to go for the jugular, the way she did in court.

"I think it's better we remain strangers," he said. "That way we won't be getting into each other's sensitive areas."

"Was Carol Lee a social climber? Is that the basis of your remark?"

"I've discovered something in my thirty-eight years. The past offers little in the way of happiness. You're always better off smelling the rose you've got, not the one you had last year."

Kelly nodded.

"Well, you rested up enough?" he asked. "I want to find us a new home before evening, and God knows how much farther we have to go."

"Yes, but I would dearly love to take a sponge bath. Do we have time for a quick dip?"

Bart looked at the meager rivulet. "You won't be able to dip much in that, but if it'll please you, go ahead. I'll rest some more. These ribs have been talking to me, anyway, and my leg has been threatening to quit entirely."

Kelly got up and stepped across the little stream to an open area on the other side. Bart was stretched out on his back. She took off her shirt, then her bikini. She didn't bother to ask him not to look. They seemed well past that.

He didn't peek, even when she stepped into the stream. The water barely covered her feet, but it was wet. She knelt and began splashing, but she wasn't able to get very wet, so she lay on her back long enough to get her hair wet before rolling onto her stomach. Once she was wet all over she sat up and glanced at Bart.

His mouth had sagged open and he was snoring. Here she was, stark naked, not five feet from him, and the bastard was sound asleep!

CHAPTER ELEVEN

AFTER BART WOKE UP, he bathed. Then they gathered their gear and started moving higher, into the uplands. They hadn't heard any helicopters for a while, but from time to time they heard a light plane circling, though they never spotted it.

With the terrain getting steeper, it was more difficult for Bart to walk, and the cooking pot had gotten a lot heavier, too. Kelly had to stop every few minutes to put it down. Bart's leg had swollen. He sat on a mossy rock, elevating it.

"This mountain's a little more challenging than I expected," he said. "We'd better find a place to camp soon—the afternoon's getting on."

Kelly looked around. At this altitude, the vegetation wasn't as dense. The plants seemed more delicate, giving the place the feel of a fern bar with an enormous skylight overhead.

"It's pretty up here, isn't it?" she said.

Bart took in their surroundings. "Yeah, but to camp we need to be close to a good source of water," he said. "Why don't we work our way around the flank of the mountain and see what we can find."

They were off again, climbing through rough, rocky terrain with only a minimum of cover. Soon they came to a small gorge with a good-sized stream running through it. The vale rose rapidly past a series of waterfalls to a small boxed canyon that formed a sort of grotto, full of ferns, lacy trees, flowering plants and the stream. At the back of the canyon a sheer rock cliff ran up to the top of the mountain.

They sat on a large, flat rock at the edge of the stream, and Kelly scooped up some water, using her leaf vessel. She handed it to Bart. "This place is gorgeous. Valhalla."

He smiled. "I'm going to poke around in those rocks and see what I can find for a campsite."

Kelly took the fruit they'd found not far from the stream out of the rice pot. She examined and smelled the piece that looked like a prickly pear, trying to determine if it would be edible. The only way to know for sure was to cut it open and have a bite.

Bart had left the weapons behind, so she took the knife and cut the fruit. It was juicy and had a green, tangy smell. She sliced off a tiny wedge and popped it into her mouth. The flavor was distinctive, unlike anything she'd had before. A second bite was no better, so she set it aside to await Bart's evaluation.

The past hour the sound of an aircraft engine had been buzzing vaguely in the background, but Kelly suddenly became aware of it growing much louder. She gazed up at the open sky above the center of the glen, expecting to see the plane.

"Kelly," Bart shouted from somewhere in the rocks above, "head for cover, quick!"

She scrambled toward the nearest clump of trees, a dozen yards from the stream, making it just before the plane passed overhead, banking and heading around the mountain.

"Did you make it?" Bart called down to her.

She couldn't see him, but his voice was easy enough to hear. "Yes, I think so."

"Let's hope you're right. I wouldn't want you sleeping with a detachment of the Thai police force tonight instead of me."

She didn't know if he was being funny or not. She walked back out into the clearing at the center of the glen. "How will we know if they spotted me?"

Bart appeared on some rocks just above the grotto. "If they come calling, we can figure you didn't get your tail feathers into the trees in time. But there's no point worrying about it."

"At least, not until I'm captured, is that it?"

She could see his smile. "There's good news, babe."

"What?"

"I found a cave. It's warm, it's cozy, it's light. No bats, no snakes. It even comes with a ready supply of canned goods."

"If that's a joke, Bart, it's not very funny."

"No joke, Kel. Come and see for yourself."

It took her only two or three minutes to make it up to where he was waiting. Taking her hand, Bart led her around a ledge to a small cave that was cut into the face of the rock escarpment. It was about twice as big as a large walk-in closet. At the back was a wooden crate with a few dozen cans of what looked like C rations, plus some medical supplies, aluminum plates and utensils.

"You wanted civilization," Bart said, "I've provided you with civilization." He was beaming.

"Yeah? So where's the toilet?"

He grimaced. "Rustic civilization, Kelly. Rustic civilization."

"To be honest, it looks heavenly."

He pointed to a small pile of gnarled logs stacked in the back. "There's even firewood."

"Do you think somebody lives here?"

"I think it's a hideout somebody set up in case they had to drop out of sight for a while. Maybe the pirates put this stuff here. It doesn't look as if anybody's used it for a hell of a long time, though. They might have forgotten about it."

She looked around. "Do you think we're safe here?"

"I don't see why not. And it's easily defended in case they come up here on foot."

"Oh, great, a siege. They can trap us and starve us out."

"They'd have to find us first. Anyway, I don't plan on spending my retirement here. I just want my ribs and leg to get a little better."

Kelly felt a burst of optimism. Bart noticed and put his arm around her, kissing her temple. She could tell he was pleased. She hugged him back, careful not to press his rib cage in the wrong places.

"All that remains is to get our stuff up here, and maybe some water."

"I'll go down and get our things. You rest that leg."

"No, I'll help."

His leg was badly swollen. Kelly shook her head. "You probably shouldn't even be standing on it and you've walked for miles. Sit down."

"Yes, ma'am."

Kelly went off to retrieve their weapons and rice. When she returned, Bart was sitting out on a rock where she'd first seen him. He pointed at the scenic vista.

"There's no extra charge for the view."

She turned and looked out at a panorama. The jungle extended like a great lumpy green carpet all the way to the bluish green sea, perhaps two miles from where they sat. The fishing village wasn't visible, but Bart told her approximately where he thought it was.

"Doesn't look so far from this vantage point," Kelly said.

"It's far enough when you have to fight your way through the jungle to get here. What remains to be seen is what the other side of the island looks like. I thought when my leg's better I'd climb up top and have a look."

The view was so pretty, Kelly could only sigh. "Hard to believe there's so much evil lurking out there, isn't it?"

"One day that beach will be lined with tourist hotels. Then you and Duncan can bring your grandkids here and tell them about the adventure you had here when you were just a girl."

Kelly couldn't tell whether he was being maudlin or if he was trying to cheer her. His tone was ambiguous. Duncan, it seemed, had captured his imagination, and she wasn't sure why. She let the remark pass.

"It does look like there's a possibility of bad weather coming our way," Bart said. "See that?"

There was a dark band of clouds low on the horizon, though they seemed far away. "How do you know it's coming this way?"

"Direction of the wind mostly."

Now that he mentioned it, Kelly did notice a breeze. Down on the jungle floor it had been dead calm.

"I have a hunch we'll be glad for our cave before this night's over. How about if I help you gather fronds to make a bed? Without them, that rock will be pretty hard."

Kelly looked at Bart's leg. "No, I want you to elevate that thing. You've overdone it as it is. I'll gather whatever we need. You take inventory of the food and work out some menus."

Bart's lips twitched. "The worm has turned."

"I hope not," she said, tapping his head. Then she walked away happily, headed for the grotto.

"Hurry home," he called after her.

Kelly stopped and looked back. "I'll watch for that plane. And for snakes. Is there anything else I should be concerned about?"

He thought for a minute. "Oh, I've read stories about some rare species of mountain gorilla that inhabits these islands, but I wouldn't put much stock in it."

Kelly smiled sweetly as she did something very unladylike, something she'd rarely done before. She flipped Bart Monday the bird.

IT TOOK FIVE TRIPS, but Kelly gathered enough fronds to make a fairly soft bed. While she'd been in the grotto, the airplane had circled the mountain again. As it passed overhead, she was careful to stay under the trees.

The last time she passed the lookout point, Kelly saw that Bart's meteorological prognostications were accurate. The front that they'd seen out at sea had moved in close to the coast. The sun had set behind it, and they could hear the rumble of thunder off in the distance.

Bart had inventoried the food and supplies. The C rations consisted mostly of vegetables and fish—twenty-year-old U.S. army rations that had probably circulated on the black market for aeons. Best of all, someone had been thoughtful enough to leave a can opener.

They decided to eat before dark. While Bart lay on the bed of fronds, his foot elevated on the wall of the cave, Kelly fixed dinner.

It was strange, but she was feeling an odd sort of contentment. Maybe the explanation was as simple as the fact that they had a solid roof over their heads, that they were no longer fleeing through the jungle in fear of being spotted. The danger wasn't over, true, but she felt more secure than at any time since they'd arrived on the island.

"You won't like hearing this," Bart noted as she worked, "but you make a damned cute housewife."

"Cavewoman is more like it." She wiped her cheek with the back of her hand. "I appreciate the compliment, but you're right. I don't like hearing it."

"Tell me, do you really like all that crap lawyers do?"

"Yes," she said. "But that shouldn't be any more surprising than the fact that you like dodging bullets and running from crooked cops."

"What I do isn't boring," he said.

She arched an eyebrow. "What makes you think law is boring?"

"I *know* it's boring."

Kelly dished the food onto aluminum plates and handed one to Bart. She'd filled a spare aluminum pot with water from the stream. Using one of the ceramic Chinese teacups that had been in the box, she scooped out water and gave it to him, as well.

"I guess that shows how different we are, Bart. When you think about it, we're from two entirely different worlds, with completely different outlooks."

She got her own plate and cup and joined him. Bart had braced himself against a rock to keep his ribs stable. She leaned against the wall next to him. He patted her knee.

"Different, maybe, but we're adrift in the same boat."

"A mere accident of fate."

"Maybe, but I don't think we're oil and water, Kelly, even if you do."

She looked at him in surprise. "What are you implying?"

"I'm not implying anything," he said, immediately sounding defensive. "I'm just not as convinced as you are that but for a chance disaster, we wouldn't have two words to say to each other."

She put down her cup and looked him square in the eye, suddenly understanding what he was driving at. "You aren't suggesting you have feelings for me, are you, Bart?"

He blinked, as though her directness was completely unexpected. "I know it's easier to pass it off as a random accident," he said, hedging, "but it's my guess you wouldn't have been...like this...with just any man who happened to be in my shoes."

"Of course not."

"Then your friendliness toward me wasn't only a token of gratitude—a reward or a bribe."

She took a bite of food, then wiped her mouth with her hand. "You're trying to get me to say I had sex with you because you're irresistible, not because you were all that's available."

Thunder rolled across the island. The sky seemed to have darkened considerably. Large drops of rain began spattering the ledge in front of the cave.

"Here comes the storm," Bart said.

For a while they watched the rain.

"You didn't answer my question," she said.

"I rather think you saw something in me apart from the fact that I'm a warm body, willing to fight to save you."

"You aren't just anybody, obviously," she said, feeling strangely satiated by their modest meal. "I think that's pretty apparent, isn't it?"

"Is it?"

Kelly folded her arms, his persistence beginning to get to her. "Okay, so you're a sexy guy and I was attracted to you. I'm capable of animal lust, the same as anybody else, and animal lust is what I felt. There! Are you satisfied now?"

He scraped the last of his food from his plate and gave her a wide grin. "I feel much better."

"Because you've eaten or because I finally stroked your male ego?"

Bart shrugged. "Both, I guess."

She took his plate from him, picked up hers and crawled over to wash them out. "Honestly," she said, shaking her head, "the only difference between boys and men is their height."

He sat contentedly as she cleaned. Once she'd finished, she returned to his side to watch the rain.

Kelly remembered sitting on the porch of her house as a child, watching the warm tropical rains that filled the air with the smells of her mother's garden. She had felt so alive then—a part of nature, yet safe in the shelter of her home. It was almost like that now. She could see and smell the rain without actually getting wet.

"I'm glad we're not out in the jungle," she said. "It would be miserable getting soaked through and having to sleep on the soggy ground."

"Our ancestors weren't called cavemen for nothing."

Bart took her hand, rubbing her fingers with his thumb. The gesture was warm and affectionate and Kelly liked it, though she knew that was an odd admission, considering.

"You have nice hands," he said, getting that distinctive tremor in his voice.

She glanced at her nails. "I could use a manicure."

"That sounds more like a lady lawyer than a cave-woman."

Kelly thought of her home, her office, her clothes, her career. "I'm not a cavewoman. Not even remotely. I'd kill to get off this island and get back to being who I really am."

"I guess I don't know the woman you're referring to," he said wistfully, "but the one I do know, the one who's here with me, I kind of like."

"You like her or you like the sex?"

He gave her a nudge with his elbow. "You've got sex on the brain, don't you, kid?"

"I do *not!*" she said, her eyes flashing. "I was just trying to understand what you really mean."

"I meant just what I said. I like you, Ms. Ronan. And not only because you've got a great bod. But I admit you could use an attitude adjustment."

She gave him a disgusted look. "What's that's supposed to mean?"

"That I wish you'd relax and not be so damned defensive. Duncan's going to be there when you get home. And I haven't exactly robbed you of your virginity."

Kelly folded her arms over her chest. "Maybe it's time to change the subject, Bart."

"Whatever you say, my love." He edged closer to her. "Whatever ends up happening, Kel, we don't have a lot of time together, so we might as well be friends."

"I suppose you're right."

He put his arm around her and she rested her head on his shoulder. Daylight was rapidly fading. They listened to the rain.

Kelly said, "My father always used to say be happy for what you've got. I guess I've never been very good about living up to that."

"Life's not easy. Like everyone else, I've discovered that over the years."

"Were you really an orphan?" she asked, looking at him. "You never knew your parents?"

"No."

"What happened to you?"

"I was adopted by some people. It didn't work out. The woman wasn't well. They had to give me up. I bounced around from one foster home to another. Got into some scrapes. Ended up in Boys' Town. The people there gave me direction. I was bright enough for college and got a scholarship to K.U."

"How did you end up in the army? Did you enlist?"

"ROTC."

"And you became a Ranger?"

"Yeah."

"Why? Did you want to be a professional soldier?"

"I wanted something unusual in my life. I thought adventure was the answer."

"It seems you still do."

He looked around the cave. "This is a little extreme, even for me. Or maybe I'm just getting too old for it."

Kelly chose to interpret the remark as a positive sign, an attempt to bridge the chasm separating their lives. Ever since she'd rescued him, she'd sensed a softening in his crusty veneer, despite the continuing jokes and sarcasm. Bart was trying, in his own way, to reach out to her, express his feelings for her. In a way, that was comforting, but in another way it scared her. She wasn't prepared to deal with the consequences.

The wind started kicking up and the downpour became heavy, the din thunderous.

"That's quite a rain," Bart said. "Would you like to have a fire—assuming the matches our friends left are okay?"

She sighed with pleasure. "Do you think it's safe? A fire wouldn't be seen?"

"There aren't any observation aircraft out in this soup. Anyway, you'd have to be inside the canyon to see anything."

"Then let's go for it."

Bart got to his hands and knees with some difficulty.

"Can I help?"

"No," he said. "You've done everything, including lugging our supplies up the mountain. It's my turn. Anyway, this won't be hard."

Kelly lay back on the bed of ferns and watched as Bart laid the fire. His movements were awkward because of his ribs, but he didn't complain. Over the course of the day his face had started turning from purple to green, but the swelling was down a bit and in another couple of days he'd start looking more like his old self.

With the coming of night, she'd begun feeling closer to him. Maybe it was instinct. Maybe their primitive ancestors were brutal to each other during the day, but when night came they would cling together, sharing body heat for the sake of mutual survival.

The matches worked, but there wasn't much in the way of kindling, making it difficult to get a blaze going. "This hardwood is a bitch to get started," he said, "but if I ever succeed, it'll burn all night."

Kelly crawled beside him and watched as he tried to coax a small flame into something more robust. He held a tiny scrap of kindling at the apex of the flame.

It seemed bizarre to her that such an elemental thing as a fire should be so difficult to effect. Around the world billions of light bulbs were aglow, and yet they had to struggle for light and heat. It made her realize anew how fragile civilization was.

Finally Bart managed to get several chips burning at the same time. Then he added the smallest of the logs, first holding one over the flame to char it a little and get it hot. When he'd succeeded in getting two logs going, he crawled back to their bed to stretch out. Kelly joined him, lying at his side.

It was dark outside. The rain was coming down steadily. The fire lit the cave, giving it a warm glow. Kelly snuggled closer as Bart slipped his arm under her and held her.

"Want to hear something stupid?" he said. "I can't remember feeling more content than I am right now."

She reflected. "You're right, Bart, it is kind of stupid."

"But I'm serious."

"Yes, I can tell."

"What do you suppose it means?" he asked.

"That you've had a miserable life up till now."

He tapped the end of her nose with his finger. "No, it's more profound than that. They say one discovers oneself through adversity. Maybe it has something to do with that."

She grinned. "After the past few days, you ought to be a regular Sigmund Freud."

He kissed her forehead and gave her a squeeze, a sort of affectionate acknowledgment. Kelly rolled onto her side, facing him. She put her hand on his stomach and became aware of the texture of his skin. His flesh seemed to come alive under her touch.

She wasn't sure why she was letting this happen, especially after the conversation they'd had, but damn if she didn't want him. She tried to nip it in the bud by thinking of Duncan, by imagining having to tell him what had happened between her and Bart during their ordeal. But try as she might, she couldn't get Duncan to stay with her. If anything, the thought of him was an annoyance.

Bart turned to face her. Then he tenderly touched her face. His eyes glistened in the firelight. She stared into them, feeling awe as well as disbelief. When he reached over and kissed her softly on the lips, she kissed him back.

It wasn't like the first night, or even at the waterfall. There was another dimension now. She knew him better. Though much of Bart Monday remained a mystery, she felt she knew his essence. There was a closeness between them, a closeness forged in the trials they'd endured.

Their kiss deepened. The heat of his body, his probing tongue excited her. Bart ran his hand under her shirt, pushing her bikini top away. He massaged her breast, kneading it, before rubbing her nipple between his thumb and forefinger. A tingling sensation spread through her.

"Oh, Bart," she moaned as her mouth slid free of his.

He began unbuttoning her shirt.

Kelly stared at the shadows from the fire dancing on his skin. The blatant masculinity of his weathered, unshaven face was offset by a gentleness in his eyes. This was a man who had shown her glimpses of his softer, more sensitive side, even as he killed for their survival. Bart Monday was a paradox, not only because of his own contradictions, but also for the conflicting emotions he elicited in her.

He had turned back the flaps of her shirt and was eyeing her breasts. She sat up and took off her suit. Still propped on his elbow, Bart began running his hand over her body. There was wonder in his eyes, and delight. A faint smile curled the corners of his mouth. His fingers went over the curve of her shoulder, where she'd been cut by the fisherman's knife, and lightly down her arm. He ran his index finger along her collarbone, then over the mound of her breast, teasing her nipple.

He passed his palm over the plane of her stomach as he began stroking her thighs, drawing his hands up them, scoring her flesh with his fingertips. She kept her eyes on his.

He stared at her golden flesh, warmed and lit by the fire. There was avarice in his eyes, but she didn't mind it because it wasn't impersonal. He was focused on her. His impetus to take was the counterpart of her desire to submit.

Bart definitely had a way with her body. His hands could make it sing like a high-voltage wire. That, more than anything, set him apart. With Bart, she was sensation, feminine energy and little else.

His fingers were toying with the curls between her legs. His touch made her legs twitch, made her throb. She was feeling warm, and she was moist with excitement, though he still hadn't touched her *there*. He was near, tantalizingly close, but still not *there*.

Bart drew the tips of two fingers up the inside of her leg, around her mound, then down the other leg and back again, once, twice, three times. The pulsing inside her had grown as steady and strong as a heartbeat. She wanted to grab his hand and press it hard against her. She wanted to make him stop the teasing. And yet, she didn't. She let the game go on.

Shifting his body carefully because of his sore ribs, Bart pressed his face close to hers. With her eyes shut, Kelly was aware of his breath on her cheek. She could almost feel the tiny hairs stand on end.

Then he skimmed his finger over her moist curls, making her gasp. He kissed her sagging lip, taking it between his teeth.

Kelly's whole body was purring. Her pelvis rocked, seeking his finger, wanting the pressure of it. But Bart denied her that satisfaction, drawing his lips across her jaw and down her neck, leaving a moist trail across her skin.

She moaned again, longingly, imploringly. Again his finger brushed her, venturing deeper than before, without quite touching her where she wanted.

"Oh, please, Bart," she murmured, "don't torture me." She lifted her pelvis against his hand, and he let the tip of his middle finger draw against her raw nerve. She gasped, almost coming to orgasm. But she didn't want to. Not yet. To stop her mounting excitement, she let her hips settle back into the bed of ferns.

Bart's hand never left her. Lightly, ever so lightly, he drew his finger up the middle of her. He found her nub and she arched against him, instinctively holding the pose before slowly dropping her hips onto the bed again, and letting the sensation flow away.

He began kissing her at the same time he stroked her, sending waves of ecstasy through her. He didn't have to caress her for long. She was already on the edge.

"I want you," she murmured as she bit into his lips.

Groaning, he moved over her, letting his belly rest against hers. Kelly opened her eyes, aware now what she had asked for.

"Are you all right?" she asked.

"I've been better," he whispered, kissing her, "but some things are worth a little pain."

Before she could protest he kissed her hard. Kelly took his head in her hands, sinking her fingers into his hair, pulling his face against hers. His penis was pressed against her, and when she opened her legs he slipped inside her, entering slowly at first, then inching deeper and deeper.

He withdrew, holding himself just clear of her opening. Kelly wanted him—she wanted him deep inside. She arched against him. That set him off and he began plunging into her, then withdrawing and plunging deep into her again.

His orgasm came quickly, but she was ready, meeting each thrust, matching each desperate clench. And when he exploded, she came as well, her body shuddering under him.

Bart tensed the instant he'd spent himself. The sound in his throat told her how much pain he was in. He was breathing in short, tentative breaths, the weight of his body entirely on his elbows.

"Are you all right?" she asked.

"Frankly, no."

"Oh, Bart, I'm so sorry."

He managed a smile. "Don't apologize. It was worth every minute." He kissed her nose. "I'm going to have to get on my back, though, before I die."

Gingerly he moved off her, turning and dropping onto the mat of fern fronds. He stretched out, flat on his back. For a second he lay breathing hesitantly.

"We shouldn't have made love," she said, feeling his misery.

"Are you kidding? This is the way I intend to die, if I can arrange it."

"Silly goose." She kissed his shoulder.

He stroked her cheek. "Damned if I've ever felt anything so good and so bad at the same time," he said.

She ran her fingers over the mat on his chest, feeling so close to him just then, so elementally attached. "I hope it didn't make you worse."

"Well, if I'm permanently incapacitated, I guess they can always put me out to stud."

"First you've got to find a way to get back to the barn. The way things have been going, you might end up in the glue factory."

He smiled through his pain. "You have such a delicate way of putting it."

She pressed her face against his shoulder, wonderfully content. Her skin was moist from their lovemaking. The heat of the fire felt good.

The rain had almost stopped now and the thunder sounded as though it had moved on past the island. Kelly realized what Bart had meant earlier when he'd expressed his happiness. She could honestly say she shared it.

At the moment there was only one reality—being in the cave with Bart Monday. Her other life seemed like make-believe by comparison. She hardly knew the woman lawyer in Honolulu, the one who lived in the beautiful condo and had wanted to be Duncan Van de Meer's wife. All that mattered was the man beside her and what they had shared.

Just as Kelly was about to fall asleep, a loud bang echoed up the canyon, reverberating off the walls.

Bart sat up suddenly, wincing.

Kelly looked at him. "What was that?"

"It sounded like a gunshot."

"Nearby?"

"Not far. Probably down in the jungle at the base of the mountain."

Her eyes rounded with despair. "Oh, Bart..."

"Maybe I'd better put out the fire. It seems like we may have company."

She watched him separating the logs and snuffing out the flames. Soon the cave was plunged into darkness. There was a small amount of smoke, but it wasn't too thick not to breathe. He crawled back to their bed, dragging the rifle with him. Kelly immediately snuggled against him, careful not to put any pressure on his rib cage.

"What do you think it means?" she whispered.

"I have no idea. Maybe the plane spotted us. Or maybe the ground force is on a sweep. They may have figured we'd head for high ground. The shot might have been a signal."

"Maybe it was an accident."

"Could be. Either way, it's bad news. Seems these boys are more determined than I'd given them credit for."

Kelly felt tears of fear and frustration. Just when it appeared fate was giving them a respite, it had plunged them back into the nightmare. Her fingers tightened on his arm. "What's going to happen to us?" she whispered.

"We'll keep going. They haven't stopped us yet, Kel. Tomorrow we'll see what we're up against and deal with it."

She was glad for one thing. He didn't seem to think it was something they'd have to face tonight. But how would she sleep, knowing that someone was out there, lying in wait?

CHAPTER TWELVE

AT DAWN BART LAY on the ledge outside the cave, surveying the jungle below. He'd seen some movement—enough to know he was dealing with an enemy who'd come in force. His best guess was that it was a paramilitary police unit and they'd probably decided they had their rat trapped and weren't going to let him get away this time. With enough food and water and ammunition, he'd be able to hold them off for weeks, but he didn't have what he needed. Capture would be inevitable once the cave had been located.

Their only hope—and it was a slim one at best—was to keep moving. But his injuries made that unrealistic, at least for the time being. He did feel much better, though. With one or two more days' rest he'd be able to walk half decently. So the real question was whether they could hold up in the cave for another day without being detected.

Bart had already decided there'd be no fights to the death. He was probably a dead man either way, but Kelly might be spared. They would beat everything out of her and it would come down to whether she knew enough to hurt anyone that mattered. He'd been vague about his mission for that very reason.

Of course, it was possible they wouldn't want to take any chances and would kill her anyway. And why shouldn't they? To the world she'd gone down with the *Ban Don*, and the police would likely just as soon leave it that way. Her best chance was for him to get her off the island in one piece, but the prospects of that were getting dimmer by the hour.

What he wasn't sure of was whether she should be told how bleak the outlook was, or if he should try to keep her spirits up. She wasn't just an innocent bystander anymore. They'd been together only a few days, but in his mind she was the love of his life. He'd never felt such an elemental gut-wrenching attraction for a woman before. It was much more than a physical thing. He could hardly describe or explain it. They simply belonged together, as unlikely and irrational as it seemed.

He knew Kelly was attracted to him, that she liked him. Obviously her sex life hadn't been sterling. To her, he was a real phenomenon, an experience, an adventure that had knocked her back on her heels. But in her heart of hearts Kelly didn't truly understand what had happened between them. He was absolutely certain of that. Hell, the woman had just gotten engaged. How could she reject all the rationalizing she'd done to get to that point on the basis of a jungle escapade with him? No, she'd explain it away, apologize for it and do her best to forget about it once she was home.

That was what made these precious hours so poignant. Bart knew their days together were numbered—either because they'd soon be captured or because they'd escape and return to the real world with hardly a look back. But so long as they were on the lam and together, he truly had her. There was not a more beautiful, intelligent, sensuous, caring, sassy woman on earth. And she was with him. For now. For as long as he could hold on to her.

"Bart?"

It was Kelly at the mouth of the cave. He glanced at her over his shoulder. Her short, boyish hair was mussed, her eyes a little puffy. She looked a bit distressed and absolutely adorable. "Morning, Kel," he said.

"What's happening? What are you doing?"

"Scouting the enemy scouting us."

She began crawling on her hands and knees toward him. "Do you see someone?"

He motioned for her to stay low. "I've seen a little activity down in the jungle."

Kelly came up next to him, dropping on her stomach beside him. "Do they know we're here?"

"I think they're suspicious. My guess is they're surrounding the mountain and will spend the day searching for us."

"Does that mean we're doomed?"

"To do it properly they'd need a battalion. My guess is they've only got a platoon, but more troops could be on the way."

"So what do we do?"

"I'd like to hole up here for another day, at least. Every hour I rest, I get stronger. By tomorrow I might be able to walk."

Kelly took his chin and turned his head so that she could see the side of his face where he'd been hit by the rifle butt. "The swelling's down, but you've got a hell of a bruise. How are the ribs?"

"Better."

"And your leg?"

"I haven't tried standing on it, but it doesn't hurt so badly and the throbbing's stopped. How are you feeling?"

She turned her face to show him her shiner.

"It's looking much better," he said. "In a couple of days you'll be perfect again."

Kelly rested her chin on her hands and peered down at the gray-green of the jungle. "Yeah, just in time to be beaten and interrogated."

"Naw, I plan on getting you off the island before then. Been thinking about that eight-course dinner at the Oriental."

She put her hand on his in an affectionate sort of way, but a bit self-consciously. "You're a real bullshit artist, Bart. I know we're not getting off this island alive. Unless it's in handcuffs. And we'd be lucky at that."

"Want to bet?"

She laughed. "What do you have to bet?"

"I get us out of here in one piece and you marry me."

Kelly looked at him quizzically. "And if you don't, we die?"

"Think of it this way—I need some incentive."

"Bart, you're a nut."

"What are you going to do when I get you to Bangkok?"

She rolled onto her side, facing him. For a moment she just stared at him, then she began fiddling with his hair. It was an affectionate gesture that took him by surprise. "I suppose I'll have that dinner with you at the Oriental Hotel, one last glorious night in bed, then I'll fly home to Duncan."

He looked into her sky blue eyes, feeling as if he was gazing at heaven. "I was with you up to that last part."

She smiled sadly and drew her finger along the stubble on his jaw. "I know the difference between fantasy and reality, Bart. You're fantasy, pure and simple."

"I don't know whether to be flattered or to spit in your eye."

"Oh, be flattered, it's much easier."

Bart looked at her mouth and wanted to kiss it. He had a terrible weak feeling, an awful pang of anxiety that shot right through him.

"You don't look very happy," she whispered.

"It's not easy being unsure whether the next day or two will bring death or bliss," he said. "I certainly picked a lousy time to become infatuated."

Kelly laid her head on her arm and looked at him dolefully. "I know the feeling."

"Infatuation?"

"I don't know if that's what it is or not," she said. "I don't know how to explain what I'm feeling. But I keep wanting to make love with you, against all logic. Almost like a death wish."

"That's not particularly flattering," he said.

"I'm not referring to you personally, Bart, so much as to what I've been doing. This is the worst possible time of the month for me to be having unprotected sex. If that isn't stupid, I don't know what is."

"Under normal circumstances those words would send a cold chill through me, but they didn't. Not at all."

"It's as if there is no future, so what we do doesn't really matter."

"But what if there *is* a future?" he asked.

Kelly shook her head. "I guess I'll just be glad to be alive. I don't know."

Bart caressed her face. "I'm going to get us out of here, babe, I promise you. Whatever it takes."

She gave him a faint smile and rolled onto her back, staring up at the early-morning sky. Bart turned his attention back to the jungle. He couldn't see anything, but he knew the time for dreaming was over and the time for action had come.

"I hate to sound practical," he said, "but we should probably stock up on water. Chances are we'll have to stick pretty close to the cave all day. It could be dangerous to venture out in broad daylight."

"Do you want me to go down to the stream for water?"

"If you want to be able to drink, it's probably a good idea."

"Should I go now?"

"The longer you wait, the more dangerous it'll be."

Kelly nodded and crawled back into the cave to get the pots. She was back in a few moments.

"Be very careful," he said. "Make like an Indian and scamper from rock to rock, bush to bush. Be out in the open as little as possible. If an aircraft comes over while you're in the open, freeze. Motion is easier to spot than shapes, even shapes as delightful as yours."

"Is that my pat on the butt, Coach?"

He rubbed her derriere. "With a promise of more if you come back in one piece."

"I bet you'd really like to zap me, know you'd gotten me pregnant, wouldn't you? That way I'd really be vulnerable, completely dependent on you."

He blinked with surprise. "Me?"

"Yes, you. That would be the crowning achievement of this little adventure."

He gave her a grin. "At least we're thinking positively."

"Ha!" She grimaced. "I ought to surrender to those guys and see if I can make a deal. Maybe I could trade you for my life."

"And leave your putative child without a father?"

Kelly glared at him. "That's not even funny."

"No, I suppose Duncan wouldn't appreciate it."

She gave him a dirty look and began crawling off to fetch their water.

LATER IN THE MORNING another tropical storm blew in and Kelly sat at the mouth of the cave, watching the rain pouring down from the dark clouds. She turned and looked back at Bart, who was dozing. He needed the rest.

At the first sign of the storm he'd said, "Good. The enemy's got to sit out there in the jungle and get soaked. If somebody's got to be miserable, it might as well be them."

They'd had rice and more C rations for breakfast. The notion of regular meals with half-real food had become a shock to her system. It was amazing to her how little it took to make a person happy after a period of deprivation.

With Bart sleeping a lot, she'd had time to think. She knew the climax of this drama was rapidly approaching. Despite Bart's good humor and his cheerfulness, she knew there was no reason for optimism, and yet she was clinging to hope. With Bart snoring nearby, she had an imaginary conversation with Duncan, trying to explain to him what had happened on Ko Pong and how she'd let herself get sexually involved with a stranger.

"All that matters is how you feel now," Duncan said in his terribly reasonable way, "how you feel about me."

"My life is here with you, Duncan," she heard herself say. "What happened in Thailand was just an aberration, a bad dream."

Of course, she wouldn't tell him about the lighter moments, or the more sensual ones. Desperate people did desperate things in desperate circumstances—she'd prefer he understood it that way.

Duncan would be a little jealous, but he'd forgive her because he'd know that the woman on this island wasn't her. It was what she did in saner times that mattered. Yes, Duncan would understand that—if she lived to explain it all.

The morning wore on slowly. Around midday there were a few loud bursts of thunder, which woke Bart up. They ate again and talked. They discussed their childhoods while the rain pelted the mountain, making life outside their cave grim.

"Do you realize we have absolutely nothing in common," she said after hearing his story.

"Mutual admiration," he replied. "We've got that in common."

"Sexual attraction doesn't count."

"I wasn't thinking of that," Bart said. "We have a spiritual connection."

"Oh? What makes you think that?"

"Haven't you noticed how we're able to talk, Kelly? I mean really communicate? Have you ever had this kind of give-and-take with anybody else?"

"Duncan and I talk by the hour."

"About what?"

"Our work, our careers, our lives. What we want to do."

"It sounds pretty sterile to me."

"You're making assumptions again," she retorted. "You have no basis for that remark."

"Well, I happen to think you and I connect on an elemental level," he said. "I feel real, like my true self when I'm with you, and I have a hunch you feel the same."

"Bart, you don't even know me."

She said the words, but her heart wasn't convinced. In an odd way, he had a point. He'd brought out a side of her she hadn't been in touch with before, a side that had been slumbering. What she didn't know was whether that aspect of her was real or something merely created by the circumstances.

Once the rains tapered off, Bart moved to the mouth of the cave to keep tabs on what was going on. Midafternoon they heard shouts in the ravine below.

"Sounds like they're searching the grotto," he whispered.

Kelly grew tense for the first time in hours. She'd gotten used to fear wedged in her throat like a fist, but now she resented its intrusion into their private little world in the cave. "Do you think they know we're here?"

"I don't know. The next few minutes should tell. Hand me the rifle, though, would you please? Might as well be prepared."

Kelly got him the rifle, which he laid across his knees. She leaned close against him, entwining her fingers with his, and waited.

There were no more sounds from outside. Bart said that chances were the troops had moved on. "Eventually they'll find us, though. Tomorrow morning we should make our move."

As darkness began to fall, they retreated into the cave. Bart told her they shouldn't risk a fire. Kelly was disappointed because she'd enjoyed it the night before, but at least it was a warmer evening. Still, she cuddled against Bart on their fern bed, watching the oranges and reds in the sky outside the cave mutating into purples and indigo.

"I have this ominous feeling, Bart, that this is going to be our last night together," she told him.

"Maybe our last night in the cave, but not our last night ever."

"You don't really believe that," she said. "Do you?"

"Sure I do."

She touched his lower lip, studying his face. "I like you, Bart. I like you a whole lot." Then her eyes filled with tears. It happened very suddenly, taking her by surprise. The next thing she knew she was crying.

Bart put his arms around her and held her. "That sounds like cause for celebration, not remorse," he whispered, kissing her ear.

She turned her face up to him. "No, it'd be much better if I didn't care." And then they kissed.

She held him close, a desperate yearning beginning to build inside her. She put her hand between his legs and discovered he was as aroused as she.

"Make love to me," she murmured.

"Are you sure?"

"I'd never forgive myself if I didn't, this one last time."

Bart held her head against his chest, stroking her. Then he made love to her tenderly. It was the most loving a man had ever been with her in her entire life. This was no longer raw passion, unbridled sex. Kelly felt his love. She felt it profoundly. And it almost broke her heart.

KELLY AWOKE the next morning to a muted gray light. She sat up abruptly, instantly aware that she was alone. The only sound was the distant *putt* of a helicopter engine.

She crept to the mouth of the cave and saw that the jungle was shrouded in a wispy mist, giving it a gray-green hue. Bart was at the observation point again, lying on his stomach as he had been the previous dawn, scanning the jungle. The rifle was at his side.

"How long have you been up?" she whispered as she crawled to his side.

"I don't know, an hour maybe." He pointed to the helicopter. "Since I first heard the chopper. They're bringing in more people."

"Are we going to leave here? Do you feel up to it?"

"I'm a new man," he said, cuffing her chin, "ready to take on a whole battalion."

In the distance, at the edge of the island, they could see another helicopter flying over the beach area.

"All right, Napoleon," Kelly said, "what's the battle plan?"

"Considering I've only got ten rounds left, we don't want to get into a protracted firefight. We resort to guerrilla warfare, hit-and-run tactics. And we travel light—one or two days' rations."

Despair clawed at Kelly's insides, but she forced herself to remain cheerful for Bart's sake. If he gave up, too, they would be lost. "Well, you're the expert. You lead and I'll follow."

"I'd like to head down the mountain, maybe do a little reconnaissance in force."

"What does that mean?"

"We search out the enemy with our entire force. In other words, you and me. We look for targets of opportunity."

Kelly couldn't help a smile. "The best defense is a good offense?"

"Hey," he said, pinching her nose, "you've read Karl von Clausewitz, too."

She shook her head with disbelief. "I don't know why I'm laughing."

"Because I've been doing my best to keep your morale up. A fighting spirit is an army's best weapon."

"So which battalion are we going to attack, Napoléon?"

"No sense wasting our ammo on troops. I was thinking a chopper might be a better objective."

Her eyes widened. "You mean you're going to shoot one out of the sky?"

"No, it's better to catch one on the ground. They've got a landing spot somewhere over the next ridge. They've been coming in there the past half hour or so. If we can get past their lines, maybe we can sneak up on their landing pad from behind. Come at them from where they think you ain't. The element of surprise."

"You want to blow up a helicopter?" she asked.

"No, why not hijack one? It's far more genteel."

"God knows we've got an image to maintain."

Bart pulled her face to his and gave her a kiss. "I want to remember the taste of those lips," he murmured.

Kelly felt herself start to choke up, but she refused to cry. She smiled as bravely as she could.

"So, what do you think, babe? Are you game?"

She nodded and pressed his hand to her cheek. That had to suffice for an answer because she couldn't speak.

CHAPTER THIRTEEN

THEY ATE A HEARTY MEAL before they headed out—there was no point in rationing. All they took with them was a bit of food, the rifle and the knife.

As they left the cave, Kelly looked back, feeling a touch of nostalgia. It had been her most comfortable quarters since she'd left her hotel on Ko Samui. And she'd felt so close to Bart in the cave, not just sexually, but emotionally.

She knew it was common for people to bond in stressful situations, especially if they were isolated. On transoceanic flights, strangers sometimes became closer than people who'd been friends for years. Was that the phenomenon at work here?

Bart took a few minutes to survey the situation one last time. Seeing no visible changes, he led the way down the escarpment to the canyon, and from there back into the jungle. Soon after they made it into the protective embrace of the vegetation, a chopper flew overhead.

Bart looked up at it through the trees. "He's headed for that landing zone I mentioned. The timing's perfect. We can follow the sound."

They struck off at a vigorous pace. Bart's leg was much improved, and he said the ribs were no longer sharply painful, merely annoyingly uncomfortable. Without the rice pot, Kelly had no difficulty moving quickly.

There was a definite difference in her spirits. Being on the offensive created an emotional lift. Kelly figured it was akin to what she felt going into a major trial. This was even more elemental and uncomplicated, though, the sensation more genuine.

She wondered if her feelings would still seem genuine once she was back in Hawaii. Everything that had happened since the attack on the *Ban Don*—including her lovemaking with Bart—had been so emotional. How would that seem to her once she was back at the office? Reading a deposition, would she look up and visualize Bart's grizzled face, shadowed by firelight? Would she remember their lovemaking with pleasure or shame?

Bart Monday was on her mind. The slapping vines of the jungle were like a metronome, desensitizing her to all but the confused ramble of her thoughts. She looked at the broad bare shoulders of the man limping in front of her, and wondered about his soul.

Kelly was so focused on her thoughts of him that when a slothlike creature loped across their path, she hardly reacted. The surprises of the jungle were becoming commonplace.

They hadn't heard the helicopter for some time, but Bart continued to press ahead. The jungle thinned and they began climbing again. Through breaks in the foliage Kelly was able to see the profile of the mountain. They had moved partway around its base. She estimated they'd walked about a mile.

Bart was moving more cautiously now, and the pace had slowed considerably. When they broke out of the undergrowth, he halted.

"My guess is that the landing zone is on top of this cliff. And there's probably a bird sitting on it right now, waiting to take you to Bangkok."

Kelly's heart soared. But it seemed too easy. "Won't it be guarded?"

"Probably, but they won't be expecting an attack."

"The element of surprise," she said. Then, turning to him, she asked, "What do we do now?"

"We go up top and have a look."

"Okay," she said, still feeling the effects of the adrenaline. "Why not?"

The escarpment was steep and laced with vegetation. In twenty minutes they made it to the top of the rocky spur, two hundred feet above the jungle floor. Peeking over the edge, they saw a white police helicopter in the middle of a slab of rock the size of two basketball courts. Two men were sitting in its shade. The one wearing flight gear was evidently the pilot, the other, in camouflage fatigues, was most likely a guard.

"How does that look to you, Kel?" Bart whispered.

"It's not United, but I'll take it."

"Yeah, but we've got the same old problem. There are two of them and I can't handle both men at once. Not in my condition."

"Oh, Bart," she said mournfully, "we can't pass up this opportunity. We may not get another."

To her, looking at the chopper sitting there in the morning sun was like standing at the window of a bakery after a week without food. She was ready to storm the thing single-handedly.

"Yeah, but we need a plan. We go off half-cocked and we'll end up riding in that thing in a body bag."

She thought for a minute. "If I distract one of them, can you take out the other?"

"I guess so. But I can't use the rifle, because there's no telling how far away the other troops are. Besides, it'd be nice to get out of here without everybody knowing we're aboard." He looked her dead in the eye. "How long can you distract them?"

"However long it takes."

"Do you have a plan?" he asked.

"How about if I take my shirt off and wander up there, like I'm dazed. I could pretend to faint. They would have to check me out, and they wouldn't be so leery of a woman alone. While they're distracted you can do your thing."

Bart didn't look enthusiastic. "Why do you have to take off your shirt?"

"I thought I might be more distracting in a bikini."

"You're probably right about that, but I don't like it."

"Do you have a better idea?" she asked, unfastening the first button.

"No."

"Then let's do it."

Bart relented, but not happily. They went over the plan again. He told her how close to the chopper he wanted her to go before she collapsed. Kelly's heart began pounding. Both men were small, slender, but she'd be awfully vulnerable on her own. God, she hoped this would work.

"All set?" Bart whispered.

"I guess."

He tweaked her chin. "Just think of a shower and a nice hot bath at the Oriental."

The thought helped. Bart gave her the thumbs-up, then assisted her over the rock.

A moment later she was on top of the cliff, staring at the chopper. She feebly extended her hands, staggering toward the men as if signaling for help. The guard spotted her first. They both stared in amazement as she took a few steps in their direction before collapsing. As she fell, Kelly heard the guard shouting to the pilot. Though her eyes were closed, she knew they were coming her way.

She heard footsteps, but judging by the sound, it was only one person. The footsteps grew tentative. The man was near, but moving slowly. Kelly moaned. She half lifted her head, trying to appear delirious. Through the slits in her eyes she could see the guard's face. His expression was full of wonder, but he had an M-16 in his hands, and it was pointed at her gut. Behind him she could see the pilot beside his helicopter. He, too, was armed.

Kelly had a sudden premonition that her plan was going to fail. When she moaned again, it wasn't acting—it was her fear and despair.

The guard took another step closer. He said something to her in Thai. He sounded angry. He repeated the phrase. When she didn't respond, he stuck the cold metal of the gun muzzle in her side. She flinched.

"You get up!" he shouted.

Kelly rolled her head and mumbled. The policeman stepped over her, and walked toward the edge of the precipice. She hadn't counted on that. Bart would certainly have to shoot him and that would mess things up.

Surprisingly, nothing happened. The guard gave a cursory glance at the jungle before returning. Kelly remained frozen. The policeman squatted next to her, his rifle across his knees. He grabbed her jaw and shook her head. "Hey," he said. "Hello, hello. You okay, missus? You okay?"

Kelly gave her best groan, fluttered her eyelids and then pretended to slide back into unconsciousness. The man stood, the gun hanging from his hand. She had an impulse to grab the barrel and wrest it from him, but Bart had told her not to resist and she was afraid of messing everything up.

But where was Bart?

The pilot began walking toward them. Ah! she thought. This is what Bart wanted, the two of them together. She fluttered her eyelids. The policeman squatted down. He poked her shoulder. Then he looked up at his friend, laughing as he grabbed the top of her suit and pulled it down, exposing her breast.

"Ah!" he exclaimed.

Kelly wanted to smack the guy across the chops, but Bart had told her not to move a muscle until he'd jumped them.

The man finally let go of her breast and was rubbing her stomach as if she was a dog. He was cooing and jabbering. Kelly didn't know what she would do if he put his hand between her legs. Where in the hell was Bart?

She chanced opening her eyes to look at them again. She saw the pistol hanging from the pilot's hand. Bart undoubtedly wanted the gun holstered before he jumped them. The pilot gave a loud command and the guard stood. They began discussing something in earnest, each pointing back toward the helicopter or gesturing toward the mountain. Her fate was obviously under consideration.

Then the pilot pointed at her, making a grunting sound and tapping her side with the toe of his boot. Then he holstered his weapon. No sooner had he snapped the cover shut than Bart came flying out of nowhere.

Before Kelly could even lift her head, Bart had knocked both men to the ground. He let out a terrible groan as he landed, but he grabbed the guard and knocked him out with a single punch. Kelly scrambled to her feet. The pilot was between her and Bart, frantically trying to unholster his pistol. Bart was lying on his side next to the unconscious guard, looking as though a horse had just kicked him.

Kelly threw herself onto the back of the pilot and knocked him to his knees. The gun dropped from his hand. He reached for it as he struggled to free himself from her grip, but Bart got to the pistol first. He pointed the gun at the pilot and spat out some words in Thai. The man stopped struggling.

"You can let go of him now, dear," Bart said to her. "I think we won the round."

Kelly got up, helping Bart to his feet. The pilot lay on the ground, wide-eyed, staring up at them.

"You okay?" she asked Bart.

"A swan dive onto my chest was not the smartest thing I've done lately. In the heat of battle I forgot about my ribs. Grab the M-16, will you, babe."

Kelly picked up the rifle. "Where's my shirt?"

"Where you left it, I guess," Bart replied.

"You didn't bring it?" she said incredulously. "I'm supposed to fly to Bangkok in my bikini?"

"Take the policeman's shirt."

"Off his body?"

"How else? But make it snappy."

Kelly put down the rifle and began unbuttoning the man's shirt. Meanwhile Bart ordered the pilot to his feet and they began discussing the helicopter.

"Hurry up, Kel," Bart said. "I'm taking this dude to the bird."

Kelly almost had the shirt off. She felt like a thief. The guard was breathing, which pleased her—she wouldn't have wanted to rob a corpse. But just as she was pulling off the second sleeve, the guy blinked. She shrieked and looked at Bart, but he was too far away to help.

Woozily, the man tried to get to his feet. The M-16 was on the ground next to her. Kelly grabbed for it and, as she tried to stand, the guard reached for her. He was still rummy, but he managed to cling to her arms and the gun.

She brought her knee up sharply between his legs. He dropped instantly, and she whacked him across the side of the head with the butt of the rifle. He fell flat on his face, out cold.

Bart had turned to watch, but had been helpless to assist her. Kelly snatched the shirt from the ground and strode toward the chopper with it in one hand, the rifle in the other. "Let's get the hell out of here," she said as she passed Bart and the pilot. "I'm getting tired of this place."

WITHIN MINUTES the lush jungle, the mountain and white sandy beaches of Ko Pong dropped away. The chopper rose steadily. Kelly knew that their problems weren't over, but she felt such a profound sense of relief, it was hard not to be happy.

Bart, in the copilot's seat, kept the pistol pointed at the pilot's head. Kelly sat behind them. She'd listened to the men conversing, partly in Thai, partly in English. There'd been some disagreement on destination, but Bart had prevailed.

As Ko Pong disappeared behind them, Bart tried to talk to her over the roar of the engine. When he'd glanced back earlier there'd been a smile on his face. Now he was positively beaming. "Comfortable?"

She leaned forward and pressed her cheek against his. "I feel fabulous."

"I told you I'd get you out of that place, honey."

"A thousand apologies for ever doubting you."

He patted her cheek and glanced out the window, gesturing with the gun. "Our friend here says it's touch and go whether or not we can make Bangkok with the fuel aboard. I told him to try."

"What if we don't make it?" she shouted over the roar.

Bart shrugged. "We don't have much of a chance anywhere else. People can help us in Bangkok. In the countryside we're sitting ducks. The real question is, where do we put this thing down? I figure as close to Bangkok as we can get. Beyond that, it's going to be a crapshoot."

"What about him?" Kelly asked.

"He doesn't matter. We'll be noticed, wherever we land. The trick will be to quickly disappear into the scenery."

"Never make it," the pilot muttered. "Never make it."

"Just fly, Charlie," Bart said. "I'll worry about whether we make it or not."

The man shook his head as though they were nuts.

"Maybe we should head for the nearest land," Kelly volunteered. "At least then we could walk if we had to."

"Sattahip, the first point of land on the east side of the gulf, is two hundred miles north," Bart said. "I told our friend to make it that far or else. Bangkok would be a bonus."

They were high enough that they could see the coast, some fifty miles to the west. There was a lot of sea traffic. Kelly could see a tramp steamer plying down the coast of the Malay Peninsula. There were smaller craft, too, some with sails, others motor powered. Occasionally there'd be a small flotilla of boats—fishermen doubtlessly, though of which variety was anybody's guess.

The helicopter followed a course parallel to the eastern coastline, which gave Kelly some sense of security. Still, fifty miles was a long way to swim if something went wrong. She wasn't going to argue, though. Bart knew the situation better than she. And if he was to be believed, officials near Ko Samui would be no less hostile than their friends on Ko Pong.

Falling into the hands of the police would be disastrous, not only for Bart, but for her. She shuddered to think of the way her rap sheet would read. Accessory to murder, assault with a deadly weapon, kidnapping, theft, resisting arrest, air piracy, aiding and abetting a felon. The list was endless.

Her euphoria waned. The old cliché was pretty descriptive—out of the frying pan, into the fire. But how hard would it be for them in Bangkok? She wanted to ask Bart what they would do, how they would survive without getting caught, but she couldn't in front of the pilot. Instead she settled back in her seat under a growing cloud of gloom, hating the fact that there always seemed to be something to worry about.

The practical problems were insurmountable. Her clothes, her passport, everything was back in Ko Samui. How would she get on an airplane? She could go to the American embassy, but there would be questions, and Bart was persona non grata there. By association, she might be unwelcome, as well.

He seemed to have a plan, though. That gave her some hope. The terrible irony was that she was probably still dependent on him—as much as she'd been when they were on the island.

Kelly closed her eyes and tried to think of something pleasant—a bath, a good meal, a few simple creature comforts. Maybe she was foolish to think too far ahead. Maybe she should be content to survive the day.

THE BATH WAS DELIGHTFUL. Heaven. Kelly felt so good that she let herself slide right under the water. She was blowing bubbles, the way she had as a little girl—her lips pooched and the air streaming from her mouth until it was all gone. Then the shouting started.

She awoke with a start. The pilot was yelling and Bart was screaming back at him. Then she noticed the erratic thump of the engine. It kept missing.

"What's the matter?" she shouted. "What's happened?"

"Engine trouble," Bart answered perfunctorily. He ripped the microphone from the pilot's hand, causing the man to hurl an expletive at Bart, who cursed back.

Kelly craned her neck to look out the window. All she could see was water. The coast was far to the west, though closer than before. The engine cut out again as the pilot frantically fiddled with the controls. Bart gestured toward the coast with the gun, saying something in Thai. The pilot banked the craft and they turned west, into the afternoon sun.

"Are we going to crash?" Kelly shouted.

Bart gave her a worried look. "I don't know. The engine started running hot a few minutes ago, then it cut out. Our friend here wants to radio for help, but that would be our death warrant."

"Well, crashing in the middle of the ocean isn't exactly drinking from the fountain of eternal life!"

They were losing altitude rapidly. Then, just when the situation would begin to look hopeless, the engine would smooth out for a bit, though the reprieve never lasted long.

"Damn it!" Bart said angrily. "People should take better care of their equipment—"

Kelly could have reminded Bart that he was the one who wanted to try to cross the gulf, but there was no point. She looked at the distant coast. How could this be happening again?

They bumped along for a few minutes more, still losing altitude. Bart's shoulders seemed to sag. Finally he turned to her, managing a smile.

"We haven't had a swim for a while, kid. What do you think, are you up to ten or fifteen miles?"

"Bart!" There was utter desperation in her voice.

"You're experienced now," he said evenly.

"I will not go in that water again. I refuse. I absolutely refuse."

"God and I will take that under advisement."

She slugged him on the arm. "I mean it, Bart! We only had to swim a few miles last time and I barely made it."

He gave her a woeful look. "That was at night."

The engine quit completely, leaving the cabin horribly quiet. The only noise was the whir of the blades, a sound much like a giant fan that had been shut down. They began sinking faster.

Bart pressed the gun against the pilot's temple and shouted. The man shook his head emphatically, jabbering in Thai.

"Shit!" Bart said.

"What's the matter?"

"This tin can's not equipped for over-water flight. No life vests. He says they never go over water."

"How does he think you get to an island? By Greyhound?"

"Well, this was an unusual operation. I guess they flaunted regulations because they considered it an emergency. Point is, we'll have to make do without."

"No!" she shouted. "I will not swim! Do something, Bart!"

He shrugged helplessly. The pilot seemed near a state of panic. Kelly wondered if they would hit the sea softly enough to survive the crash. Fighting her growing hysteria, she gripped her seat. It was all she could do to keep from screaming.

The pilot managed to get the engine started again, but it cut out right away. The cycle was repeated a couple more times. At least he was managing to slow their descent. She looked out the window again. They were only a few hundred feet above the water!

Bart grabbed her arm to get her attention. His expression was deadly serious. "These things don't float. We won't have more than a few seconds to get out." He hesitated, thinking. Then he climbed over his seat and went to the bay of the craft, where he yanked open the sliding door at the side of the cabin. A rush of air filled the bay, almost knocking him over. He steadied himself.

"Our best chance is to go out this way," he screamed at her. "Brace yourself for impact, then, when we hit, get out this door as fast as you can."

The idea of being in the water no longer terrified her—the crash was the more immediate danger. Bart looked out. The wind was blowing his hair like a flag in a hurricane.

"Eight or ten seconds to impact!" he shouted. Then he lay down on the floor of the open bay, grabbing the frame of the copilot seat to brace himself.

Kelly covered her head with her arms. She waited for the crash.

They hit the water with a terrible jolt. Kelly felt as though she'd be driven through the floor. When she looked up everything was still except for the water rushing in the door.

Bart was shouting, but she was so dazed she couldn't move. He was on his knees beside her, frantically trying to unfasten her safety belt. The water was at his waist. The next thing she knew she was floating in the cabin, her head thrust up in the rapidly diminishing air space near the ceiling. She could hear the pilot's scream before the water snuffed it out. Bart, gasping for air, was pulling on her arm. And then she went under.

The next thing Kelly knew, she was bobbing on the surface, sputtering and coughing. The salt water burned her lungs, her nose, her throat. Her arms were flailing.

"Kelly! Kelly!" It was Bart, shaking her. She knew her eyes were wide with panic, but his hands were gripping her, stifling her fear. "Come on," he shouted. "Swim!"

She glanced back at the bubbling, gushing sound. The rotor blades and a bit of the fuselage were all she could see of the helicopter. Bart gave her arm a tug and she began swimming. The swells were large and seemed to rise like a wall as they swam into them. They stopped after thirty yards. Treading water, they turned back. When a swell lifted them high enough, they could see that the aircraft was gone.

"Where's the pilot?" she asked, gasping for air.

"I don't think he made it."

She turned to him, her panic rising again. She knew the shore was an impossible distance away. They were totally alone, and the swells made the challenge seem overwhelming. Kelly felt doomed. There was no fight in her at all. "I can't make it," she said, taking in a gulp of water and choking. "I can't."

She would never forget the look in his eyes. Bart appeared immensely sad, as though he understood what she was saying and hated the fact that he could do nothing about it. The emotion was very powerful. She reached out and brushed her fingers across his face to say goodbye.

Before she could say anything else, the motion of the waves pulled them apart. Bart grabbed at her wrist but she slipped from his grasp. Yet somehow, it was okay. She could feel her body giving up. The release was wonderful, surprisingly comforting. The struggle was over.

"Eee-ah!" The voice was high and shrill. "Eee-ah!"

Bart's face appeared from behind the wall of water, his eyes round, excited.

"Eee-ah!"

Bart took a couple of strokes so that he was next to her once more. Their bodies bumped. He took her by the shoulders then and spun her around. "Kelly, look!"

A boat was coming at them like a lumbering beast, its great wooden hull cutting the waves.

"Eee-ah!"

The little man on the bow had a long white goatee and a mustache. He was dressed in black, holding a long pole in his hand.

"Eee-ah!"

"Kelly," Bart shouted, "we're saved!"

The craft stopped alongside them. Above them half a dozen smiling faces peered down. They reached out their hands, grasped Kelly's wrists and lifted her onto the slimy wooden deck. The smell of fish was strong, pungent, heavenly. It stabbed at her senses. She rolled onto her back. Two faces peered down at her. One was a boy with spiked tousled hair. He was grinning a toothy smile.

"Hello, missy. Hello." More nodding and beaming.

They pulled Bart over the gunwale. He let out a squawk as his ribs scraped the wooden rail. He landed with a thud, smiling despite the pain. Kelly got up on her elbows. There were three scrawny men and two boys, and the old man in the black pajamas who came from the bow to join the semicircle surrounding them. He was beaming and bowing.

Bart said something in Thai. The old man nodded. He gestured toward the sky, punctuating his remarks with sound effects, some of which made the others laugh.

Bart turned to Kelly. "He says they saw the chopper come down from the heavens and thought we might need help."

"He got that right."

The old man spoke again, grinning all the while. Bart translated.

"They're fishermen and they're asking if we'd like to be taken ashore."

She glanced at Bart, aware of the forest of skinny legs surrounding them. "Are they real fishermen, Bart, or is this going to be another bad afternoon?"

"Want me to ask?"

She looked up at the circle of faces. "Maybe we ought to take their word for it. No point in giving them any ideas."

"I may not be the best judge of human nature," Bart said, "but something tells me these folks are all right." He began chatting with the old man again. The conversation seemed to go on and on.

Whatever Bart was saying, the fishermen seemed pleased. Bart was grinning.

"What was all that about?" she asked.

"This might turn out to be our lucky day," he replied. "I just cut a deal with the captain here. He's going to take us right to the heart of Bangkok, no questions asked. It'll only set us back a grand."

She burst out laughing. "Where are we going to get a thousand dollars?"

"I'll scrounge it from somewhere."

"He trusts you to come back with the money?"

"No, he's going to keep you for collateral. As soon as I pay him, he'll let you go."

"*Me?* Why doesn't he keep *you* as a hostage? I'll go for the money!"

Bart shook his head. "He thinks you're more of a prize, babe. And he's probably right."

Kelly looked up at the old man and his compatriots. Nothing on their faces could confirm or deny Bart's story. How was she to know this was on the level? "I don't believe you," she said. "I bet you didn't even try to arrange it the other way around."

"No," he admitted, "you're right."

She gave him a scathing look. "Now that we're off that island, your true colors are beginning to show—is that what you'd have me believe?"

"Listen, honey, we don't want to abuse these folks' hospitality by arguing. The alternative is a very long swim."

"Bart, you're a scoundrel. And to think I was beginning to have charitable thoughts about you!"

He laughed. "You know I'll come back for you, sweetheart. We've got a date at the Oriental Hotel, remember?"

Still dubious, she asked, "What if you're killed or captured? Then what happens to me?"

A devilish smile filled his face. "I guess you'd spend the rest of your vacation cleaning fish."

CHAPTER FOURTEEN

BART WINCED as a couple of the fishermen helped him to his feet. Between the helicopter crash and being pulled aboard the fishing boat, he'd reinjured his ribs. It felt as if one of them might even be cracked. Anything more than a shallow breath sent a sharp pain through him. Kelly was on her feet next to him. She knew he was in pain.

"You all right?" she asked, taking his arm.

"I'll live."

The old man was talking animatedly. Bart was only able to make out every second or third word.

"What's he saying?" Kelly asked.

"I believe we're about to be treated to some good old-fashioned Thai hospitality."

The old man signaled for them to follow him, and they made their way toward the stern of the boat, weaving through the fish baskets scattered around the deck. At the rear was a small cabin. The man pulled back a heavy canvas flap that served as a door.

Not wanting to lose face, Bart entered first, letting Kelly follow. It seemed wise to behave in a way that was understood and respected.

The small space was dark and gave the impression of a jail cell. Three-tiered bunk beds lined the walls of two sides of the cabin. Against the back wall there was a table that served as a kind of work area. There were two canvas chairs and a couple of wooden stools tipped on their sides. The old man righted a stool and signaled for Kelly to sit.

When she saw that the chairs were for him and Bart, her mouth sagged open.

"When in Rome, babe," he explained. "In this society women have to stay in their place, and it's a different place from the men."

She sat on the stool. "Evidently. I hope they don't expect me to take over the cooking and cleaning chores just because I happen to be female."

He grinned, gingerly lowering himself into the chair. "It's amazing what a few minutes in civilization will do for the human spirit, isn't it? Only a few hours ago you were worrying about survival. Now an affront to your pride is cause for indignation." He gave her a wink.

Kelly glared. "Don't get smug, buster," she said. "I'd hate to have to disillusion you about the motives for my friendliness the past few days."

"You aren't suggesting you don't love me," he said with mock dismay.

"Bart, I'd have slept with Godzilla to get off that island."

He smiled. "Happily, though, it was me."

"Don't get too cocksure," she said. "All I need is a telephone and I can put a thousand bucks in Grandpa's hands within an hour. I don't need you to buy my freedom."

"There's only one problem with that, my love," he teased.

"What's that?"

"You don't have a telephone and Gramps is not about to lead you to one."

She looked back and forth between him and the old man. "You're taking this ransom business seriously, aren't you, Bart?"

"Yes, because he is." He glanced at the captain, who was rummaging around in a box in the corner.

The boat, which had been pitching a little, suddenly rolled, and Kelly almost fell off her stool. Bart reached out, catching her hand, but at the cost of a jolt in the ribs.

"Poor baby," she said, seeing he was in pain. She sounded genuinely sympathetic.

Bart looked at her, aware of a growing distance between them. He figured it was because they were no longer alone. He could only imagine what it'd be like once they were in Bangkok. Would she forget the way it had been between them?

The island, and especially the cave, didn't seem so very sinister in retrospect. He was actually able to look back on it fondly, though they were only a few hours removed from the place.

The old man shuffled over, grinning. He had a ragged cloth, which he handed to her, saying something. Kelly turned to Bart, not understanding.

"It's to dry your hands and face," he explained.

"How thoughtful," she said sardonically.

"He probably figures you'd be more pleasing to the eye if you didn't look like a drowned rat," he teased.

She grimaced. "Why I didn't discover that you were a male chauvinist pig before I slept with you, I'll never know."

"Weren't you the one who just said you'd have slept with Godzilla to get off that island?"

"Inner ugliness is more offensive than outer ugliness, Mr. Monday. Anyway, women have been conditioned for survival since before recorded time."

Bart knew the situation was bringing out her natural feistiness. But he also sensed an element of seriousness in what she was saying. It almost seemed as if she was trying to return to the way things had been before they were intimate. Or maybe she was preparing herself for Duncan again, if only subconsciously.

The captain pulled a square basket from under the table, opened the lid and removed a can of Coca-Cola. He handed it to Kelly, grinning like a Cheshire cat. She acknowledged the offering with a nod, giving the towel to Bart.

"Thank God," she murmured. "I'm dying of thirst."

"It doesn't look very cold," he said.

"As long as it's wet, I don't care."

While Kelly opened it, the old man handed him a warm beer. His eyes rounded at the sight of it. "Ah," he said, thanking the captain for his kindness.

He glanced over at Kelly. "It's the small pleasures of life, eh, hon?"

"I hate to sound greedy, but do you suppose they have any food on this tub? Or do women have to eat the scraps off the floor with the dogs?"

"Let me ask."

He turned to the captain and passed along Kelly's request. The old man told him he'd already given the order to bring some food. Then he launched into a series of questions, mostly about Kelly. Bart listened as carefully as he could, but was only able to get about half of what was being said. They went back and forth a few times, managing a modicum of conversation.

"Would it be too pushy of me to ask what that was all about?" Kelly asked, knocking back the last of her Coke.

"Our friend wanted to know a little about us."

"Like what?"

"For one thing, if you were my concubine."

"Concubine?"

"Girlfriend, mistress. The term can be used broadly."

Kelly put the empty aluminum can on the floor. The captain signaled for her to hand it to him. She complied. "What did you tell him I was, your lawyer?" she asked.

Bart laughed. "I hardly think that would serve our interests, Kel."

They watched the captain stow the empty aluminum can in a special basket.

"Well, what *did* you tell him?" she asked, clearly miffed.

"That you were my number-one girl." He looked down at her bare legs. "I figure it's important to establish your collateral value. I don't want him thinking I'd go off and leave you. Lawyers are a dime a dozen. A good woman is a prize."

She shook her head. "You know I don't believe a word you're saying. I bet we're going to be dropped off at the nearest port without a word being said."

"Would that it were so."

The captain asked him why he had a concubine who tried to act like a wife. Bart laughed heartily at the question.

"What did he say?" she asked.

He told her. Kelly started to turn red, but held her tongue, apparently deciding not to rock the boat, whether she believed him or not. Instead, she smiled sweetly at the old man.

"I suppose next you're going to tell me that he expects you to share me with him," she said out of the corner of her mouth. "The old Thai custom you haven't bothered to mention."

"I believe you're confusing your Thai fishermen and your Bedouins, Kel."

"So why didn't you tell him I'm your wife? Wouldn't that have made things simpler?"

Bart shook his head. "Wouldn't have been credible. Wives stay at home with the children. They don't cavort around in a bikini, even with a policeman's shirt over it."

Kelly shrugged. "Given the choice, I'd take concubine, anyway. It sounds like more fun."

The old man interrupted with another question. Bart translated.

"He wants to know how much I paid for you."

"Tell him the meter's still running."

"I can't do that. He might think I'd run off on the debt. Anyway, it's hard to put a price on you, Kelly. It's not like you were a fish or something. You're so much more than your hundred and twenty-five pounds. I mean, there's your intellect, your sense of humor . . . you're awfully good company."

"I know you're having a good time with this," she said, "but you know what scares me? I'm beginning to believe you. This guy really intends to hang on to me until you come up with a thousand dollars."

"I tried to bargain him down, but it was hard to convince him I wouldn't pay a grand for such a fine specimen."

"Oh, shut up, Bart."

The captain had more questions, and they chatted for a time, which seemed to annoy Kelly. So, to assuage her, Bart dutifully related the conversation.

"He asked if I bought you from your father or from another gentleman."

"And you said?"

"That you were in the service of a man in Honolulu who paid you well, but you ultimately succumbed to my charm."

"Do I get a rebuttal?" she said dryly.

He shrugged. "It makes a good story."

"Duncan would do whatever it took to get me home. To him, I'm priceless."

"Careful, babe, let's not drive the ransom up. We want you valuable, but definitely not priceless."

Kelly arched a brow. "Bart, I think you're enjoying this a little too much."

"Honey, how often does a man get a chance to claim a beauty like you as his very own concubine?"

She smiled sweetly and said from the corner of her mouth, "Forget the Oriental Hotel, Mr. Monday. In fact, for putting me through this indignity, you can consider our account square. No," she said, interrupting herself, "I take that back. *You* owe *me!*"

"Kelly, my sweet, don't get your loving master upset with you. In Asia, that's considered most unbecoming."

She beamed radiantly. "Screw you, Bart."

The flap of canvas over the doorway opened, and the boy with the spiked hair came in, carrying two bowls with chopsticks. He handed one to Bart, the other to Kelly. Nodding and grinning, he withdrew. Bart saw that they'd brought a kind of fish stew with vegetables over rice. He glanced at Kelly. Her expression was positively blissful.

"This smells heavenly," she said. "I take back all the mean things I said about you and Gramps."

"Then it is true—the way to a concubine's heart is through her stomach."

"Just be thinking how you're going to get that thousand bucks, big boy."

The captain left them alone. Bart watched Kelly chomp down her food. After a couple of minutes she rested the bowl on her knee and stopped to catch her breath.

"You're right, Bart. The little things are actually the big things."

He reached out his hand to her and she took it. He looked into her eyes, feeling her fingers, wanting to hold her.

"Thanks for getting us off that island," she said. "Concubine or just plain friend, I'm grateful."

He gave her fingers a firm squeeze. "Funny, I was just thinking how nice it would be if we were back in our cave about now."

"Wash your mouth out, Mr. Monday." She took another bite.

"Without the bad guys combing the mountainside for us, it might have been idyllic," he said. "I know I'm going to look back on it nostalgically."

Kelly finished chewing and swallowed. "Tell you what. If we have that ten-year reunion and Ko Pong has been civilized with hotels and golf courses in the meantime, maybe we can hike up to the cave and light a candle or something. Maybe the tourist board would make it a shrine."

He gave her an appraising look. "I don't think you're as appreciative of the good things that have happened over the last couple of days as I am."

Judging by the way she looked at him, she must have realized she'd hurt his feelings. "I didn't mean to be glib, Bart. Sorry."

He smiled to let her know that even if he was hurt, he wasn't exactly devastated. "You'd rather forget Ko Pong ever happened, wouldn't you?"

Kelly lowered her eyes. "No, that's not true."

"Tell me how you feel about it, then," he said.

"The things I said to you on the island were honest. But I believe I made it clear we were under exceptional circumstances. You know as well as I do that the world we're headed back to is very different from the one we left behind."

He studied her. "I won't hold you to your promise of one last roll in the hay before you get on an airplane and head back home to Duncan. As far as I'm concerned we're square right now. So if you've been worried about it, don't be."

"Bart, I'm not dismissing what happened. You are a fabulous lover. And a good friend. A wonderful friend."

He nodded, hearing the message she was trying to convey. He had an empty, sick feeling. It was sort of like picking up your girlfriend for the senior prom, only to be told the date would be the last. "You don't have to go on, Kelly, I get the point."

Her brow furrowed. "I'm trying to be realistic," she said. "I think it's a mistake to let ourselves get too emotional."

"Now that it's safe," he said, unable to hide his disappointment.

"Considering we still have a few hurdles to get over, it might be a little soon to be settling accounts," she said. "I foresee a lot of trouble between here and that plane ride home."

"Don't worry, I won't screw up at the eleventh hour." He poked his tongue in his cheek. "And I don't want you to worry that my attitude about the thousand dollars will in any way be affected by your behavior between now and when I buy your freedom."

She chuckled. "You're a bastard, Bart Monday, you really are."

He laughed, too. But, inside, his heart was breaking. "You're playing the hand you were dealt, the same as I am," he said.

Kelly moved from her stool and knelt on the floor next to him. She ran her hand sensuously over his bare legs and looked up at him through her lashes.

"Will you tell me one thing honestly?"

He wasn't sure what to expect. "Anything you want to know, babe."

"Just tell me straight," she said. "Was it Gramps's idea that I be left as collateral or yours?"

Bart swallowed hard, knowing that at this point only the truth would do. "It was my idea, Kelly."

She slipped into the captain's chair and folded her hands over her stomach, staring off thoughtfully. "I suppose that's better," she said. "I'd hate to think these guys really wanted to keep me hostage."

"They know you're valuable to me," he said. "And, believe it or not, like it or not, it happens to be true."

BART HAD BEEN GONE for several minutes. Kelly sat pondering their latest predicament—or maybe *her* latest predicament was more accurate. He didn't have a lot to worry about once they got back to Bangkok, other than being arrested. She'd be the one still under the gun.

At least she was sure of one thing—Bart would never abandon her. If nothing else, the man had integrity and he was loyal. And he cared. Maybe too much.

It concerned her a little how seriously he'd taken their relationship. His sentimentality was surprising. Not that she wasn't aware that there were strong feelings between them—two people couldn't be alone under those kinds of conditions without intense feelings developing. But she'd been honest when she'd said that Ko Pong was not the real world. She'd remember those days forever, but the woman she'd been on the island—the woman who'd dared to be adventurous, to test herself to the limits—was not the real Kelly Ronan.

The flap covering the doorway opened and Bart appeared, followed by the boy with the spiked hair. "All right, milady," he said cheerfully. "How about some soap and water?"

Her eyes lit up. "Don't tell me this yacht comes with a shower."

"No, but the captain offered us a bucket of water and a change of clothes. I doubt if anything will fit properly—me in particular—but it's part of the cruise package, so what the heck." Bart lowered himself gingerly into one of the chairs.

The boy had a small bucket of water and a used bar of soap, which he presented ceremoniously. Kelly looked at the soap and nearly wept. How precious a commodity it seemed.

She took it, thanking him. He responded with a smile and went to a large basket in the corner of the cabin. From it he took two pairs of pajamalike shirts and pants and brought them to her. She thanked him again, and he left. Kelly patted the dry clothing and looked down at the water sloshing in the bucket with the motion of the boat, disbelieving of her sudden embarrassment of riches.

"Shall we flip to see who goes first?" Bart said.

"No, it's always wives first, concubines second, men last. Since there are no wives present, that makes me top dog."

"What part of the Orient is this custom from?" Bart asked mockingly.

She poked her tongue in her cheek. "It's an ancient Polynesian custom—little known to the outside world."

"I bet." But he conceded. "All right, I guess you're entitled."

"Would you be good enough to step outside, then, Mr. Monday? And guard the door, if you would."

"You sound serious."

"I'm going to have a shampoo, a shower and a change of clothes. Whatever's left of the water when I'm done is yours."

Bart screwed up his face. "Don't know if I can relate to these Polynesian customs."

She smiled sweetly. "You won't need to for long."

He got up carefully. His ribs were obviously giving him trouble. Kelly decided it was a wonder he hadn't punctured a lung in the crash. On his way past her he stopped, brushed her cheek with his fingers and left the cabin.

KELLY SAT ON THE BOW of the fishing boat, letting the warm wind dry her hair. Bart was washing up in the cabin. The crew had tittered at the sight of her in the pajamas. The ankles and wrists protruding from the cuffs had told her all she needed to know about the way she looked. But the clothes were clean, and so was she. That in itself was heaven.

The old fishing boat lumbered through the water, fighting a strong wind and row after row of waves. The motion of the boat reminded her of the last hours on the *Ban Don*. That hadn't been so long ago. Less than a week. Yet a lifetime seemed to have passed in the interim.

Although they weren't out of danger, Kelly knew that her adventure was winding down. Bangkok was many miles away, but it was beginning to seem close. It was like being on a horse headed for the barn.

Bart, it seemed, had gotten over his melancholia and was his old self again—wry and devil-may-care. She was glad. That was the way she wanted to remember him.

As she stared out to sea, flashes of Ko Pong came to mind. The horrors were there, but mostly she was remembering the better things—she and Bart working together as a team, struggling to survive and maintain their sanity.

The salt air stung her eyes, making them tear. Or was it her emotion? Why, of all things, was this beginning to feel like graduation day? The happiness and expectation were there, but so was the vague sense of loss. She and Bart had shared some things that many married couples never did. For a lot of people, married life never got much beyond sleeping under the same roof, sharing a television set, meals, bills and maybe children.

And yet, there was no denying that the real world was a very different place for both of them. What would they have said to each other if they'd met at a cocktail party in Kahala instead of under the withering fire of a pirate attack? Bart was attractive and witty. He had tons of sex appeal. But that was sometimes insufficient for a successful date, let alone a serious relationship.

"Ah," Bart said, coming up behind her. "Haven't we met before?"

She turned.

"'Twas on the bow of *Ban Don,* if I recall correctly," he said. "You were a bit more scantily clad, I believe. A real knockout." He smiled at her. "Beautiful then. Beautiful now."

He was bare chested, and had an old towel wrapped around his waist. He looked down at himself.

"I couldn't get into the togs the boys had for me, so I washed out my shorts. When they dry, I'll put them back on."

"I see." She looked closely at his face and noticed that his beard was gone and that his jaw and chin were scraped and bleeding. "What happened to you?"

"I borrowed a fish knife for a shave. Didn't want to sail into Bangkok looking like a shanghaied sailor. Why do you ask? Did I miss some whiskers?"

"No, but it looks as if you cut off half your face in the process."

He laughed. "A dull blade and no mirror does not an easy shave make."

"How are the ribs?"

He sat on a box next to her. "I think they've given up trying to heal and are resigned to being permanently broken."

She reached out and took his hand. "I think you should see a doctor first thing when we get back."

"First thing? I thought you'd want me to call on the moneylender first."

"You're right. Second thing."

He kissed her hand. "We must definitely keep our priorities straight, mustn't we?"

Kelly played with his fingers, looking down at them thoughtfully. "I've been thinking, Bart. I know you don't want me to know the details of what you're doing, because it'll put me in greater danger, but I think it's a mistake and here's why. If something does happen to you and I'm on my own, I won't know what I'm up against or where I can turn for help.

"You want to be protective, and I appreciate that, but whether you realize it or not, Bart, I'm a big girl. I've taken on some powerful people in my time. True, I've slugged it out with them in court or around a negotiating table, but I wouldn't have been able to do that if I wasn't strong. Before, the details of your situation weren't important, but they are now. I really want to know."

"Maybe I have been overprotective," he conceded, looking out to sea.

"I've put my faith in you," she said. "Now I want you to do the same for me."

He sighed, looking resigned. "All right. I guess I'd best start at the beginning. I really was in import-export, as I told you. I'd been running a little operation out of Bangkok for several years when I got a call from a college buddy in the Justice Department. He asked me to visit Washington, D.C., all expenses paid. I went.

"Once I was there, he took me to see the administrator of the DEA. They were concerned about some sort of internal problem in their field operation out here—DEA agents who'd become dealers. They asked me to pretend to go into the drug export business and see what I could find out.

"I spent two years working my way into the system, trying to find out who was playing ball with the baddies. Nobody in the DEA except the administrator and a couple of his top lieutenants in Washington knew about my role. They'd tried getting the goods by working on it internally, but without success. Because I was an outsider, they figured it was unlikely I'd be compromised by someone on the inside."

Kelly shook her head. "That explains why you wouldn't deal with the embassy routinely. Now your life's at stake."

"Exactly."

"But surely you could have taken sanctuary there in an emergency, even if it compromised the operation."

"You'd be right, except that I discovered that two of the top DEA officials in Thailand were in the loop—guys sitting right in the embassy in Bangkok."

"You mean as part of the drug ring?"

"Yes. It was purely by accident that I found out. I didn't suspect anybody that high up. I was thinking field operative. I managed to get in with the local drug lords early on, but had trouble finding out who they dealt with on the American side.

"I got hooked up with a fellow named Thatree Madary, a Thai investigator out of the defense ministry working directly for the prime minister's office. The Thais were trying to root out the corruption in their police force, just as I was trying to get the goods on the rotten Americans. At first my friend thought I was one of the baddies, and I thought he was. We were pumping each other like crazy for months before we put two and two together. Thatree had some pieces to the puzzle and I had some pieces. The combination took us right to the top."

"Why didn't you take the information to the people you were working for in Washington?"

"I intended to, just as soon as I had everything I needed. Thatree was about to lay his hands on evidence connecting several high police officials with my DEA suspects and the drug lords up in the Golden Triangle. The police were alerted and Thatree told me to drop out of sight for a few days. He really stuck his neck out to save me. I went to Ko Samui and the day after I arrived I got a call from a mutual friend telling me Thatree had been arrested. When some police detectives from Bangkok came to my hotel in Ko Samui, I knew the jig was up. I had to get off the island. The *Ban Don* happened along at the right time."

"I wish you'd told me this from the beginning. It would have saved us both a lot of trouble," she said.

"You wouldn't have felt that way if you'd been captured. If they found out what you knew, they couldn't have afforded to let you live."

She could see his point. He had been trying to protect her, and she had to give him credit for that. "There must be somebody in authority you can trust."

"Undoubtedly there is. The problem is I'm a drug dealer as far as the authorities are concerned—a criminal who's probably also wanted for murder since our sojourn on Ko Pong. I can't walk into the prime minister's office or anywhere else without falling into the hands of the police. And they certainly won't give me a chance to tell my story to anyone who could help."

"Then what will you do?"

"I have a contact in the CIA. He's the only one in Thailand who knows about my undercover work. He'll get us out of here."

"How?"

"That's the problem. I tried to reach him from Ko Samui, but couldn't. As soon as we get to Bangkok, I'll get hold of him and make arrangements for a quick trip home."

"Will it be difficult to get out of the country?" she asked.

"Considering the whole police force is looking for us, it won't be a walk in the park. One thing is certain—a few top cops and some boys in the DEA are sweating it out. They'd like to see me silenced before they're compromised. The thing I don't know is what happened to Thatree or his documents. I don't know if he's still alive or not, but if so I have to do what I can for him. But it'll have to wait until I get to Bangkok."

"It seems to me somebody else can do that. Wouldn't it be smarter for you to get the hell out of here, too?"

Bart grinned wryly. "I tend to be a perfectionist, babe. I hate loose ends, especially when one of them is a buddy. Anyway, I've put two years of my life into this operation. I don't like the idea of everything slipping through my fingers at the last minute."

Kelly rolled her eyes. "I'd have thought you'd have had enough adventure for a lifetime."

"I've had a shave, Kelly," he said with a laugh. "I feel like a new man."

"And meanwhile I'm your ticket off this boat so you can go play cops and robbers."

"You'll be safer on this boat than walking the streets with me. Besides, I don't think murder and mayhem are your thing."

"I'd like to think they aren't yours, either."

Bart reached out and caressed her face, but he didn't reply.

After a while he pulled his box over by hers, and they sat, leaning against the gunwale, their arms around each other, watching the sun set behind the distant mountains. As dusk fell, the boy with the spiky hair brought them more food and a bottle of warm beer. It was the same meal as lunch, but that didn't matter. It tasted good. Anyway, Kelly was too worried to be concerned much about food. In the morning they'd be in Bangkok, and she'd find out what fate had in store for them.

CHAPTER FIFTEEN

WHEN NIGHT CAME, the fishermen offered Kelly and Bart the cabin. Bart took the bottom bunk, eager to rest his sore ribs. Kelly took the middle one. A kerosene lantern hung from a beam in the center of the cramped cabin, throwing off a dim light.

She lay there quietly, aware of the pitch and roll of the boat. Occasionally she heard the murmur of voices out on the deck, the sloshing of the waves or the purr of the wind. She expected to hear Bart's soft snores at any moment, but she didn't. Kelly wondered what he was thinking about.

"Bart," she whispered, "are you awake?"

"Yes."

"So am I." She rolled onto her side, facing out into the dark cabin. "Are you feeling sad?"

"No, are you?"

She started to say no, but thought better of it. "Yes, I guess I am."

"Why?"

"I don't know. I suppose there's always some sadness when things are coming to an end."

"Think of Duncan. That ought to cheer you up," he said.

"Don't mention Duncan."

"Why not?"

"Because I'm thinking of coming down and slipping into your bunk to be with you."

He didn't say anything.

"Unless it would hurt your ribs," she added.

"That isn't the issue," he said.

She could tell he was still carrying the wounds of their earlier conversation. And she felt badly about that because she knew she was being unfair. Yet she couldn't help herself. She had already started down the road home. "What *is* the issue?"

"You're asking *me?*"

"I shouldn't have said anything," she said. "It was selfish. Forget I opened my mouth."

"Okay."

His tone was glib and it annoyed her. He had her on the verge of begging for affection and he was making her work for it. She'd have told him to go to hell but she knew and he knew that this was likely their last night together.

"Would you be mad at me if I came down there for just a few minutes?" she asked.

"If it would make you happy, come ahead."

"Well, don't sound so elated at the prospect," she groused.

"Hey, babe, you were the one giving me the it's-been-great-see-you-around speech this afternoon. What do you think I am, a yo-yo?"

"I was trying to spare us both."

"Spare us both what?"

"Oh, Bart, you can be so damned difficult sometimes. I think you enjoy torturing me."

"*I* torture *you?*"

"Yes. You know this isn't easy for me and yet you're making me say it."

"I'm not making you say anything. This afternoon you had no trouble kissing me off on your own."

"I didn't kiss you off, Bart," she said pointedly. "I was trying to deal with the situation realistically."

"Is that what you're doing now, being realistic?"

She didn't reply. She lay in her bunk silently, wavering between anger and desperation. He was right, of course, but she couldn't bring herself to say so.

"No," she finally said, "I'm being selfish. Just forget I said anything."

The boat went through some heavy swells just then, rolling from side to side. If she didn't routinely spend so much time in and on the water, it might have bothered her. But she wasn't prone to seasickness. She wondered why Bart handled it so well. Of course, he seemed to handle everything well. He was a man of many talents, not the least of which was making love.

"So do you want to come down here or don't you?" he asked, breaking the silence.

"No."

"Okay, fine."

She drew a breath, hesitated, then said, "I mean yes, Bart. I want to come down there. Actually, I want to make love with you. But you don't have to, of course. Just say no if you don't want to."

She felt a fist pushing up through the thin mattress from below.

"Get your sweet little butt down here," he groused, "before I come up there, which I don't want to do because it would be hell on my ribs."

Kelly swung her legs over the edge of the bunk and dropped to the floor. Bart moved over and she slipped in next to him. He smelled wonderfully clean. She snuggled up against him. He kissed her forehead.

"You aren't going to hate me for this, are you?" she said.

"For what?"

"Making love with you one last time."

"You mean do I hate you for using my body?" he asked.

"Something like that."

"I've resigned myself to it," he said with a sigh. "It isn't very realistic to expect you to marry me, even if you'd be dead without my intervention, but what is, is. I'll take what I can get."

"You poor thing."

"Well, maybe I like you a little too much for my own good," he said.

His tone was teasing, but she knew there was truth in his words. She wondered if she wouldn't have been better off staying in her own bunk. But Bart was a flame and she was a moth, and it didn't seem to matter that her wings were getting singed. She couldn't help herself. She lightly caressed his bare shoulder.

"The scary part is, I could get addicted to you," she murmured.

"Why is that scary?"

"Because it's as crazy as this whole week has been. It's been insane, I've been insane, the world's been insane. And I want to make love with you so badly I could scream."

Bart began unbuttoning her shirt top. "That can be arranged," he said softly. Exposing her breast, he leaned down and kissed it, bringing her nipple to instant erection.

She ran her fingers through his hair. "I've never felt so unable to control myself in my life," she said, kissing his dry, cracked lips.

"Forgive me for saying this," he mumbled through her kisses, "but in my own crazy way, I love you, Kelly."

His words sent a jolt of fear through her, but also joy. It was not a notion she was prepared to deal with just then, so she kissed him hard and deeply, moving her hand down over his bare torso. All he was wearing was his shorts, the only thing she'd seen him in since the day she'd first laid eyes on him. She gently clasped her hand on his bulge.

"Just make love to me, Bart," she whispered. "That's all I can handle now."

"Take your clothes off," he commanded. "And you may have to help me with my shorts."

She quickly removed the pajamas the fishermen had given her. Then she helped Bart. He groaned a few times during the operation.

"You may have to be on top," he said when they were both naked.

Kelly knew it wouldn't be easy for him, but her desire was strong. Perhaps it was knowing this was most likely their last opportunity. Or maybe it was that wild, impulsive side of her coming to the fore—the side she'd inherited from her mother and had repressed so successfully all these years.

Because of the bunk above them, she couldn't sit up straight, but she managed to straddle Bart, guiding his penis into her. As she leaned over him, their faces just inches apart, she began gyrating. He seemed to swell inside her, filling her, arousing her, raising her level of excitement.

Bart began caressing her breasts as they peered into each other's eyes. He ran his thumbs over her nipples. In seconds he had her at a fever pitch. She rocked her hips violently, taking him in, consuming him.

"I'm going to come," she whispered, her breath coming in staccato bursts.

She heard a moan rise from deep within his throat, and he lifted his hips right off the bed. She came then, her orgasm racking her body with wave after wave of sensation. Tiny cries were coming from her throat as he thrust into her.

When she collapsed onto his chest, she could hear the soft laughter of the fishermen outside. She didn't care. Nothing mattered. Once again—maybe for the last time— she'd found nirvana with Bart Monday.

WHEN SHE AWOKE the eyes were only eighteen inches from her face. A toothy, boyish mouth was grinning at her. "Hey, missus, Bangkok. You want see?"

Kelly blinked. It took a moment, but she finally realized they'd returned to civilization. She looked down and was glad to see that she had a sheet over her. The pajamas the fishermen had given her were on the floor. She clutched the sheet to her chin and listened. She could hear motors and voices in the distance. The jungle, the threatening seas, were gone. Part of the past.

"Mister outside," he said, anticipating her question.

"Okay, fine. Tell him I'll be right out, please."

When he was gone, she swung her legs over the edge of the bunk and quickly slipped into her outfit, truly embarrassed for the first time about the way she looked.

She went to the door and pulled back the canvas flap. Bright morning sun glared into her eyes. She blinked and saw Bart at the bow, talking to the captain. They were on the Chao Phraya, just upriver from the mouth. As she made her way toward Bart and the captain, weaving through the fish baskets, she had her first look at civilization in what seemed like years.

Shacks and shanties on stilts were interspersed with the industrial buildings that lined the shore. There were small boats everywhere—tied up on the riverbank, bobbing in the wide channel. Most were open sided and topped with canvas or corrugated steel to protect against the sun. Some were hardly moving, others seemed in a great hurry.

Kelly marveled at the sight of so many people, the sounds and smells of city life. When she came up next to

Bart, he turned and slipped an arm around her waist. "Morning, sweetheart," he said with a smile. "Sleep well?"

"Like a baby."

"Bangkok," he announced, gesturing like Moses come to the promised land. The pride in his voice was unmistakable.

"So I see." She remembered not to squeeze him. "How are the ribs?"

"Much better, thanks. Good enough to get me to a source of funds, which is what matters at the moment."

Kelly glanced at the captain, who'd hardly paid her any attention. "I take it everything is copacetic?"

"Grandpa is a shrewd old goat. He's been asking lots of questions about our plans."

"What does that mean?"

"I imagine he's wondering if he might have sold out too cheaply."

She looked at the old man again. "You don't think he'll try playing any games with us, do you?"

"I don't think so. Not if I get right back with the money. He did change the request to greenbacks when I wouldn't renegotiate the price."

"Is that a problem?"

"It's a complication. Not insurmountable."

"Glad to hear it. I don't want to spend my life on this barge."

"No danger of that. They'd find another use for you."

Before Kelly could ask what he meant by that, the captain said something. Soon he and Bart were off on another extended conversation. She turned her attention to the high-rise buildings in the distance. City life was seeming a little less hospitable now. The snakes and other horrors of the jungle had at least posed a more honest danger.

The Bangkok she'd seen a week earlier had been a sensually exotic place, a feast for the senses. She'd done all the tourist things—seen the Emerald Buddha, the Grand Palace, the floating market on Klong Dao Kanong. She'd gotten up at dawn to watch the procession of saffron-robed monks collecting food for their day's sustenance. At the Wat Po she'd purchased a pair of sparrows in a tiny bamboo cage from an ancient toothless woman, paying twelve baht for the privilege of setting them free. It was supposed to bring her luck, which in retrospect seemed a joke.

She'd even bought a "never-can-tell" imitation Cartier watch for Duncan. She'd spent hours browsing in the markets, taking in the rich palette of color, the smorgasbord of flavors and scents. She'd been a normal tourist—innocent and unsuspecting.

Now she'd changed. And so had Bangkok. The city was filled with danger and threats she didn't fully understand, even now.

Before long the fishing boat changed course and headed for a collateral channel, a canal that led into the heart of the city. Kelly observed the scene, the metal-roofed houses propped on the banks with naked television antennae protruding like a forest of barren trees. There were mounds of dirt here and there along the shore, festooned with bursts of wild orchids. There were children naked and half-naked standing waist-deep in the murky water, bathing and splashing one another.

After a while the captain said something to Bart, who explained that the old man wanted her to go into the cabin.

"What's the matter? Is he afraid I'll jump ship?"

"He doesn't want you to be seen by anyone. Their questions might be difficult to answer. We're going to the fish market first, to unload the catch. I'll get off there. He's asked me to tell you to stay inside and do as you're told." A grin crept across Bart's face. "And he wanted me to say he may not look like a shark, but his teeth are very sharp."

"Meaning if I try anything, I'll regret it," she said with a glance at the old boy.

"That's a fair assessment."

"How long will you be gone? I'm ready to move on to the next phase of this escapade. The cruise has been nice, but I really want a hot shower and a shampoo."

"With luck I'll be back within a few hours."

"At what stage do I panic?"

"I would say nightfall would be a suitable time."

It had been the better part of twenty-four hours since she'd felt genuine fear, and when it rose in her again she didn't like it at all. She'd had enough danger. "Any suggestions about what I do if you don't come back?"

Bart arched a brow. "Got a telephone credit card account?"

"Of course."

"Give Duncan a call."

"I thought you said I wouldn't be allowed to use a phone."

"You won't," he said, "so you'll have to use your persuasive powers. I can't guarantee Gramps will be any easier to negotiate with than the corporate moguls you take on, but I don't see that you have any other choice."

"Thanks, Bart, this is doing wonders for my confidence."

Grinning, he said, "Confidence is not something you lack, my dear." Then he took her arm. "Come on, let's go into the cabin and say goodbye properly."

Once they were inside and Bart had adjusted the canvas flap, he held her face in his hands and looked deeply into her eyes. "Well, it looks like we're at the final phase," he said. "It's been a hell of a ride. I'll never forget it."

Her eyes turned liquid and glossy. "Me, either, Bart."

He took her in his arms and gave her a long, sensuous kiss. They clung to each other, hardly breathing, not wanting the kiss to end.

"I hate to say this," she said, "but this is seeming an awful lot like goodbye. Tell me you're coming back."

"Would you be terribly disappointed if I didn't come back?"

"I'd kill you, if you weren't already dead."

"If that means you'd be happy to see me, then I'd better come back ... if only to see you smile."

She touched the scab on his chin where he'd cut himself shaving, and the discolored skin on his cheek from the beating he'd taken. "You're cute as hell, Bart Monday, but right now what I need more than anything is to know I can count on you."

He kissed the end of her nose. "I haven't let you down yet, have I?" He went to the doorway, pausing to look back at her a final time.

Kelly had an urge to tell him to stop. She wanted to tell him she loved him, but she didn't want him to misunderstand, to think she was trying to ensure his dedication to her cause. Besides, what was the point? Why create unjustified hope and unreasonable expectations? And yet she wanted him to know.

"You'll be fine," he said, seeing the consternation on her face.

Kelly nodded. "Yes, I know."

Giving her a wink, he left the cabin.

IT WASN'T LONG before the boat was thumping against a dock. The boy with the spiked hair came in to keep her company. Though his face was masked with a grin, she knew he was there to keep an eye on her.

The smell of fish was very strong and there was a lot of noise outside the cabin. The unloading process was under way. Bart was doubtlessly ashore. With luck, she would be, too, within a few hours.

The boy seemed thoroughly entertained just looking at her. She figured he was curious, but conversation was impossible, so she sat in one of the chairs and waited.

After a while the boy said, "Food?"

It wasn't until then she realized she hadn't eaten. She nodded in reply. "Please."

He stepped outside and returned a moment later with a small bowl of rice. As she ate, the boy got her a Coke from the basket under the table. It was probably his concept of an American breakfast. Kelly didn't argue.

Not long after she'd finished eating, the boat's engine purred to life. The boy went to the door and poked his head out. When he turned to her, he announced, "Go home now." The communication was rudimentary, but she appreciated it.

They *putted* along the canal. Kelly had to rely on sound to tell her what was happening. The voices outside—coming from both other boats and people on the shore—seemed closer. She decided they must be on a minor canal. They were moving slowly, and the trip seemed unending. Finally they bumped against a dock, or the side of a canal, and stopped dead.

The old captain appeared at the doorway. He looked stern and spoke rapidly, as though he expected her to understand. When he was done, he gestured to the boy, who looked at her and said, "You no move, okay?"

She nodded, appreciating the succinctness of the translation. When the old man withdrew, he left the canvas flap open. That gave her more light and some air to help counteract the stifling heat. The boy continued to stare at her, seemingly incapable of boredom.

Kelly wondered how much longer she'd have to wait. She estimated forty-five minutes to an hour had passed. Perhaps Bart had been overly optimistic in saying he'd be back in a few hours. After all, his task wasn't like running down to the local bank. He was bare chested and shoeless—hardly suitable attire for a city. If only to avoid drawing attention to himself, he'd have had to find clothes. And where was he going to get a thousand dollars so quickly? He hadn't said.

One of the other crewmen came into the cabin, bringing a fan and some magazines and papers. He gave them to Kelly, grinning like the captain and the boy.

"You read, okay?" the boy said, explaining the offering.

She began fanning herself as she looked at the periodicals. One was a cheap Thai pulp, the sort of thing that was sold at the checkout counter in supermarkets at home. The other was a skin magazine, full of pictures of naked Asian women.

She glanced through the magazine. Most of the photos dealt with subjugation. Imprisoned as she was, Kelly felt an affinity with the women—an affinity she'd have preferred not to feel.

"Well," she said with a sigh, "I hope your friends don't have a dark side I haven't seen yet."

The boy grinned, again pretending he understood. He rubbed his thumb and middle finger together, making the universal sign for money. Then he pointed at her. "You very beautiful," he said. "Very beautiful. Many baht, many dollar." Then he put his bony finger on the cover girl's naked breast. "You same-same, missus."

It wasn't at all what she wanted to hear just then. Not at all.

CHAPTER SIXTEEN

THE BOY FINALLY LEFT, though two fishermen remained just outside the cabin, supposedly engaged in various chores. Kelly spent the rest of the morning in her bunk, waving the fan until she thought her wrist would break. She began to doubt whether Bart would ever return.

In the early afternoon a couple of women came on board with cooking pots and dishes and tea. They paused before entering the cabin, looking Kelly over and grinning. As they fixed her midday meal, they made several remarks to her, though it was difficult to tell whether they were being sympathetic or critical.

Kelly ate her curry and rice and vegetables, and after she finished she lingered near the door, alone, a prisoner, cared for by people she didn't know and couldn't understand. In her heart of hearts she wanted to believe Bart was all right—that he'd rescue her soon—but it wasn't easy to keep her spirits up. She was lonely and afraid.

Back in Hawaii she didn't depend on a man to make her life work, and she didn't particularly like the idea that she needed one now. But the fact was, she did need Bart. It wasn't just to get off the damned fishing boat, though. She needed to see him, to talk to him again.

All afternoon she'd struggled with her feelings, only to realize she'd been afraid to admit how much she cared for Bart. She'd fought it, convincing herself she'd be able to go home to Hawaii with nothing more than thanks and goodbye. But she knew now she'd been deluding herself.

Just how much he meant to her she still wasn't sure, but she did know she couldn't dismiss him so easily.

She lay on her bunk, growing more depressed by the minute. When her thirst became acute, she looked in the basket where the soft drinks were kept and removed the last two cans. She drank one and saved the other.

By the time the shadows started growing long, and the smell of burning charcoal grew stronger, Kelly was beginning to think Bart might not be coming back. He'd said if he hadn't returned by nightfall, she could begin to panic. It looked as if the time might have come for plan B. But what was plan B?

As soon as the captain put in an appearance, she'd try bargaining with him. Maybe if she offered him two thousand dollars, he'd listen, let her get to a phone. But of course he'd have to trust that she wouldn't use the opportunity to summon help. And then there was the little problem of communication.

Maybe negotiation would be a waste of time. If she tried to bargain, it might be interpreted as a sign that she had no faith in the prospect of Bart's return. Then what? Would that make the old man more willing to negotiate, or less?

And what did they plan to do with her if Bart never showed up? Maybe, just maybe, plan B should involve more direct measures . . . like escape.

It was clear how carefully she was being guarded. Would they be prepared if she suddenly bolted from the cabin, leaped onto the dock and disappeared into the alleys? Failing that, she might be able to dive overboard into the canal and hope she could swim away in the dark.

At dusk the women returned with her dinner. And the captain came with them, standing in the doorway as the meal was laid out. Kelly wondered if this was the time to approach him with an offer. Whether now or later, she had to be able to communicate with him, and that meant finding someone to translate.

"Do either of you speak English?" she asked the women.

They looked at her quizzically.

"Do you speak English?" she repeated.

They both shook their heads. Finishing their labors, they withdrew, leaving Kelly alone with the captain. He had a less than pleased expression on his face.

"I'd like to speak with you," she said. "Do you have someone who can translate?"

He looked indifferent.

"English," she said. "I want to speak."

The captain stuck his head outside the cabin and yelled something. A surge of hope went through her. Perhaps he did understand and would be willing to talk.

A moment later a crewman appeared. For a second she thought he'd come to translate, but then she saw he was holding a chain and manacle.

Kelly got to her feet, dismayed. The captain barked at her to sit down. She didn't understand the words but the meaning was made clear. She considered bolting right then, but it wasn't dark yet, and she wasn't absolutely certain Bart wasn't coming back. Besides, an ill-fated escape attempt would only make it more difficult later.

Still, she wasn't going to take this lying down. She put her hands on her hips. "I refuse to be chained like a common criminal," she spat at the captain, her eyes flashing.

The old man snarled a reply that sounded suspiciously like the equivalent of "Shut up, woman!"

Over the past week Kelly had dealt with a lot worse than this two-bit sea dog. She glared, refusing to back down.

Without warning the captain struck her, nearly knocking her off her feet. Before she recovered, the crewman shoved her onto the bunk and clamped the manacle to her

ankle. He secured the other end to a heavy metal ring on
the wall. The chain was long enough for her to get to the
bunk and the table, but fell well short of the door.

Kelly tried to tell herself that this was a minor setback,
that Bart would return, but she didn't really believe it. He
might already be dead or under arrest. If so, she was on her
own. She'd have to use her wits if she wanted to save her
hide.

SHE AWOKE IN THE MORNING to the sound of crowing
cocks and the realization that Bart still hadn't returned.
His absence had a feeling of finality to it. Desperation
washed over her.

An hour later breakfast came, but the manacle and
chain remained. After she'd eaten, the boy with the spiked
hair brought her a pail of water and a bar of soap. He also
brought a clean shirt and a freshly threaded string of jasmine for her to wear around her neck. Apart from Bart, he
had been the closest thing she had to a friend.

Kelly thanked him, but the boy avoided eye contact. She
decided he must be embarrassed by what had happened to
her. As he was about to leave, she stopped him, taking him
by the arm. "What's happened to the man I came with?"
she asked.

The boy looked at her dumbly.

"Mister," she said. "Where mister?"

He shook his head, a vaguely sad look on his face.

Bart, she decided, wasn't coming back.

Late in the morning she heard a commotion on the deck,
the sound of voices. The curtain flew open and the captain appeared. With him was a stocky Asian gentleman in
a suit and tie. He was middle-aged, wore wire-rimmed
glasses and a somber expression. Two younger men in
white short-sleeved shirts followed him. The group spread
out before her, staring. Kelly stared right back.

"Good morning," the Asian gentleman said in perfect English. "Miss Ronan, isn't it?"

Kelly was so startled she could hardly reply. "Yes...who are you?"

He barely smiled. "That's hardly important. The point is I'm going to get you off this old fish barge." He glanced around with a smirk of disdain. "Hardly a proper setting for a lady of your sophistication. It's stifling in here."

"Glad somebody besides me noticed."

The man looked at the manacle and shook his head. "This is most unfortunate," he said, his accent impeccably British. "I regret that in Bangkok such a thing could happen." He turned to the captain and barked a command in Thai.

The old man said something to someone outside, and the crewman who had chained her the evening before came running in. His fingers fumbled with the key as he removed the manacle, and quickly withdrew.

Kelly rubbed her ankle and stood. She looked into the new arrival's eye. "Now what?"

He glanced at her pajamas. "I take it those are not your clothes."

"Hardly."

"We shall get you something decent, then. This is shameful. You have my apologies. Truly."

"Do you mind if I ask who you are and what you intend to do?"

He allowed himself a slight smile. "For the moment, consider me your benefactor. I'm taking you out of here."

Kelly's eyes narrowed. "Before I go anywhere, I'd like assurance of some sort."

"You aren't suggesting you'd prefer to stay here, are you, Miss Ronan?"

She eyed him. "How do you know my name?"

"I make it my business to know what's going on in this town. It's in your interest to cooperate. Believe me."

She smiled thinly. "You've made a few good moves, but being a lawyer I'm naturally suspicious. Perhaps you could tell me what's happened to Bart."

"Mr. Monday."

"Yes," she said, "Mr. Monday."

"I should like to know his whereabouts as much as you, Miss Ronan."

Her brow arched. "Why is that?"

"This is not the place to discuss it. If you'd be good enough to come with me, we shall see that all your needs are tended to."

"Right now my only need is to be free."

"In good time you shall be."

She folded her arms across her chest. "In good time?"

"We'll discuss it later," he said a bit more curtly. He gestured toward the door. "Shall we go?"

"I'm not going anywhere until you tell me what's going on."

The man's polite façade vanished. "Miss Ronan, my associates are skilled in martial arts. They are here to protect me, but their talents can be used to subdue you. I would like you to accompany us peacefully, but I will take whatever measures are necessary to ensure your compliance. Do I make myself clear?"

"I don't like being threatened."

"I don't like being disobeyed."

"Well, Mr. Whoever-you-are, we obviously aren't compatible. It's been a fun conversation, but maybe it's time for us each to go about our business."

"You have a delightful sense of humor, Miss Ronan, but my patience is wearing thin."

She tried to feign the same resolute expression she used in court. "If you're a drug lord, you may as well shoot me because I'm not going with you."

A grin played at the corners of his mouth. He pushed his glasses up off his nose. "I am a businessman, not a drug lord."

"Oh? What kind of businessman takes a woman under threat of force? If you were an upstanding citizen, you'd help me go free, call the police, whatever."

"Is that what you'd like me to do, Miss Ronan, take you to the police?" He shook his head. "I think not."

Kelly put her hands on her hips. "Who *are* you?"

He sighed. "No wonder the Japanese are running circles around you Yanks. You don't understand discipline. And American women, especially, don't understand their place."

She glared. "I'm not interested in your sexist jingoism. Just tell me your role in all this."

"All right, but this is my last concession. Mr. Monday is indebted to the captain in the amount of a thousand dollars, and the captain is beginning to doubt Mr. Monday intends to make good on his obligation. Having no use for you, he has offered to sell you to me for eighty cents on the dollar. In brief, Miss Ronan, I have purchased you for eight hundred dollars."

"Purchased me!" she sputtered. "That's illegal! I'm not a chattel!"

"I don't think either you or Mr. Monday are in a position to raise matters of illegality. You're rather fortunate, actually, that I've come to claim you, not the police or the drug lords."

Kelly swallowed hard.

The businessman smiled benevolently. "Should your ego need a boost, you might be pleased to know that your collateral value has now increased tenfold. Should Mr. Monday wish to redeem you, it will cost him ten thousand dollars."

"You can't be serious!"

He nodded, letting his eyes drift slowly down her body. "I paid that for a weekend with a starlet in Hong Kong not long ago. I must say, the young lady wasn't half so attractive as you."

Kelly wiped her damp brow with the back of her hand and looked down at herself.

"Yes," the man said, "even in your peasant clothing." Again he gestured toward the door. "Now, shall we go?"

Kelly could see no point in resisting. What difference did it make who held her prisoner? Anyway, she doubted conditions could get much worse.

They left the boat, entering the crowded byways of Bangkok. Their procession must have looked singularly comical—a smartly dressed businessman with his two thugs escorting a gangly blonde in ill-fitting peasant clothes. They walked no more than fifty yards through the tangle of *sois* and alleys adjoining the canal before coming to a black Mercedes with tinted windows.

Kelly glanced up the street, jammed with noisy three-wheel *tuk-tuk* taxis, *samlors* and brightly painted trucks, before the bodyguards guided her firmly into the back seat. Her benefactor got in next to the driver. Kelly was sandwiched between the two men in the back.

They started down the street, which, though full of shops, wasn't a tourist area. Kelly was curious about her surroundings, but what struck her most was coolness. The air conditioning was incredibly luxurious. She felt pampered, despite the fact that she was being carried off by three strange men.

The boss turned to look at her. "Be good enough to lower your head to your knees, Miss Ronan. For security reasons, I'd prefer you not know where we're taking you."

Kelly complied, seeing she had no other choice. To assure her full cooperation, one of the bodyguards put his hand firmly on the back of her neck, pressing her forehead against her knees.

"I hope you know this is kidnapping," she said through her teeth.

"Not at all," the Asian gentleman said. "I'm simply securing collateral. I assure you, this will be a good deal more pleasant for you than it would have been had you stayed on the fish barge."

Kelly didn't know about that. "What happens if Bart doesn't come for me?" she asked. "Or if he can't for some reason?"

"I'm an optimist by nature," he replied. "Besides, there's no point contemplating dire developments. Let's hope he does."

The realization hit her then that having her face shoved into her knees was the least of her worries. Kelly began to pray that Bart was alive and well and readying his charger for combat.

THEY DID NOT DRIVE FAST. The streets were crowded, the honking incessant and the stops frequent. Kelly couldn't see a thing, but the motion of the car told her all she needed to know. They drove for fifteen minutes, but she estimated they didn't go more than a couple of miles.

Eventually they entered what seemed to be a narrow street. She could tell because it got darker in the car and the ambient sound seemed to close in. When the Mercedes came to a stop, she was allowed to sit up. They were in a dead-end alley with a few lines of laundry overhead and not much else. There was no one in sight. The buildings on either side rose three or four stories.

The businessman turned to her, a self-satisfied smile on his face. "My apologies for bringing you to the service entrance, as it were. However, discretion is in both our interests."

The car door was opened and Kelly climbed out on the heels of a bodyguard. The dank air was tinged with the pungent smell of urine. She glanced around and tuned her ear. She could hear the voices of hawkers touting "look-look" shows. A week earlier she'd ventured into the bawdy district around Patpong Road, and she wondered if that wasn't where she was now.

Her escorts didn't give her long to contemplate the matter. They stepped to a heavy metal door and entered a small hallway with barely enough room for the four of them to stand. One of the guards pushed a button next to an elevator.

The door opened and they squeezed into the car, although the limit was probably three persons. Kelly was aware of two scents—the jasmine hanging about her neck and a very strong, tangy cologne. Though she couldn't be sure, she decided the cologne was the businessman's. The other two men made no eye contact. They were both her height, perhaps three inches taller than their employer. Their faces had a menacing quality that indicated they took their jobs seriously.

Kelly's putative benefactor made no attempt to avert his eyes. He stared up at her, shifting his glance to her breasts once or twice during the elevator's slow ascent.

They got off and stepped into a second corridor. This one accessed only one door. The businessman opened it and led the way inside.

They entered a kitchen. An old woman who was chopping vegetables stopped what she was doing and bowed. The businessman ignored her and proceeded through the room.

"Again, my apologies, Miss Ronan," he said over his shoulder.

They came to a plushly appointed sitting room. The walls were covered with red silk, the furniture was teak. Though not large, the room was sumptuous, with jade carvings, porcelain vases and hand-painted screens.

The businessman gestured. "This is where you'll pass your time as my guest. I hope you'll find it comfortable."

Kelly looked around. "It's an improvement over what I'm used to," she said, managing to keep her tone bland.

He gestured toward a tailored white sofa trimmed with red piping. "Please make yourself at home, Miss Ronan."

Kelly plopped down, feeling like a pauper in a palace. She couldn't help running her fingers over the fine silk pillow next to her. Her benefactor sat in a carved wooden chair across from her, looking thoroughly pleased with himself.

"I think you'll be comfortable here," he said.

"You live here?" she asked.

"I spend time here. Let me put it that way."

"No one normally lives here?"

"My, you're full of questions, aren't you, Miss Ronan?"

"Most prisoners know their jailers. I don't."

He contemplated her, weighing his thoughts. "My name is Wong," he announced. "My friends at Cambridge called me Norman. If you wish, you may call me Norman."

"I was wondering where you learned to speak English like that."

The indirect compliment obviously pleased him. "I run many enterprises, in Bangkok and in other places. I got my start as a money lender, and I suppose my heart is still in the business. As a rule, when a fisherman wishes to factor a loan, the request would not come to my attention. However, one of my associates thought the proposition a bit unusual in that the collateral in question was a beautiful blond American. The matter piqued my curiosity. I investigated, and here we are."

She studied him. "That doesn't explain how you know who I am."

"As I told you, there is little in this town that I do not know. When a foreign gentleman and his lady friend are wanted not only by the police, but by virtually the entire criminal establishment of the country, it is not difficult to learn their names."

"So you plan to sell me back to Bart for ten thousand. And that's how you're justifying this song and dance?"

Wong's brow furrowed. "It struck me as a favorable return on my investment. Dealing with desperate but decent people tends to be profitable, more profitable and usually safer than dealing with unsavory characters. However, having learned a bit about Mr. Monday's difficulties, I have my doubts about his ability to perform. Frankly, I think he will be fortunate to live through the week."

There was something about Norman Wong's unbiased observation that hit her right in the gut. Bart, she suddenly realized, was almost certainly in serious trouble. But that fact hadn't seemed to dampen Norman Wong's enthusiasm for the venture. "So where does that leave me?" she asked.

"Your value, need I say, is immense." He smiled. "The old saw about supply and demand applies—everybody wants you, there's only one genuine article, and I've got it."

Kelly hated his smugness. "You're saying if Bart doesn't come through, you'll sell me to the highest bidder, is that it?"

"Common sense would dictate such a course. However, I find you so charming that I'm in no hurry to part with you." His eyes drifted down her body. "You're lovely and bright, and I haven't had a decent conversation with an educated woman in so long that I might...shall we say...savor your pleasures for a while before collecting my profits."

"Conversation I don't mind, Wong. You can forget anything beyond that."

He beamed. After a long pause he said, "Charming, indeed."

Kelly looked around. "So tell me, where's the girl you usually keep here?"

He grinned. "You're very astute, Miss Ronan."

"A simple deduction, Norman. You don't keep this place to have a quiet corner in which to read Byron."

"Quite right. The young lady in question has gone to visit her family."

"When did she leave?"

"This morning."

"How convenient."

Norman Wong pushed his glasses up onto the bridge of his nose. "The maid has been cleaning out the boudoir. I'm sure all evidence of the previous occupant won't be expunged, but we shall do our utmost to make this your home, Miss Ronan—at least for the duration of your stay."

The way Wong kept looking at her made Kelly think his plans were evolving even as they spoke. What she didn't know was how far he was prepared to go. He appeared to be civilized, which gave her some hope, though there was no disputing her situation was desperate.

"Well, here I am, abusing you with conversation," Wong said, "while you've been living in hardship for days. No doubt you are eager for some pampering. This apartment is furnished with any convenience you could possibly desire. If I may, I'll show you around." He got to his feet and Kelly did too.

He led the way into the adjoining bedchamber. Unlike the sitting room, it was entirely Western in decor. Dominating the room was a four-poster with a yellow chintz bedspread. There was an elegant dressing table and chaise longue and a tall mahogany armoire. The paintings were impressionist.

"I saw this in a British magazine and had it replicated," he said, beaming with pride. "It goes nicely with my fantasies." Wong reached out and touched her arm. "How about yours?"

"Thank you, Norman," she said, pulling her arm away, "but my fantasies are confined to my bedroom at home."

"Do you have a lover?"

Kelly was thrown off balance by the directness of the question. She thought carefully before answering, since it wasn't clear what response would best serve her interests. "I'm engaged to be married to a man in Honolulu," she said, taking what looked like the most profitable course. "Let me put it that way."

"Marriage," he said, a bit taken aback. "I must say, Miss Ronan, you don't strike me as the marrying type."

She didn't know whether to be offended or not. "Well, I'm definitely not concubine material, Norman. I want to be clear about that right up front."

He stroked his chin. "I've learned over the years that people are a product of their circumstances. You may not have fancied yourself a prospective concubine in America, but this is Thailand. And you, my dear, are no longer an ordinary tourist."

It was, Kelly realized, the truest thing he'd said yet.

Wong pointed toward the open door to the bathroom. "The facilities need no explanation. A woman will arrive momentarily with a selection of clothing. I've also made arrangements for a manicurist and hairdresser." He checked his watch. "They should be here at any time, but there's no rush. Have a leisurely bath—I have business to attend to. I'll return this evening. We can talk then, have an intimate dinner, see what common ground we can find." The last was delivered with a slight arch of his brow.

He started toward the door, and Kelly stopped him. "Norman, I have a question, if you don't mind."

"Of course."

"If I can get some money wired here, how much would it take for you to put me on a plane headed out of the country?"

He shook his head woefully. "I'm afraid, my dear, it's no longer just a question of money. I'm taking a tremendous risk, protecting you from the wolves." He raised his hand in caution. "But don't worry. There's something else I've learned in life—all good things are worth their price." He smiled. "It's a lesson you might be well advised to learn."

Kelly watched him go, telling herself not to despair. There was no way on earth an educated woman, a partner in the best law firm in Honolulu, could be forced into servitude as a concubine to a smug little dandy in Bangkok, Thailand. At least, that's what common sense dictated. The problem was, nothing made much sense anymore.

As the door closed, Kelly said aloud, "Damn you, Bart Monday! Why didn't you let me drown?"

CHAPTER SEVENTEEN

THE GLEAMING WHITE TILE of the bathroom almost made Kelly forget her troubles. She opened all the cabinets and drawers. In a small closet next to the shower she found a carton of perfumes, creams and makeup. She wondered if the maid had placed them there in a last-minute attempt to hide the personal effects of Norman Wong's mistress.

Over the tub was a small window that afforded a view of the nearby rooftops. It was too high for her to look directly into the alley, even when she climbed onto the ledge and craned her neck. Like the window of the bedroom, which faced the wall of the adjoining building, it promised no route of escape.

Having checked out the place, Kelly decided to take a shower. The hot water felt so good she washed her hair three times, once with each of the shampoos she found. Then, after toweling her hair, she decided to use the Jacuzzi. She poured in bath crystals, then climbed into the tub, leaning back and staring at herself on the mirrored ceiling. Lying there, she understood why a girl might choose to live in such luxury. It certainly beat the hardship she'd lived through during the past week.

Of course, Kelly would never remotely consider being kept, but it wasn't hard to see the issue through the eyes of a twenty-year-old Thai flower who had grown up bathing in the Chao Phraya river.

The sensuousness of lying in the Jacuzzi inevitably led her thoughts to Bart. It was getting harder and harder to ignore the fact that he might not return. But there had been one positive note. Norman Wong had said nothing of Bart's demise. Since he seemed to know a great deal about everything that was going on, it seemed logical to assume he'd know if Bart had been killed or was arrested. On the other hand, Norman might be aware of bad news and had elected not to send her into a fit of despair.

To think that Bart might be dead tore at her heart. It would be the cruelest sort of irony considering all they'd been through—the chances they'd taken, the adversity they'd faced. But until Bart's fate was clear, she had no alternative but to make do. If it was truly a question of money, Norman Wong could probably be bought off. Or could he? It was beginning to appear that for Norman, money wasn't the issue.

An opportunity to escape would come along eventually. The real problem was, she didn't have anyplace to go, anyone to turn to. Even if she got hold of Duncan, how would she get out of the country with the police looking for her? No wonder Norman acted as though he held a pat hand.

In a way, Bart was still her best chance, assuming he wasn't dead. She pictured his face, battered from both the beating he'd gotten at the hands of the pirates and the hatchet job he'd done on himself trying to shave. The poor baby. After all they'd been through, he just couldn't be dead!

Kelly heard someone in the bedroom. She tensed. There were no locks on the doors—she'd checked that out already—so she knew she was vulnerable. What if it was Norman? There was a soft knock on the bathroom door.

"Who is it?"

The door slowly swung open and a young, barefoot woman in a long straight skirt and white tank top appeared. She had the demure expression of a kitten, with shy, soulful eyes. She wasn't pretty—her nose was flat and wide, her face irregularly shaped—but she had a smile that was endearing. She took no notice of the fact that Kelly was naked.

"Sorry," she said, just above a whisper. "Ladies here. For hair—" she touched her head "—and for..." She held up her hand and pointed to her fingernail.

"The manicurist. Yes, I understand. Thank you."

The girl stood waiting, as if for further instruction. "You want they come in here, or you go out?"

"I'll come out."

The girl nodded and went to get a large white fluffy towel from a cabinet. She stepped to the tub and held it unfurled for Kelly to step into.

It was the first time she'd ever been attended at her bath, but the girl was so unassuming that Kelly found it easy to overcome her modesty. She stepped into the towel. "What's your name?" Kelly asked.

"Anura, miss."

"Do you work here normally, Anura?"

"Yes. I am the maid."

"The maid of the lady who lives here?"

The question brought a deep blush and averted eyes. "I am the maid of the house," she said so softly she could barely be heard.

"In other words, you work for Mr. Wong."

"Yes, miss."

Kelly saw little prospect of an ally, but she considered ways she might enlist Anura's assistance. Could she bribe the girl to phone Duncan? Kelly imagined him receiving the call in his plush corner office in the firm's Honolulu tower. A frail voice in broken English, muttering words like kidnap, police, money. No, it would never work.

Anura lifted her eyes, appearing as uncertain of their relationship as she. Kelly reassured her with a smile. "Tell the ladies I will come out shortly."

"You will need something to wear," Anura said. "Wait, please."

The young woman snatched the fisherman's clothing from the floor and stepped out of the bath, returning a moment later with a long silk kimono. When Kelly had put it on, she went out to meet the hairdresser and the manicurist, two nondescript women in their forties. Neither spoke English, or at least they pretended not to. What communication was necessary was accomplished with Anura's help.

With three women hovering over her, Kelly felt like a courtesan. She looked at her image in the mirror of the armoire and wondered what had happened to the sassy lawyer in the navy and gray suits who wasn't afraid to slug it out with the big boys in a tense courtroom encounter, or stare down an opposing counsel who dared to play chicken with her client's money.

"Very pretty, miss," Anura said several times, implying that Mr. Wong would undoubtedly be pleased.

Kelly's emotions ebbed and flowed from desperation to awe. She felt as though she was in some sort of Hollywood fantasy—one as troubling and frightening, in its own way, as the pirates and snakes of Ko Pong.

When the repair work was nearly complete, a Mrs. Lui arrived with the new wardrobe. She reminded Kelly of the cunning dragon lady in a Charlie Chan film. Like Norman Wong, she was Chinese, not Thai.

Mrs. Lui was somewhere between fifty and sixty, with a tall black lacquer bouffant, bright red lips and black penciled brows. She wore a tight cheongsam. The dress matched her lipstick and nails—tiger claws as long as the first joints of her fingers. The syrupy ennui with which she dealt with her customer came, it seemed, from long years of waiting on self-indulgent women. If she found Kelly a curiosity, she didn't betray it.

"The choices in your size limited, madam," she said in clipped, staccato English. "This the best I can do, so short notice."

Kelly, who was in the middle of her pedicure, looked at the dresses held aloft by Mrs. Lui and her assistant, a young Chinese girl. After a week in the jungle, anything short of a flour sack would do. But a decision was called for, so she made herself contemplate the choices. On reflection, she rather liked the black cheongsam with gold dragon embroidery.

"That one, I think," she said, pointing with freshly painted nails.

"Will madam try for size?"

Kelly realized she had no underwear. She considered a face-saving fib about lost luggage, but elected to be direct. "I have nothing to wear under it."

A click at the assistant brought a case of undergarments. Kelly's eyes widened with delight at the cascade of lingerie. A couple of pairs of panties were quickly selected, but a bra posed a greater problem. Mrs. Lui went through the selection like a fishwife at the market, tossing rejects aside left and right. Finally she stood upright. "I think you too big." Her eyes dropped to Kelly's bust. "No matter. You hard. Tits stand up nice."

Having little choice, Kelly accepted the judgment. Then, while the manicurist fanned Kelly's freshly polished toenails, Mrs. Lui's assistant brought a dozen shoe boxes from the other room.

"How big your foot? Maybe eight? Maybe nine?"

"Eight and a half."

A pair of black silk evening shoes with three-and-a-half-inch heels was quickly produced. Kelly couldn't try them on because of her wet nails, but Mrs. Lui pronounced them perfect. She, of course, wouldn't have to wear them.

Kelly took the underwear and dress to the bathroom. The silk underpants were heavenly. The dress, except for the fact that it came two inches below her knee, fit perfectly. The blonde looking back at her in the mirror was startlingly pretty. Kelly wished Bart could see her.

She called Mrs. Lui into the bath. It was a long shot, but the dragon lady was probably her best hope. Stern faced, the woman stood with arms folded, waiting for Kelly to express her desires.

"Mrs. Lui," Kelly said, eschewing preliminaries, "if I give you five hundred dollars, will you make a phone call to Honolulu for me?"

The sober mask on the woman's face didn't break. "You don't have five hundred dollar."

"I can get it very quickly if you'll make the call."

"Ask Mr. Wong."

"He won't agree. I want you to do it. He needn't know."

The dragon lady stared back impassively.

"A thousand dollars," Kelly said, anticipating a signal of the desire to bargain.

"What good a thousand dollar if they break my hand?" She held up her fingers, twisting and gnarling them to illustrate the point. "I don't think so," she said, shaking her head. "Better you pillow with Mr. Wong one, two months. Then he let you go. I bring you many pretty dresses meantime. Everybody happy. And I keep two good hands."

Kelly was beginning to see it was hopeless.

Mrs. Lui showed her first signs of compassion, though. "Mr. Wong not so bad. Many girls say he okay. He fast. Maybe ten minute. Not so bad. Ten minute, three, four time a week. Nothing too dirty. You don't mind. Easy. Better than sell dresses."

"I'm not so sure about that. Cross-examining hostile witnesses is no picnic, either, but somehow though, I think it beats spending thirty minutes a week at work on my back."

"Huh?"

"Nothing, Mrs. Lui. Forget it. Just giving myself a little pep talk."

The dragon lady knew the negotiations were over. She said, "Turn around, please, madam."

Kelly complied, turning full circle.

The long red nails waved at her. "Mr. Wong like short dress. This too long. Like wife." She extracted a straight pin from the collar of her dress, bent over and tacked the hem six inches above Kelly's knee. "Okay, take off, please."

Kelly looked down at the hem of the skirt. "I was thinking maybe the middle of the knee."

Mrs. Lui shook her head. That seemed to be the last word. She waited while Kelly stepped out of the dress and wrapped a towel around her bare midriff.

Then, taking the cheongsam, Mrs. Lui said, "Only take me a few minute to sew hem. You wait, please." She went to the door.

"Oh, Mrs. Lui..."

The woman turned.

"If I'm going to be here for a couple of months, I might be needing something besides one cheongsam and a pair of heels."

The dragon lady nodded. "Now I know your size, I send many clothes."

"Could you include a jogging suit and a pair of Reeboks?"

The woman arched a brow.

"I like to do aerobics in the morning," she explained disingenuously. "Come to think of it, a VCR and a workout tape might be nice."

The mask on the woman's face betrayed a hint of skepticism. "I talk Mr. Wong."

Kelly shrugged as the bathroom door closed. It was hard to tell whether the circumstances she was in were simply bizarre or deadly grave. Perhaps the only way to find out for sure was to size up Norman Wong.

WONG ARRIVED at the cocktail hour wearing a flashy silk suit and rakish tie. He greeted her decorously. It had been raining since late afternoon, and his cuffs were slightly damp. He left his umbrella by the door, next to the bodyguard who stood there to discourage any thoughts Kelly might have entertained about escaping.

Norman kissed her hand, then presented her with a dozen red roses. "You look absolutely stunning!" he said. "Remarkable." He grinned so broadly that Kelly thought his cheeks would lift his glasses right off his nose. When he glanced up at her shiny blond hair, he had to crane his neck because the spike heels gave her seven inches on him, at least.

"Thank you," she said nervously.

Over the course of the afternoon her concern about Norman Wong had built to a quiet terror. Despite the faux charm, he didn't strike her as a man who'd accept rejection lightly. Thus far, he'd been no more offensive than a slobbering puppy, yet she had no doubt he intended to have sex with her. And those proposed ten minutes of bliss were out of the question as far as she was concerned.

Beaming, Wong had the guard take the flowers to the kitchen. He then led her to the sofa, sitting beside her, his short legs coming to rest firmly against her thigh.

She scooted a few inches away, more uncomfortable than indignant. It was time to confront the situation head-on. "Norman...we have a few things to discuss."

He threw up a hand to interrupt. "Excuse me, Kelly," he said, using her given name for the first time, "but we should first have a drink." He called to Anura, and the maid promptly appeared. "What may I offer you?" he asked.

She could have used a stiff vodka, but she didn't want to send the wrong message. "Water would be fine."

"Water? Do you think this is the Sahara, my dear? How about French champagne?"

"I don't like champagne."

"What do you like?"

She kept her tone light. "Water."

"A little wine won't hurt. You'll enjoy it, I'm sure."

Kelly opted for a tactical retreat. "I'm sure champagne would be fine," she said, unable to mask the sarcasm.

He dispatched Anura with their drink order. When the maid was gone, Norman put his hand on Kelly's knee. She promptly removed it. "Norman, I—"

"No, my dear, not until our champagne comes." He waved his finger like a potentate. "But tell me, how was your afternoon? It seems you were well taken care of."

"The service was quite good."

"Your day was pleasant, then?"

"Uneventful."

"I trust, my dear, that your evening will be more event filled." He grinned, puffing out his cheeks.

Kelly looked at him, trying to judge the balance of malevolence and compassion in his soul. He was a hard man to read. The simplest thing would be if he'd jump her bones. Then she could kick him in the groin and be done with it.

She cast a wary eye at the bodyguard. A second man was in the kitchen. She'd heard his voice. They were probably capable of anything. What happened to her would undoubtedly come down to what Wong decided.

"There's no reason why we can't enjoy ourselves," Norman said. Then, at the sound of a cork popping, he winked. "In my view, the best is yet to come."

Was he alluding to his intended ten minutes of ecstasy, or to his company in general? And did he really think she'd go to bed with him because he'd spent a little money on her, or was he relying on her desperation? Regardless, Kelly chose to ignore the remark.

Anura returned to the sitting room with the wine in an ice bucket and two chilled glasses. She put the tray on the coffee table, and Wong shooed her away. He immediately poured each of them a glass of champagne.

"Have you heard any news about Bart?" she asked, wanting to get what information she could.

"No, I'm afraid I haven't," he said, handing her a glass.

"He hasn't been arrested?"

"Not to my knowledge."

Kelly's spirits lifted. Then she realized that wasn't proof of anything. Even assuming the cops hadn't gotten Bart, there were other pits out there that could have claimed him. Still, she felt a spark of hope. Her hand trembled.

"Does that please you?" Wong asked, noticing. He held up his champagne flute, waiting for her answer.

Kelly wanted to say that Bart was her lover, that she was madly in love with him and would have put in ten years in the jungle to see him again, but that didn't square with what she'd told Norman earlier. And it would hardly serve her cause now to seem too easy. "Actually," she said soberly, "I love Bart like a brother. We're very dear friends. He was an orphan, you know, just like me. We have a great deal in common."

Wong reflected. "Mr. Monday is a man with many problems. A smart woman would not throw in her lot with someone in such dire straits. And you, Kelly, strike me as a smart woman." Apparently assuming he'd had the last word on Bart Monday, Wong lifted his glass. "To the loveliest flower in all Bangkok." He grinned at her through his thick glasses.

Kelly knew without any doubt that she would endure a beating rather than spend ten easy minutes with him.

"Norman, I must be brutally honest. I have absolutely no desire to be your mistress. You'd be better off to call the girl who lives here and let me go home to my fiancé."

"No, no, no, my dear. You haven't given me a chance."

She took a healthy quaff of champagne, feeling tears well. "No offense, Norman, but it's true. I really do want to go home."

He shook his head. "A little wine, a pleasant supper, some music and you won't feel that way at all. Trust me."

"I know my heart."

"The human heart is malleable, Kelly. There are ways." With that, he took what looked like a pillbox from his pocket and placed it on the table next to the champagne bucket.

"What's that?" she asked.

"Colombian cocaine. I had some imported for special occasions. In America it's the yuppie drug of choice, is it not?"

She blinked. It took her several moments to get control. "Norman, I'm not into drugs...of any kind."

He smiled and put his hand on her knee again. "That's what you said about champagne."

Kelly was forced to play her second trump. She picked up his wrist and removed his hot little hand.

"Pity," Wong said, his eyes narrowing to slits. "I'd hoped this would be easier."

"Sometimes," Kelly said, shrugging, "a girl just has to say no."

Wong drained his champagne and poured himself some more. He ignored the cocaine, and he ignored her. Anura brought in the roses and, at Wong's instruction, handed him a bud. He took it, touched it to his lips and then to Kelly's. The gesture seemed so incongruous it made her almost feel sorry for the poor little devil.

She took another sip of her champagne, wondering why in the hell she was concerned about him. Before the evening was over he'd probably try to rape her. She glanced at his pudgy face. He was quaffing champagne like water. Maybe if he drank enough, he wouldn't be able to manage two minutes, let alone ten.

After finishing his third glass, he set the empty flute down. Without looking at her, he walked two fingers down his thigh and over to hers. Kelly sat there, incredulous, as the puppet fingers walked up her black cheongsam. When the fingers made clear their intention of scaling her breast, Kelly grasped his wrist.

But Norman wasn't going to be thwarted. With surprising agility he threw himself on top of her, pressing his mouth hard against her lips. Kelly was so stunned it took her a minute to push him away.

"Norman, for God's sake!"

He fell back in the sofa, smiling drunkenly. "There's a secret to unlocking your heart," he said. "I must discover it."

"The secret is named Bart Monday!"

"What?"

"I mean Duncan Van de Meer."

Norman seemed thoroughly confused.

Kelly got up abruptly. From the corner of her eye she saw the guard tense. She went to the other side of the table. Her hands on her hips, she glared. It was time, she decided, to lay her cards on the table.

"Norman, we've got to negotiate a mutually acceptable resolution of our differences."

Just then Anura came out of the kitchen and said something. Norman righted himself, straightening his tie. "Dinner is ready," he said. "Have you ever had fried catfish salad?" He got to his feet with some difficulty.

Kelly felt thoroughly frustrated. Dealing with Norman Wong was like trying to pick up an eel. She sighed. "If you don't mind, I'm going to the powder room first."

She stomped off toward the bedroom, her frustration welling, her heart pounding. In Mrs. Lui's three-and-a-half-inch heels, she felt like a two-bit whore. Why had she been so stupid as to play along this far? As soon as she got into the bedroom she closed the door and kicked off the shoes, sending one crashing against the headboard.

When the small crew-cut head rose from the other side of the bed, Kelly almost screamed. She stood frozen, mouth agape as the boy, perhaps ten or eleven, rose to his full height, his index finger pressed to his lips. He quickly came around the bed, casting a wary eye toward the door. He was in a white short-sleeved shirt, dark blue shorts and sandals. He was soaked from head to toe, water running down his face.

"Good job," he whispered. "I hope you come in alone."

"Who in God's name are you?"

"Bart said come pick you up. Not so easy, huh?"

She still couldn't believe what she was seeing. "Bart sent you?"

"Yeah. My name Thep. I Bart's main man. You know?"

"You're his main man?" A half smile formed on her still-gaping mouth.

"Bart say give old captain a thousand dollar and bring you home. No sweat, huh?" He pulled a roll of hundred-dollar bills from his pocket and held them out. "This job not so easy. Maybe I keep for a tip." He giggled. "What you think?"

"I think I'm hallucinating, Thep." She shook her head. "How did you get in here?"

"No sweat. You left bathroom window open."

"You came in that little window, four stories above the ground?"

"Pretty tricky, huh?" He glanced again at the door. "You want to go now, or have dinner first?"

"Go? How?"

"Out bathroom window. No sweat." He marched into the bath and Kelly followed. Thep pointed at the window.

Kelly climbed up on the tile shelf and peered out into the dark, rainy night. There was a wooden plank extending from the windowsill to the roof of the adjoining building, fifteen feet away. It was shimmering wet from the rain. She looked down at the boy. "You don't expect me to walk on that thing."

"Why not?"

"That's four stories above the ground!"

"No sweat. Don't look down."

Kelly rolled her eyes. "Easy for you to say."

Thep shrugged.

"So that's the choice . . ." she said as much to herself as to Thep. "Dinner with Norman or walk the plank."

Just then there was a loud knock at the bedroom door and Norman's inquiring voice. Kelly swallowed hard, then called out, "Just a minute, Norman. The champagne made me a little dizzy. I'll be out in a while." She closed the bathroom door and looked at the urchin, who was grinning at her.

"You number one, all right," he said.

"Why didn't Bart come himself?" she asked.

"Not so easy. He got bullet right here." He pointed to his thigh.

Kelly felt her stomach drop. "Oh, wonderful!"

"No problem. Pretty soon he walk again. No big deal."

She looked up at the open window again and felt sick. She could hear the patter of rain on the plank. "I hate heights," she said.

"Okay, then," Thep said. "I go first."

As the boy scrambled up to the window, Kelly gritted her teeth. A wooden plank four stories in the air. It was either that or ten minutes with Norman Wong. She pictured Bart with a blood-soaked leg. "I could kill that man," she said aloud.

Thep, perched on the windowsill, looked back at her. "Mr. Wong bad news, all right."

"I was referring to Bart!"

The boy giggled. "Yeah, he say you in love with him. Bart number one. Always same, same. Every lady fall in love."

From the next room came the imploring sound of Norman Wong's voice, followed by a knock on the bathroom door. Kelly climbed up on the tub. She peered out the window at Thep, who'd started crawling across the plank on his hands and knees, then she looked heavenward and groaned.

CHAPTER EIGHTEEN

WITH HER HANDS GRIPPING the edges of the eight-inch plank, Kelly shifted her gaze to the alley. Raindrops were spattering the mirrored surface of a large puddle. A single light over a doorway cast long shadows from the cans and boxes stacked against the buildings. There was a hum of traffic in the nearby street, an impatient honk now and then, and the soft drumming of the rain against her skull.

Her hair was already pasted against her forehead; her heart was tripping like a jackhammer. Across the chasm, Thep held the end of the board, watching her with wide, uncertain eyes. Behind her Norman Wong was thumping on the bathroom door. Kelly held herself together by cursing her fear.

She inched farther into the void, her knees clamped together on the slippery surface of the wood. She felt a bit of spring in the plank and wondered if it could support her weight. Thep wasn't even half her size.

"Will this thing hold me?" she whispered to him through her constricted throat.

"No sweat. You have big boobs maybe, but you skinny lady."

The observation almost made her smile. She inched farther into no-man's-land, her inner thighs pressed together, her teeth clenched.

"Kelly, Kelly," came Norman's plaintive voice through the door. "Your soup will be cold."

She inched out some more. A wind seemed to come up. Was the board swaying? No, the rain was only coming down harder. It was tattooing the board like a snare drum.

"Shit!" she said. "I'll never make it."

"You better," Thep said. "Bart be really pissed if you fall."

Thump, thump, thump, came Norman's insistent knock behind her. "Kelly, you come out or I'll be obliged to come in," said his muffled voice.

"If I fall," she said to Thep, "I want you to tell Bart it's all his fault."

"I not say it *my* fault," Thep said. "You be damn sure of that. But too much talk, Kelly-san. Hurry up, okay?"

"Not okay!" she snarled, chancing a glance up at the boy. "This is the worst thing that ever happened to me!"

"Then why you stay so long? Let's go!"

"Kelly?" Norman's voice was no longer muffled. "Kelly, where..."

"Oh, damn," she said, and made a flurry of caterpillar steps toward the waiting boy.

She could hear Norman climbing onto the tub. She looked at Thep, who was only a few feet away.

"Kelly, you idiot!" It was Norman, in full indignant voice, at the window. She could almost feel him staring at her fleeing derriere.

"Norman," she said, "go back inside and eat your salad!"

"Come here at once!" he shouted. He thumped the plank with his fist. "I insist!"

"Damn it, Norman, if you make me fall, I'll never speak to you again." More caterpillar steps.

"Return at once. I command you!" he roared.

"Can't you see she don't got reverse?" Thep interjected.

Apparently afraid she was about to make good her escape, Wong switched from bluster to decisive action. He shouted to his men. Kelly could almost taste the safety of the rooftop. Thep's hand was in front of her nose. She didn't know whether to grab it or continue on. She decided on the latter.

"Come on, Kelly-san," he said. "No time. Fat man plenty pissed."

Her hands were now on the part of the plank that extended onto the roof. Only her legs were left hanging. Thep reached out and gave her butt a slap to hurry her along. She lunged forward, landing face first in a puddle on the flat roof. She rolled over and looked up at the disgusted face of the boy. He was standing now, his hands on his hips.

"You think we got all night?" he said.

Kelly jumped to her feet. Thep led her along the slippery roof to a fire escape. He scrambled over the side and started to descend. Grabbing the rails, Kelly blindly followed, preferring not to look down.

The ladder stopped at the second floor, next to a window. Thep tried to push it open, but it didn't budge. "Damn," he said. "Somebody lock."

He looked around and so did Kelly. They were still twenty feet above the ground, a cobbled *soi* that didn't promise a soft landing. To one side was a three-foot pile of trash, mostly papers and garbage.

"We jump," Thep said. It wasn't a question.

Lowering himself to the last rung, he swung his body back and forth until he had the momentum he needed. Letting go, he landed in the pile, sinking partway out of sight. He bounced up right away and waved for her to follow.

"No sweat!" he said.

Kelly wasn't exactly a gymnast, but she figured she could handle that. The trouble was the tight skirt of her cheongsam. Holding the ladder with one hand, she pulled her skirt up over her hips with the other. Then she lowered herself to the bottom rung.

The door immediately below her opened just then and a little old man stepped into the alley. He wore a massive white apron that extended from his armpits to his ankles. First he saw Thep, then he sensed something overhead and looked up at Kelly, hanging like a side of beef from the fire ladder. He let out a yelp and jumped back inside the building.

Thep doubled over with laughter.

"This isn't funny!" Kelly screamed through her teeth. She'd managed to work her body into a swing. The rain became a deluge.

"Let go!" the boy shouted.

And she did, landing in a heap in the garbage pile.

Thep was helping her get to her feet when they heard a shout from one of Wong's bodyguards. There was another shout from the opposite end of the alley, from the second guard. Kelly and Thep were trapped between them. "Not so good," Thep said in a surprisingly calm voice.

All Kelly could think of was that she'd crawled across that plank for nothing. "This is so unfair!" she moaned.

The door in front of them burst open again, and the old man reappeared. This time he had a companion, a taller, younger man who wielded a meat cleaver. He waved it menacingly.

The old man pointed at Kelly and Thep, shrieking. His friend raised the cleaver just as Wong's guards started toward them from opposite ends of the alley. Thep pulled a hundred-dollar bill from his pocket and threw it at the cooks as he rushed past them into the building, pulling Kelly behind him. He paused just long enough to slam the door and throw the bolt. Almost simultaneously fists crashed against the metal door. Thep looked up at Kelly, wiping the rain from his face.

"So far, so good."

Kelly sagged against the wall. "I think you really are Bart's main man."

The pounding stopped. "No time now," the boy said in a businesslike tone. "They go around to front. Come on."

Taking her hand, he led her through the restaurant kitchen. It was hot and it smelled like curry and coconut, mint, cilantro, ginger and grease. There were steaming pots, mounds of fish and vegetables, sizzling grills and utensils hanging from the ceiling. The sous-chef backed away as they ran past him into the crowded dining room. Customers with strands of noodles strung between their bowls and mouths looked up with amazement as Kelly and Thep sprinted through the room and out the front door.

As they stepped onto the sidewalk, Thep looked each way, then plunged into the crowded street. A chorus of horns rose like the squawks of angry geese. They wove through the vehicles and stopped again on the far side of the street. The bright neon lights gave their soaked skin a bizarre hue. Thep was apparently trying to decide which way to go.

Kelly, aware for the first time that she was shoeless, looked down at her feet. Then, in the window of the car parked beside them, she saw her face and plastered-down hair. Passing pedestrians looked up at her from under their umbrellas.

Suddenly Thep jerked her arm and pointed up the street. "They over there."

Kelly spotted Norman Wong's two bodyguards at the corner at about the same time they saw her and Thep.

"You run pretty good?" the boy asked.

"Damn good."

"Let's go, then."

Kelly hiked up her skirt and they took off, weaving their way through pedestrians on the crowded sidewalk. There was more than one collision along the way. At times Thep lurched into the street when the going was easier there. Then he sprinted back onto the sidewalk, around a corner, through the traffic to the other side, all at full tilt.

They cut through a short alley that led them to another, wider street. Rounding a corner, Thep narrowly missed a man transporting a tall stack of boxes on a hand truck, but Kelly hit him broadside, sending him and his load tumbling to the ground. Recovering, she continued to follow Thep while the victim angrily shouted at the top of his lungs.

The rain had let up some, and traffic was moving at a fair clip. Kelly ran comfortably. The time she'd spent barefoot in the jungle had toughened her feet. Her long strides had hiked up her skirt to the top of her thighs, but it hardly mattered.

A glance back told her the bodyguards had begun to fade. One had dropped considerably behind the other. Thep was slowing, too, and Kelly began to feel a stitch in her side. The chase was taking its toll on them all.

At a lamppost the boy made a sharp turn into a dark side street that seemed to end in darkness. She'd been following him blindly, but now she wondered if Thep hadn't led them into a cul-de-sac with no escape.

A hundred yards from the street they came to a large, closed gate. It was wrought iron and forbidding. At the side was a pedestrian gate. As Thep worked it open, Kelly, her chest heaving, looked back up the dark street.

The guards were silhouetted against the bright lights of the boulevard. The first one had traversed half the distance to the gate, the second was still trailing behind.

Thep opened the gate and they slipped inside. It was pitch-dark, but Kelly could tell that there were trees—tall palms—and shrubs. They were in what seemed like a courtyard. The rain slowed to a drizzle. Kelly was aware of the silence. It was as though the city had suddenly evaporated. A parrot shrieked nearby. If it hadn't been for the cobblestones, she would have thought she was back in the jungle.

Kelly grabbed Thep's arm. "Where are we?" she whispered.

"Temple."

Suddenly she understood. They were in one of the many wats that were spread throughout Bangkok. Thep seemed to know the place, for he walked without hesitation. Behind them, they heard the clank of the pedestrian gate. Their pursuers hadn't given up.

Thep pulled Kelly into some shrubs. The damp air smelled of vegetation, but there was another odor, too. If she hadn't known better, she'd have thought she was in a barn. Overhead a parrot screeched again. They heard footsteps and shrank deeper into the shadows.

Hunched down, listening, Kelly had a funny feeling that they weren't alone. She heard a sound—a grunt, a groan; it was the deepest baritone she'd ever heard. Slowly turning, she looked back.

First she saw the eyes. They were rolled up, so that the whites glowed hideously. Then she noticed that the horns seemed to fly from the skull like the wings of a bat. And when it belched on her, Kelly screamed.

Suddenly the silence was rent by a ghastly bellow. A water buffalo, thrown into full panic by the scream, charged, nearly knocking her over. Another one rushed from the undergrowth, followed by a third. Dogs started barking from every corner of the courtyard. A horse neighed, the parrots screeched, the buffalo bellowed. It was total pandemonium.

Kelly stood amid the chaos, dazed. She saw Norman Wong's bodyguard in the center of the courtyard, his white shirt like a red flag for the buffalo. He was darting this way and that, like a rodeo clown without a barrel. Finally he took off the way he'd come.

"Not bad," Thep said to her over the din. "Come on, Kelly-san. You number one." The glimmer of his smile made Kelly feel good.

She followed him through the shrubs to the temple, which they entered. They walked over the stone floor of the candlelit sanctuary, past a Buddha flecked with so much gold leaf that he looked like a half-scaled fish. A moment later they were going out a side entrance, across a garden to a different gate and into another street. They walked at a brisk pace, but the urgency had abated.

"You knew that place pretty well," Kelly said.

"Good place to steal watches."

"You're a thief, then."

He grinned. "When I was little. Now, too many important things to do."

"I appreciate what you did for me, Thep. I don't know what would have happened back there with Norman, but I infinitely prefer your company."

"No problem, Kelly-san."

She would have given the kid a hug, but she doubted his pride would have allowed it. Instead she patted him on the shoulder. "Thanks."

They were nearing another boulevard. The sounds of traffic began to reclaim the silence of the temple grounds. When they came to the corner, Kelly said, "What now?"

"Boss worried, I think. Maybe we go say hello."

Kelly beamed, feeling joy for the first time in two days. "I think that would be a darned good idea."

Thep waved down a *tuk-tuk* and slid into the banquet seats. Thep gave the driver instructions and lowered the canvas sides of the passenger compartment. Then he patted Kelly's knee. "Pretty romantic, huh?" He laughed heartily.

"I think you've been hanging around Bart Monday too much," she said.

"Bart number one." The boy grinned. "He say you number one, too."

Kelly put her arms around his shoulders and silently watched the traffic. Thinking of what they'd been through together, she felt her eyes get misty. There was no doubt about it. She'd made another friend.

THE *TUK-TUK PUTTED* through the crowded streets. They went for what seemed like miles. Occasionally they'd take on another passenger—a woman with her purchases wrapped in newspaper and stuffed in a plastic shopping bag, a skinny young man who chain-smoked acrid cigarettes, a uniformed worker dozing on his way home, an old man with a duck under his arm. But they also had a chance to talk.

Thep explained that he'd arrived with the ransom money just as she was leaving in Norman Wong's limo. He'd followed her to the apartment, but it had taken him hours to discover where in the building she was being kept and to plot the escape. Kelly wasn't so concerned about that as she was about Bart.

"Who shot him?" she asked the boy.

"Some police, I think. He trying to get in building where he live. Bad news. Police waiting. Bang, bang. Boss pretty smart, pretty lucky. He get away." Thep told her Bart had made it to safety with friends, and had gotten hold of him to deliver the ransom money.

"How serious is the wound?"

"No big deal. Boss say only bad thing, maybe, is infection. He pay lots of money to doctor to fix him and keep mouth shut." Bart, the boy said, complained of hemorrhaging money more than he'd complained of hemorrhaging blood.

After a while they found themselves in a modest neighborhood on the outskirts of Bangkok. The semipaved streets were covered in potholes filled with water. The rain had stopped and the streets were teeming with people, despite the late hour.

"We home soon," Thep said, nudging Kelly with his elbow. "Bart want me tell you something before we get there. Don't worry about lady you see there, okay? Sumaree old friend. Don't mean nothing now. Just friend."

The communication was direct, but Kelly read a much richer story between the lines. "You mean we're going to the house of Bart's girlfriend, is that it?"

Thep shrugged. "Something like that."

"I see."

Her surprise must have been obvious, because the boy immediately tried to smooth things over. "Hey, no problem, Kelly-san. Sumaree very pretty, but not so pretty as you. Lots of girls don't mean nothing to the boss. No sweat, huh?"

Thep didn't know it, but the more he talked, the worse he made things sound. Kelly was hit with the realization that she knew absolutely nothing about Bart's private life. It shouldn't have been surprising that he was a ladies' man, though—not considering his skills as a lover.

And that made her think. Not once during their time together had she thought of Bart in his normal environment, pictured the life he led. How could she have been so naive?

Kelly looked at some children playing in the street, despite the late hour. She told herself that Bart's private life was his business. She could hardly hold his past against him—nor, for that matter, what he chose to do now.

"Don't think so much," Thep said, reading her silence. "Bart pay good money for you. I think he love you. You don't believe me, you ask Sumaree," he said.

"His girlfriend?"

"She say same thing. Boss love you, Kelly-san."

As the *tuk-tuk* bumped along, she was bemused by the thought that Bart had briefed his friends on what to say to her. It was rather endearing, actually. Still, she couldn't help wondering if this Sumaree wasn't deserving of her pity. Kelly pictured a devoted little flower watching with a heavy heart as Bart's latest "friend" arrived on the scene.

The *tuk-tuk* came to a stop just as Kelly was at the height of her self-doubt. She wasn't sure if she was ready for Bart in his real life. She'd never been a coward, though. Whatever and whoever Bart was in reality, she had to face him.

Thep jumped down to pay the driver and Kelly got out. She stood in the street, looking at a score of faces turned her way. A scraggly dog sauntered up and sniffed her knee. She looked down at her dress, now a wet rag. The side seam had ripped open. She ran her fingers through her hair, but could tell she was a mess.

The *tuk-tuk* sputtered off and Thep took her arm. "Come on, Kelly-san. Let's say hello to boss."

A curtain covered the front door to the house, which faced directly onto the street. Adjacent to the door was a spirit house, brightly painted, its lone flickering candle serving both to ward off evil spirits and to invite guests.

Thep announced them as he pushed the curtain aside. The first room was small and crowded with furniture—simple wooden tables and chairs, shelves with knick-knacks, pictures and a Thai Airways calendar on the wall. A single light bulb hung from the ceiling. The sole occupant was a woman in her early fifties. She was snapping snow peas at a table in the corner. Seeing Kelly and Thep, she immediately put down her bowl, rising and bowing, her smile genuinely friendly.

"That the mother," Thep said with the officiousness of a tour guide.

A curtain at the back slid aside, and one of the most beautiful girls Kelly had ever seen appeared. She was twenty or so. Her dark eyes were almond shaped, her smooth skin a rich nougat. A serene smile was on her perfect lips. There was no judgment, no accusation. Only open, quiet beauty. She wore a long wraparound skirt much like Anura's. Her hips and bare shoulders were perfectly proportioned to her height. She wore thick, solid silver ankle bracelets and, when she half turned, inviting Kelly to enter, a silver barrette glimmered in the dark hair hanging to her waist.

"This Sumaree," Thep said unnecessarily.

"Please," the girl said softly, beckoning Kelly to come into the room.

Kelly took a deep breath, knowing it would hurt to pretend it didn't matter that Bart had a girlfriend. But she didn't want to embarrass him or Sumaree, so she had no choice but to swallow her pride. Their adventure on Ko Pong had been a fantasy, anyway. But even though her mind was half prepared to believe that, her heart told her she was a liar.

Kelly moved toward the curtain and ducked under the low doorway into the tiny candlelit room. Bart was on a mattress wedged in a corner. He was propped up. One leg—the bandaged one—was lying flat; the other was bent at the knee. He'd shaved, and he looked clean in a white short-sleeved shirt. When Kelly looked at his face, she saw the expected smile. Beside him, on the sheet, playing cards were spread out, indicating an interrupted game.

"Ah, the prodigal daughter," he said cheerfully. "I was beginning to get worried." His eyes slid down over her soaked and tattered cheongsam. "Where've you been?"

Kelly was rooted to the floor, in the grip of an unexpected paralysis. She'd been in reasonable control of her emotions until then, but seeing him, it was all she could to keep from crying.

"Kel," he said, "what's the matter? Where'd you get that dress?"

"From an admirer. I've been on a date," she managed, her voice breaking. "Of course, I looked better earlier. About all that's left now is the manicure." She self-consciously held up her hands to show him.

He looked at her hands, her dress, her wet hair. "What are you talking about?"

"We had a little problem, Boss," Thep said from the door behind her. "Somebody else buy Kelly-san before I get there. I do big big business to get her back. Almost not make it. Right, Kelly-san?"

She nodded.

Bart beckoned her. "Come here and tell me about it."

Kelly glanced over her shoulder and saw that Sumaree and Thep had slipped silently from the room. She padded slowly over to the bed and looked down at Bart. He reached up and took her hand. She instantly dropped to the bed and put her arms around him, holding on to him but not saying a word. It took all her willpower, but she managed not to cry.

Kelly wasn't sure why she was so emotional, why, after all she'd been through, she was on the verge of breaking down now. Maybe it was the relief—a sense that she was with Bart, safe at last. She pulled herself together and sat upright, taking a deep breath.

"When you didn't return, the captain proved he meant it when he said he was an old shark. He put me on the auction block, if you can believe it. A little bastard by the name of Norman Wong was the highest bidder.''

Bart sat up. "*Norman Wong?* That twerp? How'd he get involved in this?''

"He originally planned to resell me to you for ten thousand, but he changed his mind and decided I might be worth keeping." She smiled bitterly. "Can you believe it? In a bad month I make ten thousand practicing law, but on the white slave market that's all I'm worth, period!''

"Ten thou's not exactly peanuts, Kelly. But I agree, you're worth more. I'd have gone to twelve or thirteen easily.''

"Go ahead, make light of it," she said, "but I came this close to becoming that little gangster's concubine. If it wasn't for Thep, I'd be listening to Norman snoring this very minute.''

Bart pulled her to him and stroked her head. "My poor angel," he said. "I had no idea.''

"I don't expect Norman is too pleased right now," she said. "Chances are, he and his henchmen are looking for us—in addition to everyone else.''

"Far be it from me to snub anyone. He can join the party.''

There was a knock and Kelly sat upright. Sumaree stuck her head in. "Please excuse me, but you wish something else to wear, Kelly?" she asked in a voice as soft as the petal of a flower. She held out a loose kimono. "This maybe more comfortable. You are too wet, I think.''

Kelly stepped over and took the robe. They exchanged tentative smiles. "You're very kind.''

"I maybe find clothes for tomorrow," Sumaree said to Bart, as if asking for his concurrence.

"Good idea," he said. "Do you need to measure her?''

Sumaree giggled. She looked up and down Kelly's long frame. "No, I can see." She withdrew.

Kelly quickly wriggled out of the wet dress and put on the silk kimono. As soon as she'd tied the belt she turned to Bart, who'd obviously been watching with great interest. He smiled with admiration.

"Where'd you get the fancy pants?"

"A gift from Norman," she said. "He's *very* generous."

"I'm glad to see you were able to rise above it. Does this mean that love conquers all?"

"I wouldn't get too cocky if I were you, Mr. Monday. I'm still a free agent, you know."

"Free, but wanted by the police, the drug underworld and Norman Wong."

"Is that supposed to be a reminder of how desperately I need you?" she said, returning to the bed.

He reached for her hand and she sat next to him. He shifted, groaning slightly.

"Thep told me about your leg," she said, looking at it. "Are you all right?"

"Same old, same old. I'll live."

"You seem to be well cared for," she said. "She's very pretty—beautiful, in fact."

Bart looked momentarily perplexed, then made the necessary deductions. "Sumaree, you mean."

"Yes. I can hardly blame you."

"Didn't Thep explain?"

"Yes. He explained very well."

Bart's brow furrowed. "What did he say?"

"That she's an old friend."

"And friends look out for each other," he said evenly. "Like you and me?"

"Yes, like you and me." He took her hand and drew it to his mouth, kissing her fingers. "Though you and I might do a little more than just look out for each other."

Kelly looked into his golden eyes. She watched the shadows from the candle dancing on his face. She remembered the lean-to, the cave, the waterfall. She remembered making love with him as if there was no tomorrow. But now tomorrow had come.

"Don't things seem different to you now that we're back in the real world?" she asked.

Bart continued to engage her eyes. He slowly shook his head. "No. Does it seem any different to you?"

She shrugged. "Well, I've had a bath, a shampoo and a manicure, so I feel a hell of a lot better."

"That wasn't what I was referring to and neither were you."

She bit her lip and looked up at the shadows dancing on the ceiling. "I'm not sure how to answer you," she said. "I guess I'm not back in the real world yet—not *my* world, anyway."

He grinned as if he was amused. Spying her knee sticking out from the opening in her kimono, he put his hand on it and began to caress her thigh. "You're so beautiful," he said. "I can't really blame Norman for wanting you."

She sighed woefully, looking down at his fingers entwined with hers. "Mr. Monday, Mr. Monday, what are we going to do?"

"About what?"

"Us. The games and fantasies are over. We've got to start thinking like adults."

Bart took her face in his hands. "Before we get too sober and responsible, I'd like to say one thing." He gently rubbed her cheekbones with his thumb.

"What?"

"I love you, Kelly Ronan. Like it or not, believe it or not, I love you. And I probably always will."

A lump formed in her throat and her eyes filled with tears. She could hardly see because of them. Soon they ran over her lids and she couldn't speak.

CHAPTER NINETEEN

BART LAY IN THE DARKNESS, more aware than usual of the warm spicy air tinged with a vague hint of incense and charcoal smoke. Kelly had been sleeping peacefully for an hour. He hadn't slept at all. The pain in his leg kept him awake, but that wasn't all—he hadn't been able to shut his mind down. Kelly still didn't know what would happen in the morning, and that bothered him.

As soon as Thep left and Sumaree had gone to her mother's place down the street, Kelly had blown out the candles and lain down beside him. She wouldn't let him make love to her because of his leg. "I don't want the last time to be painful," she said, kissing his chest. He'd pointed out that he hadn't been in the best of shape the past two or three times, but she'd insisted that it would be better if they simply held each other. It was, she'd said, more poignant that way. And she was right.

She'd wanted to hear about his plans for getting out of the country and he had told her he'd been in touch with his CIA contact. A special flight had been arranged for the following night from an air base up-country. "All I have to do," he'd said, "is get you there."

Kelly had been thrilled. She'd kissed him, more excited than at any time since they'd hijacked the chopper. He hadn't had the heart to tell her the rest of the story. The way he figured it, morning would be soon enough.

He stared at the ceiling and tried to ignore the pulsing in his leg. It was killing him, but he'd already taken the few pain pills the doctor had given him. All he could do was put it from his mind.

Beside him, Kelly turned in her sleep. There was enough moonlight coming in the window that he could see her face. She was so lovely, so exquisite. The thought of another separation was almost too much to bear. And yet, he couldn't walk away from his commitments. That wasn't his nature.

Kelly purred, evidently dreaming. He touched her cheek and she cuddled against him. Her hair was soft, fragrant, making him weak with longing. She was a pleasure to his senses, and had been from his first glimpse of her. When she'd arrived at the bedroom door in her cheongsam, looking long-legged and sexy as hell, he'd momentarily lost his resolve, vowing never to allow her from his sight again.

For the past hour he'd been torturing himself, asking how important self-respect truly was. If he got on that plane with her tomorrow night, would he wind up resenting her and hating himself?

Pain shot through his leg and he flinched. Kelly stirred. She lifted her head and looked around. Her eyes focused on his face.

"Bart?"

"It's okay, honey. Go back to sleep."

"Did you say something?"

"No, it's just my leg. It's all right now." He stroked her head. "Go to sleep."

She lay back on the pillow, but she didn't close her eyes. She put her arm across his chest. He could see the hazy contours of her face in the moonlight.

"Can I get you anything?" she whispered.

"Just having you with me is all I need," he said softly.

She was silent for a time, but she caressed his chest, gently digging her fingers into the mat of hair. He could see she wouldn't be sleeping anytime soon.

"Bart, where are we flying to tomorrow night, anyway?" she asked. "Or is it a state secret?"

"I'm not sure, but my guess is either Hong Kong or the Philippines."

"And how long do you propose we stay there?"

He didn't answer right away. He just stared at the ceiling, wondering if he didn't owe her candor at this point. He hadn't exactly lied, but he'd allowed her to think they would be leaving together.

"Kelly," he finally said, "I won't be getting on that plane with you. I'm not finished with what I've got to do here."

She looked up at him. "What? You're joking, aren't you?"

"No, I'll be staying on here awhile longer. Thep will go with you to the air base. My contact in the CIA will ensure that you get off all right. I'd take you myself, but with this leg I'd probably cause more problems than I'd solve. Besides, you'll be less conspicuous without me."

"Bart, this is insane. You've got to leave Thailand—for your own safety."

"Last night, before you arrived, I got another piece of information on those documents Thatree Madary uncovered. It's all but in my hands. When I get what I need, we'll have these guys cold, and the case can be wrapped up."

"How can that be as important as your life?"

"It was important enough to Thatree that he died for it, assuming the word on the grapevine that he's 'disappeared' is accurate. He was counting on me to carry on and I can't let him down. Besides, I'm not dead yet."

"*Yet* being the operative word."

His fingers lightly trailed over her jaw. "I love you, Kelly, but I've got a duty to finish this thing."

She turned from him. "You don't have to justify yourself. You don't owe me anything."

He heard the hurt in her voice. "I owe you my life."

"And I owe you mine," she replied. "So we're even. It's a wash. No obligation either way."

He didn't respond immediately. The last thing he wanted was ill feeling between them. Not at the eleventh hour. "A week, babe," he said. "Two at the outside. Then I'll be in Honolulu, bright-eyed and bushy-tailed. I promise."

"You know," she said, "I was almost beginning to think I knew you, but this shows me I don't."

"Oh? Who was the Bart Monday you thought you knew, Kel? A guy who was a quitter? Who ran from trouble? Who didn't finish the things he started?"

"After what you've been through, you could hardly be blamed for wanting to leave Southeast Asia, Bart. No government could expect more of you than you've given already."

"I'm right at a critical juncture in the operation. Nobody else can step in and take over without losing months of effort. People have died, Kelly, so we could get this far. It's almost within our grasp."

She was silent, and he could tell she was unconvinced.

"What if the shoe was on the other foot?" he said. "You're as devoted to your work as I am. Would you just walk away from your responsibilities, especially knowing a lot was on the line, something that affected the life of a client? You say we don't know each other yet, but I know that about you. You aren't the type who turns her back and walks away, and neither am I."

She still didn't say anything.

"Are you not speaking to me?" he asked.

"Maybe I just learned something about you," she said.

"Good or bad?"

"Good, assuming that knowing you choose to put yourself in danger can be good. But I admit I admire what you're doing—not that I don't still think it's crazy."

He cuddled her against him. "I haven't signed on to do this for life," he said. "A week or so and it will be over. Hardly any longer than it will take you to unpack and get the sand out of your hair." He kissed her forehead. "You might want to tell Duncan I'm coming. I imagine that won't be the easiest thing you've ever done."

"You got that right."

"So you see, you have plenty to keep you busy while I clean up the mess here."

She smiled. "You're very confident about how this is going to turn out between us, aren't you?"

"You knew that about me from the day we met."

"If you're referring to the way you flirted with me on the *Ban Don,* you might as well know I thought you were a lecherous bum and I was dreading the prospect of you making a pass at me."

"And I thought you were an angel sent from heaven."

"So what does that say about us?" she asked.

"Either that I'm more perceptive or that you make a better first impression."

She laughed and raised her face to him. He kissed her. It was a sensuous kiss and he immediately became aroused. She broke it off.

"Don't get any ideas, big boy."

"You can be very harsh at times, Ms. Ronan."

"I've got my faults, believe me."

"And I'm going to delight in discovering them."

"If you live that long."

"Yes," he said, stroking her head, "if I live that long."

She dropped back down on her pillow and looked away. He watched her eyes glisten in the moonlight.

Kelly rolled her head toward him. "Come with me tomorrow," she whispered.

"I want to...more than you can imagine, but I can't."
He thought he heard her sniffle but he wasn't sure. He
kissed her again. "I'm a man of my word, Kelly."

She hugged him. "You have been so far," she said. "I
have to admit that."

Bart eased himself back down on the mattress and
sighed. "You'd better get some sleep, honey. Morning's
coming early."

She nodded. "It won't upset you if I cry a little, will it?
Sometimes it's the only way to deal with the tension."

"I don't mind, as long as you promise to give me that
beautiful smile of yours in the morning."

"I promise," she croaked.

Bart held her as she cried softly. Her tears lasted only
four or five minutes and then she was sound asleep.

BART, HOLDING A CANDLE, woke her before dawn. Kelly
blinked as he sat on the edge of the bed. He handed her a
pile of neatly folded clothing and a pair of rubber sandals. "Sumaree's mother arrived a few minutes ago and
brought you these."

She sat up and took the clothes. There was a long wraparound skirt and a simple blouse. They looked as if they
would fit.

"Mama-san's making breakfast," he said, "and something for you to take with you on the trip. You'd better get
dressed. I've got some things to do in the other room." He
touched her cheek affectionately and got to his feet, in
obvious pain.

"How's your leg?"

"Feels like hell, but what else is new?"

"Shouldn't you be in bed?"

"I'll rest after you've gone." He smiled and, leaving the
candle on the floor, limped from the room.

Kelly dressed, then went to the front room. Sumaree's mother was working at the table. Bart was sitting on a straight chair across from her. The woman smiled at the sight of her, bowing and mumbling a greeting in Thai.

Bart looked Kelly over. "Not bad. I kind of like the demure touch."

She made a face. "If you ever saw me in a business suit, you wouldn't recognize me."

"If the skirt was short enough, I would."

The woman gestured for Kelly to sit next to Bart. A breakfast of fruit, bread and tea was laid out. They ate in silence while Sumaree's mother puttered around the kitchen.

When they'd finished, the woman brought Bart a plastic shopping bag, putting it on the table. As he removed a package from the bag, she shyly glanced at Kelly and picked up the dirty dishes.

Bart tore off the plain brown paper wrapping, exposing a shiny, nickel-plated automatic. He examined the weapon carefully and took a box of shells from the sack. Laying the gun on the table, he loaded the clip and put a half dozen extra rounds in a pile on the table.

Watching, Kelly felt her stomach clench. She remembered him coming below deck on the *Ban Don,* going to the closet and taking a gun from his bag. He'd displayed a cool professional demeanor that day, and she saw it again now. This time, like the last, he scarcely paid attention to her. She was seeing the man in his element. Yet a big part of her refused to accept that this was the real Bart Monday.

After a few minutes he set the gun aside and said something to Sumaree's mother, who began putting some food in the sack.

"I'd better outline the plan for the day," he said. "I've hired a *songthaew* to take you to the base. It's a small truck they use to transport people in the countryside. I figured it would be the least conspicuous way to go. The driver can be trusted. He knows the terrain and can take back roads if there are roadblocks. He's well paid, so you won't have to worry about him abandoning you. Thep will ride along and, as you already know, he's pretty capable for a kid.

"Kit Jensen is my contact in the agency. He'll meet you at the base and smooth the way from there. I don't know if you've dealt with the CIA before, but they like to play little games to justify themselves. The best way to handle them is to play dumb and not ask any questions. The less you discuss what I'm doing, the better."

"I understand."

"Kit's actually harmless, but he'll put on his act for you. Don't let him bully you into any commitments. They're taking you out of Thailand because I made it a condition. Their obligation is to me—you won't owe them a thing."

"What would they want from me?"

"They'll ask you for your silence on what you've seen and learned. Tell them you'll keep your mouth shut, but you don't have to sign anything or submit to questioning beyond that."

"Don't worry, Bart, I've dealt with demanding people before. I've sued a number of them, as a matter of fact."

He squeezed her hand affectionately. "I keep forgetting that in real life you're an ambulance chaser."

"That's me. Counselor-at-law, barrister, attorney, pettifogger. And believe it or not, I wear navy blue suits and pumps and I can look very stern if I have to."

"Yet such a gentle creature otherwise." He gave her a wink.

"Keep that up, Mr. Monday, and the reception you get in Honolulu won't be very friendly."

"Want to know something, Kel? There's one vivid image of you I'll carry in my mind forever. It's sustained me the past couple of days, and also when the police had me on Ko Pong.''

"What's that?"

"It's the way you looked that day, kneeling by the stream, completely naked. The image is indelibly burned into my brain."

He said it so lovingly that her eyes misted, even though the notion was embarrassing. "Remember it if you must," she whispered, "but I'll always be grateful you didn't have a camera."

He sighed wistfully. "I don't need it on paper." Then he touched his temple. "It's here for good, just as you're in my heart."

"You're sentimental, aren't you?"

"Only when it comes to you. I'm going to miss you, babe."

"And I'm going to miss you."

Thep arrived a few minutes later. He was all smiles, greeting everyone in turn. Kelly wondered where Sumaree was, but decided not to ask. The woman fed Thep. Bart and Kelly watched the boy eat in silence. They both were feeling the pain of their impending parting.

As Thep was finishing his breakfast, a vehicle pulled up in front. Bart hobbled to the window and looked through the shutters. "It's your ride," he announced.

Kelly's stomach sank. He turned and faced her. "You ready, honey?"

"Yes."

"How about you, Thep?"

The boy got up, stuffing a tangerine into his pocket. "Sure thing, Boss."

"Let's go, then." Bart stood in the doorway as Thep trooped past him.

Sumaree's mother stopped Kelly before she got to the door. She took an amulet hanging on a string from around her neck and put it over Kelly's head, mumbling something in Thai.

"It's for luck," Bart explained. "Mama-san says it will protect you."

Kelly thanked her and they embraced briefly. The woman said goodbye and went into the back room. Then, as Kelly fingered the amulet, Bart reached out and touched her face. He was leaning against the doorframe, looking into her eyes. She felt herself getting misty and stepped over to hug him, so he wouldn't see her emotion. He kissed her hair.

"I'll talk to the driver if you want to wait here," he said.

Kelly stood in the doorway as Bart hobbled into the street. The driver, a dark-skinned man with a narrow jaw, stood next to a small Japanese pickup that had a canvas canopy stretched over the bed. He greeted Bart.

While the men spoke, Kelly glanced around. There were a few people in the street, a dog or two, no other vehicles. A film of wispy smoke hung over the low buildings. The muted gray light of early morning gave the neighborhood a torpid air, but in less than an hour the heat would rise and the community would be buzzing with activity.

There were apparently no temples in the area, because Kelly saw no Buddhist monks. The dog that had sniffed her leg the night before ambled toward her, and despite her brief stay, she felt strangely sentimental about leaving.

Bart concluded his conversation with the driver and dragged himself back to her. Thep was already seated on a bench in the back of the truck. Bart leaned against the doorframe to take his weight off his leg. He took her in his arms and nuzzled her neck, and Kelly bit her lip. When her tears began running down her cheeks, he wiped them with his thumb. "I hate this," he said.

Kelly gave a laugh that was nearly a sob. "*You* do?"

He caressed her fingers, looking down at her hands. "Well, at least you got a free manicure out of the trip. You can't say it was a total bust."

She nodded, drawing a ragged breath. "I'll never forget you, Bart."

"Well, I hope the memory lasts a couple of weeks. After I get to Honolulu, I won't give you a chance to forget me."

She smiled, not even sure why she was acting as if this was goodbye forever. When she lowered her head, several tears fell onto the front of her blouse. She wiped her eyes.

Bart leaned over and kissed her lips. She stood as motionless as a statue, afraid to breathe, afraid to move, afraid to love him. Just afraid.

"I love you, Kelly," he said.

"I love you, too." Her voice was tiny. Her willpower was rapidly dissolving. "I guess I'd better go. I wouldn't want to miss the plane after all we went through."

"No," he said sadly, "that would be a tragedy."

Kelly touched his arm. "Go inside and rest that leg. You've got to be well enough to take me dancing when you get to Honolulu."

"Do you like to dance, Kel?"

She nodded. "Do you?"

"Yeah. I love it." He beamed. "See how compatible we are!"

She kissed him fiercely, then she went to the back of the truck. Thep helped her onto the bench that faced Bart. He was leaning against the doorframe, and it was light enough to see his face clearly. He waved. She waved back, tears running down her cheeks in streams.

The driver started the engine, and the *songthaew* began moving up the street. "Bring a bottle of wine!" she called to him before they were beyond hearing.

Bart gave her a thumbs-up, then stepped to the edge of the street, where he stood watching as they drove away. Kelly kept her eyes on him until he faded into the haze of the early-morning light.

A long block farther up the bumpy street, a *tuk-tuk* with a bad muffler passed them, going in the other direction. It sounded like a lawn mower. She had a glimpse of the pretty girl in back, seated in the shadow of the canopy. It looked like Sumaree. If so, Kelly imagined she was going home to nurse Bart. The image of that unfinished card game came to mind, and she had a sudden and certain premonition that she would never see Bart Monday again.

CHAPTER TWENTY

KELLY LEFT THE OTHERS and went to the bow of Duncan's yacht for some air and a look at the moon. Inside the cabin, her mother's birthday party was going strong. Everyone was having cake and champagne. She could hear Duncan's laughter. He was having a good time and had taken it as a favorable sign that she'd wanted to include him in such an important family occasion. "God knows I need to win a few points with the old girl," he'd said when Kelly had told him how sweet it was of him to volunteer to host the party.

They'd known it was a bad time for her when the party had been planned back in July, but Kelly figured her mom would only be sixty-five once, so she'd gone along with Duncan's suggestion. He'd promised they'd stay close to shore. They wouldn't go any farther than Diamond Head—no more than twenty minutes from the Ala Wai boat harbor. And so they'd cruised at a sedate pace just beyond the reef, back and forth between Kapiolani Park and Sand Island. Enough for Beryl Ronan to feel she was at sea, something she dearly loved.

"I hate to be such a drag, Mother," Kelly had said while they'd had cocktails on the deck before dinner. "I feel as though I've put you on a leash."

"Don't be silly," her mother had replied. "The point is, we're all together. Duncan wouldn't have to sail halfway to Tahiti for us to have a good time, you know. Besides, the last thing I want to do is endanger my first grandchild for the sake of a silly old birthday party.''

Over the past nine months her mother had been like that—incredibly supportive. It had started the moment Kelly had told her she'd gotten pregnant during her adventure in Thailand. Beryl had blinked with surprise, but hardly missed a beat. "Well, I wanted you to have a good time, dear, but I hardly intended this. Do I want to know about the lucky father?''

Kelly had told her everything. Not unexpectedly, the illicitness of it all had appealed to Beryl Ronan, especially when Kelly told her she intended to have the child. "If you were eighteen or twenty, I'd say you were a fool, but a baby at your age strikes me as the perfect jewel in your life, dear.'' Kelly suspected her mother's response had more to do with her feelings about Duncan than the potential joys of motherhood, but she was glad for the support either way.

Beryl had helped her turn the second bedroom of her condo into a nursery, and she'd offered to take care of the baby after Kelly went back to work. At first Kelly had thought that was a bad idea—it seemed unfair for Beryl to give up her freedom like that. But her mother had pointed out that Skip and Patti had no intention of having kids, which meant that Kelly's child would be her only shot at grandmotherhood.

Kelly leaned back in the deck chair, smoothing the hem of her black muumuu splashed with white orchids that matched the one in her hair. Now that she was out in the breeze, she was glad she was alone. The kona winds had been blowing out of the south for a couple of days, bathing the islands in warm, sultry air that reminded her of Thailand.

Kelly couldn't look at the sea at night—especially when there was a full moon like the one coming up over Diamond Head—without remembering that terrifying swim with Bart from the *Ban Don* to the shores of Ko Pong. She'd gotten a whiff of the sea while Duncan was pouring champagne, and perhaps the truth was, she'd wanted to sit on the deck . . . and remember.

There was more laughter inside the cabin, and she glanced back, seeing the glow of the master's cigarette as he stood at the wheel up on the fly bridge, calmly surveying the night. Off to the portside were the lights of Waikiki, not much more than a mile away. The big hotels seemed close enough to reach out and touch, though Kelly knew she would be hard pressed to swim as far as the reef in her condition. Ever since her experiences with Bart in the Gulf of Siam, she couldn't be out on the water without calculating swimming distances.

A minute later Duncan came out of the cabin and made his way along the port side toward the bow. He was in a dressy blue-and-white aloha shirt and white linen trousers. He beamed happily, still imbued with the gaiety of the party.

"How is our young mother doing?" he asked.

"Still only a prospective mother, Duncan, but inching closer by the moment."

"Are you feeling all right, darling?"

"No labor pains, if that's what you mean, but that's as much as I'll admit to."

Duncan grabbed another deck chair and pulled it around to sit next to her. He stretched out, clasping his hands behind his head, and sighed. With his deep tan, he seemed the picture of health, though over the past six months or so his hair had grayed noticeably, and his worry lines seemed deeper. Seeing the woman he'd loved and wanted to marry pregnant with another man's child couldn't have been easy for him.

Rough as the past seven or eight months had been for Duncan, they had been worse—much worse—for Kelly, and they both knew it. First she'd faced the long, fruitless wait for Bart to show up, followed by the ensuing battle to get word of his fate, then finally receiving the tragic news of his death.

The baby squirmed, pressing against her lungs and taking her breath away. Kelly was glad that November had finally come. Her Thanksgiving baby, as she called him, had been restless all day. Her doctor had said it was only a matter of days now.

"You know, darling," Duncan said, "I only have one regret. I wish we'd gotten married before you left for Bangkok. That way the baby would have a father and I'd have you."

"Duncan, we've discussed this ten times if we've discussed it once. Giving the baby a name isn't a good enough reason to marry you."

"But—"

"But nothing," she interrupted. "I learned something very important in Thailand. I wouldn't have fallen in love with Bart if you'd been the right man for me. As it is, we were lucky to find out in time."

When Duncan didn't answer, she looked at him. The moonlight reflected off his tanned skin. There was still enough light for her to see the blue of his eyes. He had a pout on his face, the look of a thwarted child.

She sighed and turned to the lights of Waikiki.

"He's gone for good, Kelly," Duncan said. "He's dead. You've got to accept that. It won't do you any good to dwell on it, to pretend otherwise."

"You might be right about that," she said, laying her hand on her stomach. "But it still doesn't change anything between us."

"I don't see why not. He can't rise from the dead. Clinging to your memories only blows the man out of proportion. You've got to get on with your life."

She didn't like to admit it, but Duncan was probably right. She knew Bart was dead, yet something deep inside kept her from letting go of him. Probably because she didn't trust anything she heard after the runaround she'd gotten from the DEA and the Department of Justice.

The first two weeks after she'd returned to Hawaii had been the most nerve-racking of her life. She hadn't known whether Bart was alive or dead, whether he'd come back to her or forsake her. She'd tried to prepare for the worst, but even as her zeal had waned with each passing day, she'd never quite given up hope.

By the end of the second week, her spirits had really begun to lag. She'd also come to the realization that she'd missed her period. Bart's failure to appear, and the suspicion that she was pregnant, had been a double blow—the worst possible combination.

At first she'd been worried sick, sure he was dead, or even worse, lying wounded someplace, suffering terribly. Then she'd been angry, blaming him for risking his life by staying on to finish his job. She'd decided early on not to be passive. When three weeks had passed and the pregnancy had been confirmed, Kelly had begun her campaign to find out what had happened to him.

She contacted Peter Staub, the U.S. attorney in Honolulu, who'd gone to Harvard Law with her, and asked his help. Even if Bart had chosen voluntarily not to come to Hawaii, she thought it only fair to let him know he'd fathered a child.

Peter conveyed her requests to Washington, but little came of it. Everyone denied knowing who Bart was. It wasn't until she threatened to take everything she knew to the media that the DEA made an effort. Kelly got a letter from the deputy director informing her that Bart had been unaccounted for over a period of several weeks. The agency no longer carried him on their rolls as a contract employee. They regretted that they could not be more helpful and trusted she understood.

Kelly hadn't understood—she was outraged. Over the next month she exchanged harsh letters with the agency, accusing them of malfeasance and dishonesty. In the end, they promised an accounting. Not long after that, Kelly returned home to find Kit Jensen, the CIA agent who'd put her on the plane to Hong Kong, waiting for her in the lobby of her building.

Jensen, in a rumpled seersucker suit, stood when he saw her. His ruddy complexion and fleshy face made him appear to be on the verge of heatstroke. Kelly remembered him that way in Thailand, too, always mopping his brow and perspiring profusely.

"It's about Bart, isn't it?" she said.

Jensen nodded. "Since I knew him better than anybody else in the government, they wanted me to talk to you."

Kelly's chest felt as though it had been crushed in a vise. "Is he dead?"

The CIA man lowered his eyes. "Yes, I'm afraid he is."

She took him up to her unit, and they sat on the white sofa in her living room as Kit explained how Bart had gone north to Chiang Mai on assignment, then disappeared without a trace. A month later his body had been found in the wreckage of a small plane on the Burma-Thai-Laotian border.

Kelly wanted to know if it was certain Bart had been on the plane. Jensen admitted there'd been doubt at first because Bart wasn't a regular government employee, and therefore not as thoroughly documented. Accordingly, they'd been unable to get complete medical records. But his passport had been recovered from the crash site, along with the body.

She wept and, with tears streaming down her face, she asked if he'd talked to Bart again after she'd left Thailand.

"Yes," Jensen replied after a hesitation.

"Did he say anything about me?"

"The day after your departure he contacted me to make sure you'd gotten off all right. I assured him you were safely on your way home."

"Is that all?"

Jensen shrugged helplessly. "Monday and I didn't talk about much besides our work. We had other conversations, but you didn't come up."

"Was he going to leave Thailand within a week or two after I did? Was that really the plan or did he just tell me that?"

Jensen got up and paced partway across her living room. "I'm not at liberty to discuss operational matters, Miss Ronan."

"I just want to know if Bart intended to see me again."

"He went to a lot of trouble to get you out of the country. I don't know if that translates into wanting to see you again or if it doesn't. You'd be a better judge of that than I."

Then she asked him what they'd done with Bart's body.

"My understanding is that it was shipped to Nebraska for burial."

The image was more than she could bear. As Kelly cried, Jensen left. She had no further contact with anyone in the government. The file on Bart Monday had apparently been closed.

Duncan took her hand and gave it a friendly squeeze. "Well, no point in bickering. I understand that you've made up your mind, and I respect that. It's just that I still care.''

"I know," she said simply.

They sat in silence then as the boat moved through the water. Kelly looked at the lights and the dark profile of the Koolau mountains beyond the city. The ridge line against the night sky reminded her of Ko Pong.

There were other pleasure craft in the waters off Honolulu that evening, but they were mostly larger vessels of the sail or power variety, so the distant sound of a racing speedboat was a surprise. By day the things were everywhere, towing water-skiers and parasailors or simply running pell-mell over the deep blue waves of Mamala Bay. Duncan stood and looked astern, in the direction of the marina.

"Some fool must have had too much champagne, or else he's trying to impress his girlfriend," he said disdainfully. "I'm surprised he remembered to put on his running lights."

Kelly craned her head to see the boat that was raising such a commotion, but it had circled behind them and was heading farther out to sea. Duncan looked up at the fly bridge.

"Who is that, Jack?" he called to the master.

"Don't know, sir. It's a big inboard of some kind. Maybe a rental craft. He seems to be buzzing every boat. Kind of acts like he's looking for something."

"Well, if he's a pest, the Coast Guard ought to be alerted. Anything on the radio?"

"No, sir. Not that I've heard."

Duncan went to the starboard side of the yacht and gazed out to sea where a large sloop was sitting at anchor half a mile or so away. The speedboat had looped around it, then moved farther south, toward a cabin cruiser that was lit up festively.

After a minute, Duncan returned to his chair next to Kelly. "Silly cowboy," he muttered.

She patted his hand to calm him. Duncan was no hothead, but he had a clear sense of propriety. Everything was meant to work a certain way, and everyone had his place and his obligations within the system.

"Do you think Mom's having a good time?" Kelly asked to distract him.

"Are you kidding? When I left, she and Skip were singing show tunes from the fifties." He shook his head. "You know, I really appreciate the fact that your mother let me have the party, especially since she never cared for me."

"I think she really appreciates the way you've stood by me, been so supportive about everything."

Just then the speedboat began to make its way in their direction. Duncan turned to watch. "I wonder what in the hell that guy's up to."

The inboard was running parallel to them, about a hundred yards off the stern. When it was just about abeam of the yacht, it angled closer. Duncan again got to his feet and stared at it.

"Maybe we should go back inside," Kelly said. "I'm sure Jack can handle things."

"No, I want to see what this joker is up to." Duncan stepped to the other side of the boat and stood watching with his hands on his hips.

Kelly turned for a better view. The speedboat was no more than thirty yards off the bow. The moonlight was bright enough for them to see that only one person was in the boat, a man. He waved, but Duncan didn't return the salute. Instead he turned toward the fly bridge.

"Shut her down, Jack!" he hollered. "I want a word with this clown."

The yacht's engine dropped to idle. The inboard's motor also died down, bringing comparative calm to the surrounding waters.

"Is there a Duncan Van de Meer aboard?" the man in the speedboat shouted.

Duncan looked over his shoulder at Kelly, then he waved in a gesture of acknowledgment. "I'm Van de Meer," he hollered over the water. "What can I do for you?"

Curious, Kelly got to her feet. She stepped over to Duncan, taking his arm. The powerboat was about fifteen yards away and continuing to close. The driver's face was obscured, but there was something in the sound of his voice that sparked a recollection.

Before the man replied, a spotlight from the fly bridge flashed on, illuminating the powerboat. The face Kelly saw jolted her. "Oh, my God!" she murmured.

Duncan looked over at her.

"That's...Bart...."

The driver of the speedboat was shading his eyes against the bright spotlight. "Kelly? Is that you?"

"Dear God," she said, feeling her knees start to buckle. She clung to Duncan's arm.

Duncan looked back and forth between her and the man in the boat. "Monday? Are you Bart Monday?" he called.

The two craft had drifted nearly together. Bart was still shading his eyes against the light. He had a bottle of wine in his hand. Kelly's heart started pounding. She could see him clearly. He was in a plain white shirt and khaki pants. He was much thinner than when she'd last seen him.

Bart reached out to cushion the blow as the two boats came together. He glanced up at them both. "Yes," he said, his eyes now on Kelly, "I'm Monday."

"I thought you were...dead," she said, her voice frail, unbelieving.

Bart stared up at her, holding on to the railing with one hand, the wine bottle in the other. "Several people did, honey." He turned to Duncan. "Mind if I come aboard?"

Duncan pulled himself together. "No...uh...toss me a line. I'll tie you up amidships. There's a ladder down there." He glanced at Kelly. "Will you be all right for a moment, darling?"

She took hold of the railing, nodding. Then she looked at Bart. Her breath started coming in spasms and she felt dizzy, but she was determined not to pass out.

Duncan moved back toward the middle of the craft, holding the line. Within a minute Bart climbed aboard.

Neither man said a word. Bart immediately began walking toward her, moving with a limp, his eyes fixed unerringly on her. When he got to her, he stopped. Kelly braced herself, disbelieving. Then his mouth broke into the familiar grin that was burned indelibly in her brain. "I told you I was a man of my word."

She threw her arms around his neck, her full body bumping hard against him. Bart held her for a minute, pressing his cheek against hers. She began to cry. Duncan, standing several feet away, merely watched.

"I can't believe this," she murmured. "How...did you..." Her head was spinning and she lost her sentence, so she inhaled him instead, trying to make sense of the sensations buffeting her.

Bart eased back to get a better look at her. His eyes scanned her swollen body. "There seems to be an unexpected development." There was a trace of anxiety in his voice. "Who...should I be congratulating?"

"It's yours, Bart."

He broke into a broad grin, the relief on his face palpable. "Hot damn!" He put the wine bottle down on the deck, took her face in his hands and kissed her squarely on the lips.

"Kelly? What's happening?" Beryl Ronan came out on the deck. She looked from Kelly to Bart to Duncan and back to Kelly again. "What's going on?"

"We've had an unexpected visitor," Duncan said glumly. "Bart Monday."

Her mother gasped. She looked at Kelly, who nodded.

Beryl rushed forward, beaming. She took Bart's hands in both of hers and looked into his eyes. "Good Lord," she said. "We thought you were dead."

"Bart," Kelly said, "this is my mother, Beryl Ronan."

He grinned broadly. "There were times when I thought I was dead, too, Mrs. Ronan."

"Call me Beryl, for heaven's sake. You're practically family." She looked at them both, giddy as a schoolgirl.

Behind her Duncan cleared his throat. The three of them looked at him. After an awkward moment Beryl went over and stood next to him, taking his arm.

"Duncan, dear," she said, "there are times when events are simply ineluctable. I have the utmost respect for you, just as Kelly does. Could I call on your honor as a gentleman and ask you to escort me back into the party? This lady and gentleman have things to discuss that are probably best said in private."

Duncan, his face ashen, stared at Kelly, then seemed to bow to the inevitable. "Certainly, Beryl," he said. Then, addressing Kelly, he added, "If you need us, we'll be just inside."

Kelly nodded, and Duncan turned smartly on his heel, offering Beryl his arm. Together they went into the cabin.

Kelly looked at Bart, wiping her eyes. "I can't believe this. I truly can't."

"I'll do my best to make a believer of you, sweetheart."

He kissed her hard. When their lips parted, he glanced down at her stomach, placing his hand tenderly against the bulge.

"This will take some getting used to," he said, a smile twitching at the corners of his mouth.

"Considering what you've done to me, you deserve a surprise of your own." She put her hand on his shoulder. "I've got to sit down before I faint."

They went to the deck chairs where she and Duncan had been sitting. Bart helped ease her down, then sat himself. He took her hand. "I know I'm late getting here," he said sheepishly, "but it couldn't be helped."

"Late! That's a hell of an understatement!"

"I've been held prisoner in Burma the past eight months by some guerrillas. I was just released a week and a half ago. I got here as fast as I could, but I stopped long enough to buy a bottle of wine in the duty-free shop. I promised to bring the wine, remember?" He grinned. "My worst fear was I'd be too late." He looked toward the cabin. "I was glad to see you haven't married him, but are you still engaged?"

Kelly shook her head. "No. I broke it off after I got home from Bangkok."

Bart sighed. "When I got to the marina this evening, the harbormaster told me Duncan was throwing a party. I thought . . . maybe it was an engagement party."

"Oh, no. It's for my mother's birthday." She paused to think. "How did you know we were out here?"

"I went to your place, and when nobody was there I called Duncan's. The houseboy told me where he was. I went to the marina, and here I am."

He was playing with her fingers, suddenly looking weary and very gaunt. She caressed his hollow cheek, tears forming in her eyes.

"You must have lost thirty pounds, poor thing."

He glanced down at her belly, again laying his hand affectionately against it. "About as much as you've gained, by the looks of it. By the way, are we having a girl or a boy?"

"A boy. I had every test in the world because I couldn't even get your blood type out of the DEA. Medically, this was practically an immaculate conception."

His eyes danced in the moonlight. "I don't remember it as being very immaculate. Rather sensuous, as I recall."

"Bart, you haven't changed."

"Then I'm forgiven?"

"Yes, but when you didn't show up, I was ready to kill you . . . until I found out you were dead, of course!" Kelly looked wistful. "I had such lovely plans—a place picked out for dinner and dancing, a new dress. I was going to be so pretty. Now look at me! It practically takes a crane to get me on and off the boat."

"To me you're the most beautiful creature on earth, Kel."

"You have no idea what it's like to be nine months pregnant, do you?"

"I have a feeling I'm about to find out."

"This is pretty convenient for you, Bart Monday. You zap me then go off to let me suffer through the pregnancy alone."

"I wasn't exactly the guest of Conrad Hilton, you know."

She took his hand. "Was it terrible?"

"You were all that kept me going, Kelly."

"I didn't even have that, because I thought you were dead."

"Believe me, I had every intention of being here in a week. The documents I needed were supposed to be in Chiang Mai, but it was a trap. I was ambushed, then traded twice before I finally ended up in guerrilla hands.

My friends in the DEA claim they didn't know I was alive, so the guerrillas had trouble finding somebody to make a deal with. At least, that was the story. Truthfully, I don't know what to believe.''

"At least you're safe." She sighed. "But finding me like this must be a big shock."

He contemplated her and she felt a wave of doubt.

"Tell me what you're thinking, Bart," she insisted.

"Kelly, honey, I think you look terrific."

"I'm fat and ugly. You've never once seen me looking decent."

"You've never been more beautiful."

She put her arms around his neck and they kissed, this time more deeply. The feel of his lips brought back a cascade of memories that even her condition couldn't spoil. But as their lips parted she felt a sharp pain and she flinched.

"What's the matter?" Bart said.

She rubbed her side. "I don't know.... I felt ..." Then it returned, a distinct pain, a sharp pain. "Oh, Lord, don't tell me this is it."

"What? The baby?"

"I don't know for sure." A vague feeling of nausea washed over her. "I don't feel well, I can tell you that much."

His brow furrowed. "Does that mean you're going to have the kid now?"

"I don't know, Bart. I've never had one before."

"Well, you read a book or something, didn't you?"

"It could be a false labor pain."

"But you aren't sure?"

"It's hard to tell. Maybe you should call Duncan."

"What do we need him for?"

"It might be a good idea to start heading back to the harbor."

"I've got a powerboat, it's a lot faster."

Another pain shot through her. "I don't know...."

They heard someone on the deck and turned to see Duncan walking toward them.

"I don't mean to intrude," he said, "but I thought I'd see if everything is all right."

"Everything's copacetic," Bart replied, "but Kelly and I'll be leaving now. I thought I'd get her back ashore."

She looked up at Duncan. "I may be starting labor."

He gulped. "Well...we'd better turn this thing around, then."

"No need," Bart interjected. "It's my kid. I'll get them both back all right. And more quickly." He got to his feet. "Come on, Kel."

"Kelly," Duncan said, "are you sure this is what you want?"

She looked back and forth between them. They both waited. She drew a long breath. "I started this with Bart," she said. "I suppose it's only fair that I finish it with him."

Bart went over, snatched up the bottle of wine and handed it to Duncan. "We won't be needing this tonight. You might as well have it." Then he offered his hand. "You're a decent man," he said, "and I want you to know I respect that." Then, taking Kelly's arm, he led her to where the powerboat was tied up.

As Bart went down the ladder into the speedboat, Kelly felt another pain. It seemed like the real thing. Bart carefully helped her down into the boat. She dropped heavily into the passenger seat with a groan.

Bart untied the boat, then fired the engine. He kissed her cheek. "Do you want a siren and flashing lights, or is it that urgent?" he said over the roar of the powerful motor.

"Bart Monday, you're impossible," she shouted back. "I have no idea why I came with you."

He eased the throttle forward, made a graceful loop around the yacht, then headed back to the marina at high speed. The wind and the exhilaration sent a rush through her.

"I think that's obvious," he said, giddy with delight. "It was the same impulse that got you into this mess to begin with!"

"Maybe, but just because I'm going with you to the hospital doesn't mean I'll be willing to traipse through any more jungles with you. I can't go through that again."

"Me, either," he shouted over the roar of the engine. "I'm officially retired. Matter of fact, I'm thinking of settling down here in the islands if I can find the right girl and the right kid."

She reached over and squeezed his neck.

"Does that mean you accept?" he asked with a laugh.

"Accept what?"

He throttled back, so that the boat slowed. "Maybe we should negotiate this while I've still got some leverage."

Her eyes rounded. "What a brute!"

"Just say you'll marry me and I'll take you ashore."

"I'll do nothing of the kind!"

"Why not?"

"Wouldn't it be a good idea if we got to know each other first?"

"Well, if that's all that's bothering you..." He pulled on the throttle, and the boat took off again. Then he looked over at her, noticing her baffled expression. "What's the matter now?"

"Bart, I mean it. Getting to know each other is no small thing!"

"Kelly, honey," he shouted as the ocean spray kicked up over the bow, "after what we've been through, getting to know each other is going to be a piece of cake!"